DI

To my beloved Valerie.
Who tolerates me spending
so much time on other planets

AMARA'S DAUGHTER

E H HOWARD

www.shudalandia.co.uk

ehhoward@shudalandia.co.uk

First published by Ozcreative in 2013

www.ozcreative.co.uk

ISBN: 978-0-9926223-0-5

Chapter 1

Maryan pressed her toes into the arena floor and held her sword ready for Nasty Asti's inspection. Checking her grip, she glanced at the tower on the arena perimeter. Weapons class would end when the sun reached the tip of the spire. Until then, she had to endure the attention of Asti the Red, legendary warrior and one-time companion of her mother.

"By Thrippas, would you all look at this?" The tutor rocked back and sneered. "Is that the best the daughter of Amara the Magnificent can do?"

Asti hitched her signature red cloak over her shoulder revealing her gleaming breastplate. A deep scar creased her face, contorting her once-beautiful, ebony features. A single plait ran from the nape of her neck, the badge of the legendary virgin legion. Her good eye opened wide, whilst the full horror of her puckered eye socket poured scorn onto Maryan.

"Fleur, come forward," Asti commanded.

The Queen's daughter stepped out of line. "Yes, Class Leader." Ash blonde hair scraped severely back from a high forehead, her willow-thin neck showed every sinew. Maryan always envied Fleur's slim figure and dancer's grace.

"Attack!" Asti commanded.

Without hesitation, Fleur's sword leapt into her hand. A well-placed thrust forced Maryan back. Her eyes glinted as she ducked inside Maryan's defence. "I'm going to carve …"

"Silence," Asti said. "Speeches are for sagas and men. A true warrior concentrates on the job, not the chatter."

Maryan parried, but felt her sword almost whipped from her hand. Fleur attacked from every direction. A shadow moved and somebody stepped clear of the circle around them.

"Notice how Fleur's economy of movement practically removes recovery time," Asti said. "There! Maryan's flawed grip means she cannot offer the cutting edge."

Maryan blocked out the commentary. She realised that Fleur dipped her head slightly each time she intended to strike. One feint, another and then another, she waited for the telltale dip. It came and instead of raising a parry, Maryan drove her balled fist under Fleur's jaw. Fleur staggered and Maryan leapt forward. A foot slipped between her ankles, tripping her. She rolled, thumping her head into the arena floor. Twisting, she saw one of Fleur's cronies, Violet, grin.

Asti's commentary droned on, hammering home her humiliation. "The problem with the training ground is that we focus on a single foe. Note, in battle a simple foot soldier can bring the greatest warrior to her knees." She barked a harsh laugh. "Not that we are actually witnessing a great warrior fall in this case."

Fleur glanced to check Asti wasn't watching before drawing her sword back. Her head dipped and Maryan could see she was going to follow through. Powering her leg straight, she crashed her heel against Fleur's crotch, folding her double and leaving her writhing in agony.

Shaking with rage, Maryan rolled upright and raised her foot to stomp on Fleur's face.

"Back off." Asti pressed her sword against Maryan's throat. "Is there no end to your vile tactics?"

"Tell *her* to hold back!" Maryan pointed at Fleur.

"You really think the Queen's daughter would assault a vanquished foe?" Asti's words fell slowly. "You respect law and honour less than your damned mother did." Her fingers strayed to the grotesque scar. "Amara the Magnificent, yes, I can see something to remind me of her." She glanced at the tower. "Class dismissed."

Glad to escape from the sycophants around Fleur, Maryan hurried through the single exit from the arena, the Tunnel of Heroes. Even without the torches that would light the passage for a contest, the air reeked with the stench of tar.

Alone in the changing room, she securely racked her weapons and body armour before entering the steaming bathhouse. Grateful to hide, Maryan leant back in an empty corner. A cascade of whys poured onto her. Why was life so hard? Why did she have to be the daughter of a famous mother? Why had her mother vanished so mysteriously that she'd remain a legend forever? Her tears mingled with the sweat running down her face.

The chatter of the other girls making their way from the changing rooms into the bathhouse intruded on her misery. Most of them shared a common look, that of a lean, taut-muscled warrior. A few stood out as different. Small and dark, her blade-sister, Sami, came from the handmaiden caste, the first girl from her family to switch to warrior training. Even in the steam, Maryan could pick her out. Her unruly hair bounced in a curly halo. Her feminine curves outdid the statues adorning the palace corridors. At the other extreme lumbered Rose, another of Fleur's cronies, barrel-like and quick with her fists against Fleur's enemies.

Not that many confessed to being Fleur's enemy. She ladled charm thicker than honey on any who might aid her clamber for the throne. Unlike other lands, Serenia didn't have hereditary royalty. The people selected their queen from the best of the nation. The last two queens had been of Fleur's bloodline and she intended to make it three.

Unable to face anybody, Maryan peeled away from the tiles and headed for the cold plunge. Steam swirled, following her into the antechamber. She opened the exit and gasped at the chill. The plunge stretched out in front of her, a pool continually refilled by the icy streams flowing from the mountains. Without pausing, she exploded into an arching dive, attempting to reach the mid-point before touching the surface. The cold crushed the breath from her lungs, but she completed the mandatory length underwater. Her hand brushed the far wall and she scrambled out.

"Serenian warriors are women carved from ice with blades of fire," she muttered through chattering teeth. Not for the first time, she wondered if her sire had come from warmer climes.

In the dressing room, she quickly dragged her clothes on over her damp skin. Her head was still trapped in the folds of her robe when she heard the tap of sandals approaching.

"Come on, let's get out of here."

Maryan forced herself free of the clinging robe and watched Sami's flail become an almost invisible circle before slapping into the leather holster she wore on her thigh. Retaining her handmaiden traits, Sami always dressed more extremely than the rest of the cohort. Stretched tight by the swell of her hips, her skirt hung cut to a point below her knee on one side, opening in a gaping slash high on the other leg.

"Should you take that?" Maryan nodded at the flail.

"It's not a weapon, just a training aid." Sami wrinkled her nose. "It helps my coordination." She reached up tilting Maryan into a kiss.

The twinkle in Sami's dark eyes forced Maryan to laugh. Although they were too young to swear the blade-sister oath, she knew their bond was for life. "Where are we going today?"

"My sister, Arlaine, is training at The Centre and I said we'd meet her. We can head for the docks to look at the trade goods before they reach the market. Maybe pick up something."

Maryan followed, puzzled by her friend's constant need to browse shops, but glad of the company. She leapt at any chance to visit the docks where she'd last seen her mother. On that occasion, she'd been part of the academy guard. Her mother had turned at the top of the gangplank to wave at the cheering crowd. She'd been destined for the Baraland Games with the honour of the Serenian nation resting on her shoulders. After weeks of competition, Amara had defeated all-comers and been crowned Ultimate Warrior. On the night of her final victory, she'd vanished. In the following five years, not even the vaguest rumour of her fate had emerged. The incident had soured international relations, confirming Serenia in their status as an isolated feminine state.

Sami tugged Maryan's hand and they escaped the forbidding confines of The Academy. Their route took them through the imposing black doors of the main entrance and around the side of the arena down into the main town.

Where The Academy remained formal and black, The Centre, the home of the Handmaiden caste glistened. Clad with sparkling white marble, a wide staircase led up to a golden doorway. A queue of boys waited outside the doors and Maryan slowed down to eavesdrop on their whispered conversation.

"They don't hurt us, do they?" a pale-faced boy said. He was peering along the line winding inside the building.

"Don't be daft," a much larger lad scoffed. "They take you, break your heart and rip it still beating from your body," He grabbed at the young boy's chest and raised his hand pretending to hold a pulsing heart.

Maryan shook her head. Each school for boys had to provide 'volunteers' for the trainee maidens to practice seduction and allure. The experience proved a source of sniggering amongst both genders.

The square outside The Centre heaved with people milling around the chaotic assembly of market stalls. Farmers from the country brought everything from bread to live pigs for sale. Stalls selling clothes made of stout Serenian wool had also started to display lighter, linen garments ready for the brief summer that still seemed an age away.

Arlaine appeared at the entrance and all eyes turned to her. Where Sami barely reached Maryan's chin, her sister easily matched Maryan's height and moved like a cat. Draped in a sumptuous fur coat, she swept an armful of dark curls back over her shoulder and grinned. "Sami, Mari," she squealed, wrapping them in a double embrace. Maryan felt awkward. Warriors didn't hug, but Sami's family did. They hugged, kissed, stroked and generally seemed to be touching all of the time.

"We have to get along to the docks. I hear there's a delivery in from Bara. They have the most heavenly perfumes arriving." Arlaine linked Maryan's arm to guide her through the market square. "We'll find a cup of something first, I think."

Men stood behind many of the bustling stalls. Some risked a flirtatious call to get the attention of the three women, but their words died when Sami glared in their direction.

"Don't do that," Arlaine chided. "One day you might seek a husband."

"And one day a dragon will toast my bread."

"It doesn't hurt to practice." Arlaine granted one of the men an eye-fluttering smile, laughing when he flushed red. "They're so predictable."

The chatter that usually lifted her dark thoughts niggled at Maryan. "I don't feel well," she said, pulling free of the two sisters.

Sami stopped mid-stride and reached for Maryan's forehead. "You look alright. Are you hot?"

Maryan brushed Sami's hand aside. "I just feel odd. I'm going to head back to school. You stay with Arlaine."

She walked away, imagining the sisters' stare drilling into her back. Once out of sight, she headed to the docks. She didn't want to visit the safety of the trading house, but wanted to go into Portside, close to the sea.

"Hey, Maryan, what are you doing here so late?" the guard shouted.

As most of the merchant vessels were operated from Walsholm, guard duty on Portside was only assigned to the toughest warriors. This guard, Trista, had so much scarring that her face looked like a jigsaw with some pieces missing. In addition to her twin blades, she carried a hefty quarterstaff. Maryan knew it would be stained with blood before dawn.

"Hi Trista, it's just a quick visit. You know how things can get." She attempted a forlorn expression. Amara had been the hero of the nation, beloved of all the warriors. No matter how tough the guards were, they usually took pity on her.

"Be out by sundown. We've had two whores killed. There are some bad types in port this week."

Maryan made her way through the ancient side streets. At one time, Portside had been part of the city. Now, as a partitioned enclave, the place was home to foreign prostitutes and drug traders, leaving the laws of Serenia suspended at the gates.

Maryan didn't care. Having spent so much time gazing out to sea, she felt safe amongst the ramshackle warehouses. Dangling her feet over the edge of the wharf, she was hypnotised by the lapping water. It hurt that her mother was a fading memory. Did she really have blonde hair and had she ever worn it unbound from its tight plait?

The sun dipped towards the horizon and the coarse laughter of the seedier denizens of Portside warned her to leave. Numbing cold had seeped into her legs, making them wobble. She tried to stomp life back into them as she made her way through the shadow-filled alleyways. A girl of The Academy, one year from graduation, shouldn't fear the dark.

"Hello, sweet pea."

A punch bounced her head off the wall. Rough hands hauled her around. Drink-laden spittle flecked her face as a sailor pushed against her.

"Grab her arms." His fingers folded over her robe and tugged. The fabric ripped, biting into the back of her neck, jerking her head against him. "See that? Desperate for a kiss from her new friend, Thomas. Just wait, sweet pea, you'll be introduced to all the lads."

Maryan screamed and kicked out. Punches rained, snapping her head sideways. She started to fold.

"Spread her on that barrel," one shouted. The sailors dragged her onto the rough wood. Strong hands yanked her legs wide. The ringleader leered, tugging at his belt and opening his breeches. "Sweet pea, you and me are gonna dance a jig now." Fumbling, he pressed between her thighs.

His eyes widened. A torrent of blood coughed from his mouth, washing across her breasts and stomach.

"Get down." A hand pushed her roughly, slamming her head against the ground. A shadow flickered and a steel blade gleamed. Lights flashed behind her eyelids. She could see feet moving. The sailor lay alongside staring flat-eyed and motionless.

What had he said? They were going to dance. Feet scuffled before one and then another attacker fell. A fourth scrambled to run, but something stopped him.

Ungentle hands gripped Maryan and sat her against the wall, a red cloak swirled and Asti dropped in front of her. She tipped Maryan's head back. "Are you awake?"

Maryan tried to speak, her mouth felt numb. "I'm okay."

"You don't look it. What were you thinking, coming here alone? If Sami hadn't raised a warning, you'd be tiger-fish bait."

Trista stood to one side, watching as Asti wiped her blade across the chest of a dead man. Grunting, she helped Asti haul Maryan to her feet and wrap the red cloak around her. "Try not to bleed on it, or you'll pay for a new one," Asti said.

"I said I'm okay," Maryan protested, her numb fingers struggling to hold the cloak shut.

"Sure you are." Asti hitched her shoulder beneath Maryan's arm. "You don't need any help, do you?"

Chapter 2

Back at The Academy, Asti marched with Maryan through the deserted passageways to the dormitory she shared with three other students. At this time of night, few torches remained lit. The echoing slap of Asti's sandals vanished along the gloomy corridor.

"You're more of an idiot than your damned mother, you know that?"

"Were you ever really her friend?"

Asti's hand strayed to her scar. "She was a total pain all her life and continues to be one in her death."

"Dead, you believe that?"

"Got to be. Your mother almost certainly suffered the same fate you nearly had, beaten and dragged off for pleasure. It happens anywhere the Walsholm traders turn up." Asti shrugged. "Hasn't Steppis ever said anything?"

"What would Steppis know?"

"The stupid woman probably believes that if she doesn't talk about it, then it can't have happened. She was there. She helped take Bara apart searching the town for any sign of your mother, ask her."

At the dormitory, Asti swung the door open. "I'll send somebody to tend to you."

"No need, Kait is my roommate."

"The Magic Wielder?" Asti sucked in sharply. Although other lands accepted sorcery as commonplace, it was rare in Serenia. Kait, the only magician born in a generation was destined to be the greatest healer Shudalandia would ever produce. At least that was what she told anybody who would listen. Asti nodded her approval and walked away, leaving Maryan swathed in the red cloak.

The comfortable smell of four people growing up together greeted her the moment she opened the dormitory door. Stella's perfume, Sami's oils and Kait's herbs gave the room a unique signature.

It had been her home for the last twelve years. The beds, two on either side, had felt large to a five year-old, but they'd shrunk over time. Close to Kait's bed, stood an ancient table forever buried beneath the debris of her studies. On the left, close to Sami's bed, their communal dressing table and mirror. A huge shared wardrobe dominated the centre of the far wall.

Her home was a collection of furniture accumulated by the hundreds of girls who'd grown up in the room before them. Each generation of students had added their mark, with every wooden surface bearing the scars. Partially visible murals of ancient dragons peeped from beneath recent additions. A life-sized picture of a naked man that she claimed was art brooded above Stella's bed.

"Gorath and Friggit, what happened to you?" Kait sprang up from her work, her white nightdress wafting around her thin limbs. She dragged Maryan across to the table and pushed her into a chair.

"I'm alright," Maryan protested.

Opening the red cloak, Kait gasped at the torn robe and the blood smeared on Maryan's skin. She tilted Maryan's head to examine the bruising. "Is this something Fleur did? If it is, you have to complain."

Desperate to blame somebody else, Maryan's thoughts raced. She shook her head. "No, this was my own fault."

“I need some things. Don’t move.” Kait crashed out of the dormitory, heading in the direction of the Infirmary.

Her fault? Maryan sat with the cloak gaping open and wondered how she’d been so stupid. The door creaked and Maryan thought it was Kait returning.

“Acting out fantasies with your playmate?” Fleur’s voice grated through Maryan’s reverie. Violet slipped out of Fleur’s shadow and Rose grinned from behind them.

“Looks like they’re playing slave girl and barbarian,” Violet said.

Maryan tugged the cloak around her. “If you’re after another kicking, send your friends away and we’ll discuss it.” She tried to sound calmer than she felt.

Rose cracked her knuckles against her palm. The three girls moved forward and Maryan sprang up clattering the chair across the floor.

“Another beating? I don’t think so.” Fleur snapped her fingers and Violet flourished a studded leather glove. “You laid a hand on my royal personage and now you’re going to feel the weight of my wrath.” Moving with dramatic slowness, she eased the gauntlet onto her hand. “Besides, from what mother has been saying, I doubt I’d have a chance to deliver it on the arena floor. Something about ‘might serve as a handmaiden,’ was her suggestion.” She let the words hang.

A whistling fireball the size of a sparrow screamed across the room and exploded against the wall. “What will it feel like when every hair on your head goes up in flames?” Kait said from the doorway.

Fleur spun to face her. “You wouldn’t dare, freak. Even if you are spoiled rotten, you can’t use magic without supervision.”

“And nobody ever breaks a rule …” Kait snapped her fingers and Violet’s plait burst into a yellow flame billowing green smoke. Rose tipped the pot from beside Sami’s bed over her. Smelling the urine, Violet screamed and dashed for the door.

Maryan took two strides and swung all of her weight into landing a punch on Rose’s jaw. The big girl’s eyes rolled back and she dropped into a dead heap. “And then there was one.” Maryan stalked closer to Fleur forcing her to back away.

“Going somewhere?” A fireball exploded close to Fleur’s heels blocking her retreat. Kait flicked her straight red hair back over her shoulder, fixing Fleur in her wide-eyed stare. “I think our royal guest should be leaving.” She nodded at the barely moving Rose. “And take your rubbish.”

Rose struggled to her feet and started towards Kait, but Fleur restrained her. “You two have a problem.” Her face became pinched and she turned to each of them, flexing the studded glove. “The royal decree shall be that you both suffer for this. Using weapons and magic are forbidden.” She pulled herself tall and glided from the room.

Maryan and Kait held their breath and waited for the door to close before exploding with laughter. Kait raised her hand and a phantom gauntlet appeared around her slender fist. Holding her head painfully high, she forced her eyes to bulge from her face. “By royal decree I have an entire broom stuck up my rear.” Stiff-legged, she paraded the length of the dormitory, waving regally at an imaginary crowd. The gauntlet vanished and she straightened the chair, motioning for Maryan to sit down. "Let me take a look at these cuts." At her glance, the bag she had been holding when she'd entered slid across the floor to snuggle against her ankle like a dog seeking a treat.

She started to clean the cuts with a ball of lamb's wool doused in fluid from a purple bottle. The strong smelling spirit bit into the wounds.

"Can't you numb it?" Maryan muttered.

Kait moved Maryan's head to catch the light. "I'm scared that if I make your head any more numb, you might stop breathing. What were you doing?"

"Yes, what *were* you doing?" Steppis, the housemistress had entered the room. "I'm sure we all want to know." Solid as a sack of grain, she wore a grey woollen dress that clung to her every bulging contour. Her thick girth made the tales of her past exploits seem unlikely, but her warrior skills remained legendary.

"I went to the dock," Maryan said. "I must have fallen into a kind of dream thinking of my mother." Asti's comments sprang into her mind. "Asti said you were with her the day she vanished. Why couldn't you find her?"

"Girl, if she'd been there, we'd have found her." Steppis sank onto the edge of Kait's bed. "We almost got ourselves thrown into prison for the riot we kicked up. I was supposed to be a steadying influence on the young blades. Instead, I fear that I was the worst. I took the town apart. I kicked the door out of three embassy buildings, I …" She stopped and ground her stumpy fingers into her short grey hair.

"Finally, the Emperor himself 'escorted' us from the city. I don't know where she is, but I'd swear she was not in Bara."

"Asti says she's dead."

"Well, those two …" Steppis leant forward to put her hand onto Maryan's knee. "You've been assigned to royal duties. The Queen herself asked for you." She stood and squeezed Kait's shoulder. "Get her fixed up and mend all these scuffs. She's going on show in the royal apartments. Remember, young healer, she must appear unblemished and bruise free. Gorath, anybody might think her a warrior or something."

"Are you commanding me to use magic without supervision?" Kait's mouth dropped open in mock innocence.

"And that would be the first time, wouldn't it. Don't play the fool with me, just get her fixed." Steppis turned to Maryan. "Be at Dorrat's door tomorrow morning." The old warrior spun on her heel, leaving with the ponderous grace of a warship nudging out of harbour.

Kait pursed her lips before turning her attention to Maryan. "I hate looking at you magically," she said, wrinkling her face in distaste.

"Why?"

"I can see a presence. A dark evil's going to try to hurt you. I can feel it getting closer."

"Don't you think what just happened with Fleur is dark enough?"

Kait wrapped her arm across her face, peeked over her elbow and wriggled her fingers melodramatically. Her voice became the croak of a stage witch. "No, my dearie, evil approaches and it's coming closer. It is malevolent and mystical, not bile-filled and blonde." She snapped her head back and used magic to project a deep laugh echoing around the room. A tiny bolt of lightning flashed accompanied by an impressive thunderclap.

Something scuffled inside the wardrobe and the girls froze. "Come out," Kait shouted. The noise stopped.

"Another prank by Fleur?" Maryan frowned. She tugged the cloak back onto her shoulders and crept across to the closet.

"You pull the door open and I'll handle whatever emerges." Kait folded her arms, waiting for Maryan to raise the latch. A terrifying screech wailed. Something pounded against the inside, rattling the hinges. Maryan flipped the door open and Jasper, the castle cat, an enormous, black-furred feline sprang free.

Kait fell over backwards in a tangle of white nightdress. The hissing animal landed on her chest, his claws dug deep, powering him over her head as he headed the door. "Cursed cats! I hate the things." She twisted to throw a fireball, but Jasper had already vanished.

Maryan returned to the chair so that Kait could finish working on the bruises. "What's your problem with Jasper?"

"Magic can be harsh. Just as I see this presence coming at you, but can't identify it, I know a cat is linked with my death. I don't know when or where, but I know it will happen. Whenever I see one, I think of dying."

Waiting for Kait to do her work gave Maryan too much time to think. What had Fleur heard the Queen say and what did assignment to the royal chambers mean? She laid her hand on her friend's waist, almost too scared to speak. "These futures, can you see other things? Am I being re-trained to be a handmaiden?"

"I doubt a great clump like you would be much use for dance and allurement," Sami's cheerful voice rang shrill across the dormitory. She crashed through door and fell onto her bed, tilting her hands into what she'd told them was the first position of seduction. "A handmaiden needs a delicate touch. What are you talking about?"

"I've been assigned to serve the Queen and Fleur says I'm getting kicked out of warrior training."

Sami rolled off her bed and rushed across to wrap Maryan in a perfumed hug. "They couldn't kick out the daughter of Amara the Magnificent, there'd be a riot." Her dark eyes flashed. "Fleur might not like you, but you're too important for them to lose." She studied the bruises fading under Kait's ministration. "What happened?"

As Maryan repeated the story, Sami listened in disbelief. "Saved by Nasti. I bet that stuck in old scarface's throat. I think she's been jealous of your mother since they were babes. Imagine living in *that* shadow."

Maryan nodded, well aware of the weight of her mother's shadow.

"I knew something was going to happen. I'm never letting you out of my sight again." Sami smothered her. "You missed such a time. I came back looking for you. The council have passed Arlaine. She's now part of the official staff at the centre, free to practise and serve. Mum says people are already suggesting she could compete with Fleur for the royal title."

"Queen Arlaine?" Kait spat out the ball of wool she'd been using to clean the cuts. "That would answer some problems. The nation always prospers when a handmaiden holds the crown." She patted Maryan's shoulder. "All done."

The door clattered open framing Stella in the corridor torchlight. She held her sandals in one hand and wore a shimmering black robe that clung to her curves. Golden paste a shade lighter than her tanned skin highlighted her brown eyes.

"You'll not make the virgin legion creeping around dressed like that," Sami said.

"But I never sleep with them … Not a wink." She swept back her tousled black hair, hooked her fingers into her shoulder straps and dropped her robe to the floor. With a flick, she kicked it into Sami's face. Laughing and naked, she stretched languidly onto her bed, before propping herself up onto one elbow. "Go on then. What's happening?"

In the pitch black of night, Sami slipped into Maryan's bed and kissed her shoulder, rolling her into an embrace. "It must have been awful."

Confined against Sami, Maryan tried to shrug, "It was all over so fast."

Sami chuckled. "Mum say's it usually is with a man. Did he …"

"Gorath no! His thing was so sad and grubby. I don't know what pleasure they can be."

"I doubt he was thinking of giving any pleasure at all."

Night crept past and Maryan lay cradled in Sami's embrace waiting for the sunrise. Yesterday, life had seemed so organised. Sworn as blade-sisters, she and Sami would be fighting in the legion. Kait would move to Idrahail to learn from the wizards. Stella? Well, three out of four seemed organised.

What would happen if she didn't finish her training? She'd linger, like a ghost in the corridors, tormented by Fleur, lost amongst a new cohort. Maybe worse, sent away to find a husband and work on the farms. Why would the Queen be asking for her?

Uncurling Sami's arm from around her shoulders, she lifted the edge of the blanket to slip out into the chilled morning air. Her friend's unbound hair filled half of the tiny bed. Hesitant with fear, Maryan washed in cold water before tugging her best robe over her head. She started to gather her hair into bunches, but her hands shook so much the strands kept escaping her grip.

"Let me do it." Sami appeared behind her. She pressed Maryan onto the low bench in front of the communal mirror. Although sleep filled Sami's face, her fingers worked quickly to gather a complex plait from the crown of Maryan's head to the nape of her neck. "Don't worry. It's probably a great honour rather than the punishment Fleur suggests." She kissed the top of Maryan's head, before tumbling into her own bed.

Maryan crept out of the dormitory to the passage that separated The Academy from the Royal Palace. Although joined, it was obvious where the Palace started. The practical stone floor changed to plush carpet and the pictures of stern-faced heroes gave way to pastoral scenes of rolling landscapes. Ahead of her, golden tables arrayed with objects of infinite delicacy lined the passages. Maryan kept her elbows close to her sides. Always in fear of damaging anything fragile, she imagined a whisper running through the precious ornaments. Watch out, the ox is about.

The palace housekeeper possibly wielded more power in the residence than the Queen did. Maryan smoothed her robe before knocking on the white panelled door to Dorrat's office.

"Come." The single word hammered through the wood.

Dorrat's face was creased with folds. She wore her grey-streaked hair pulled into a severe bun. Her head twitched like a hawk checking for mice. "You know why you're here?"

"No …" Maryan didn't know how to address her, "Class Leader?"

Dorrat smiled, but little warmth came from it. "Housekeeper, or Madame, followed by Dorrat."

"No, Housekeeper Dorrat, Steppis told me to be here, but nothing else."

"Secrets and need to know." Dorrat shook her head. "These warriors will be the death of me. We have important guests and Queen Etelan believes that showing off the daughter of Amara the Magnificent will impress them."

How could they show off the worst student ever to pass through The Academy? "You mean I'm still to be a warrior?"

"Of course you are, stupid girl. What else could you be? Now follow me."

She led Maryan into a storeroom stacked with clothes. “These are the uniforms you will require. Wear this during the day and this for evening service. You must return them to my assistant, Lucy, at the end of each week for replacement.” She plucked items from the shelves and then swivelled on her heel. “Are you listening, child? If you have questions, spit them out, we don’t have all day.”

“I’ve never worked in service.” Maryan shrugged and caught a shelf, tipping the contents onto the floor. “I’m clumsy. Famous for it,” she said, struggling to lift the board back into place.

“You will have training, Lucy will see to that. Change and report to her immediately.”

Chapter 3

“**Why** do the gods hate me so much?” Lucy, Dorrat’s assistant, stood in the corner of the small training room. She grimaced and rapped her polished black cane on the wooden floor. “Glide, girl, glide!”

The rope tying Maryan’s ankles pulled taut, almost tripping her. She glanced across hoping Lucy hadn’t noticed, but the housekeeping assistant saw everything.

“If the rope binds, you’ve stepped too wide. Walk, don’t prowl.” Lucy glared. “Why on earth were you carrying a tray of dishes along the main corridor in the first place?”

“I had to get from the kitchen somehow, didn’t I?” Maryan almost added more, but held her tongue under the stare.

The cane swept out to the panelling just below waist height. “Use the servant passages.” Lucy tapped on a small section, clicking open a concealed door. “You’re not the first clumsy servant. The builders of The Academy worked these passageways throughout the fabric of the building. You’re supposed to use them.”

Maryan peered inside. Although narrow, the passage was wide enough for a servant carrying a tray to make their way along. There was an alcove to pass in and tiny grates filtered light into the passageway from outside.

“Three bars of veneer a shade lighter than the rest indicate where they are, you’ll notice these concealed latches placed where you can activate them either like this.” She swung her hip, to demonstrate how and then tapped a latch close to the floor inside the passage. "Or set above ankle height where you can use your foot. Keep your eyes open." Her face wrinkled, almost smiling. "I'm sure the Sudaland Trade Minister will survive his near brush with death."

The memory of the small man covered in soup haunted Maryan. His screams had almost broken the ornaments in the corridor and the event had resulted in Maryan receiving extra tuition.

"You're supposed to be in the kitchens," Lucy said. "Hurry, but glide. Go!" She punctuated her last word with a sharp rap of the cane.

Maryan adored the luxurious air of the palace. Thick pile carpet covered the corridor floors and the ceilings sported murals depicting the ancient gods in heroic combat. The walls were powder blue, decorated with white plaster mouldings highlighting important pictures.

Although late, Maryan paused at a quiet corridor ideal to practice her servant's walk. Shortening her stride, she forced herself to float 'like a petal dropped on a tranquil pond.' She counted twenty paces, turned right and fifty paces brought her to another right turn.

Puzzled, she glanced back. It should have gone left and had the exercise ground visible through windows. It didn't add up. She shrugged and set off to the right.

Panic gripped her. From somewhere close by, she could hear Queen Etelan talking with the Sudaland Minister. Dorrat had sworn she'd roast Maryan alive if she ever went near the poor man again. She needed to escape without being seen, but also had to reach the kitchens.

Now they'd been pointed out, she could easily spot the concealed doorways leading into the servants' passageways. She clicked one open and slipped inside. Trailing her hand along the wall, she hurried through the gloom until she came to an open doorway where she stopped to peep inside.

The wooden floor showed through holes in the ragged carpet. Light spilled from the dust coated windows on the far side. Holding her breath, Maryan crept on tiptoe to look out. She'd been right, she could see the exercise ground.

Envious of the naked freedom of the girls below, she tugged at the high neck of her serving blouse. Hoping to catch Sami's eye, she waited with her forehead pressed against the window.

Down in the square, Sami kept her attention focused on her whirling flail. Fleur ran gracefully around the perimeter, stretching her pace into a fluid, mile-eating lope. In the centre of the exercise square, Rose bent over, legs straight, her white backside thrust out to heave weights in a curled rowing position.

Prompted by the numbing cold of the glass, she left the window and wandered along a narrow corridor. It led into a room with more pictures and dusty ornaments. One painting caught her eye, a large canvas depicting two women, beautiful, but serious. She recognised her mother instantly, her slim waist and rigid-backed posture, the feminine curves of her moulded armour. Unmarked by the awful scar, Nasti clasped her mother's forearm in unmistakable friendship. Beneath the image, the artist had written the words 'Strength through eternal love.' At the top of the canvas, a sequence of indecipherable runes arched above their heads.

Mesmerised by the tranquil beauty, she settled on the window ledge facing the picture. Even to an untrained eye, every brush stroke whispered of a loving union. At one time, they had posed for this painting apparently in perfect friendship, but now every word Nasti uttered about her mother was venomous.

A shout from the training ground startled her. "Gorath!" she muttered. The sun was setting, meaning she'd be in serious trouble. Slapping the dust from her uniform, she cast a last glance at the picture. What could have soured their friendship?

The heat of the ranges made the royal kitchen feel airless. During the day, the high windows gave some light, but for evening meals, the illumination came from oil lamps hanging on ornate iron brackets.

Although tiny compared to the main kitchens, the room easily serviced the needs of the palace. Assisted by four under-cooks, Madame Ferani, the Baraland master chef, orchestrated the chaos with a voice that could split stone. During service, she always kept her dark hair tied back and wore a long brown dress.

When Maryan joined the end of the line waiting to carry the first course, Madame Ferani was at the far end of the kitchen helping an under-cook to apply the final embellishments to a dish. She spun and shouted, "Service."

Maryan moved up the queue. The broad-faced cook paused. "I was about to send out a search party for you. It takes most people no time to walk from The Academy to the kitchen, you, it takes an extra day." She touched a spoon against the back of Maryan's hand. It burnt and Maryan leapt back sucking at the scald. "So you are awake. Tomorrow you will be serving at the banquet for the Garalandian Ambassador. If I send you off with a plate of hot food, I expect it to reach the guests before ice forms on it."

By clever use of screens and sectioned tables, the palace dining room could accommodate different sized parties and moods. Tonight, the tall, dark wooden panels created an intimate dining room. The large chandelier remained unlit. Instead, elaborate candlesticks had been placed along the tables, their flickering light cast dancing shadows all around.

Queen Etelan sat at the centre of one table. An older, slightly heavier version of Fleur, tiny wrinkles touched the corners of her eyes. The neckline of her blue dress plunged deep, flowing over the slight contours of her body. She wore her silver-blonde hair caught in a loose plait covering her ears.

Breastplate gleaming with a parade ground shine, Asti sat alongside the Queen. Her almost purple skin matte and smooth, her thick black hair, shaved away from her ears, formed a thin strip along her skull. Sensing somebody staring, her scowl coalesced into simmering fury. Maryan quickly turned away to concentrate on not making a fool of herself.

After service, Madame Ferani always called the team together to discover if anything had gone amiss. "Take this to warm you up," she said, passing out small glasses of Sudaland brandy. After running from the kitchens to the tables, Maryan didn't need warming up. She coughed at the fumes rising from the drink.

The spirit burned and she rocked forward, choking. Madame Ferani slapped her back, startling Jasper from his cosy slumber above the ranges. Hissing wildly, he flew at Maryan. She barely caught the frenzied cat and had to fight to keep him at arm's length away from her face.

"Don't hurt him!" Madame Ferani claimed Jasper and smothered him against her voluptuous chest. Her hand bent over his ears to prevent him from listening. "Don't you know the Queen herself sometimes rides inside his head? She looks through his eyes and uses his ears. Never mistreat him, or you might be punishing Etelan herself."

Back in their dormitory, Kait sat opposite Maryan across the solid wooden table. She grabbed Maryan's hand, her eyes wide with intensity. "You've been sneaking where?" Her voice escalated. "Have you any idea how many tales of ghosts and vanishings centre around those rooms?"

Stella sat upright on her bed. "I'm more interested in the arrival of the Garalandian Ambassador. What does he look like?" She licked her lips. "Will he have any young guards with him?"

"Ignore that and listen to me," Kait said. "I had to study the folklore of The Academy. Too many unexplained incidents centre around those rooms and the caves in the rear garden. You must have heard of Mad Queen Morgan."

Maryan shrugged, sharing a wink with Stella.

"She had her head chopped off. It floats in front of her wailing as her corpse staggers behind seeking victims to throttle."

"How does her head wail when her lungs are still in her body?" Stella asked.

"I don't think things like that apply to ghosts." Kait sniffed.

The atmosphere of the dining room felt colder than a winter night in the high mountains. The Queen dominated the centre table. She wore a blue dress, with complex folds hanging over her shoulders. Its stiff bodice cupped and pushed her breasts into a tight cleavage. She appeared immersed in animated conversation with the richly dressed man beside her. Eyes glowing, Etelan swept back her unbound hair with a flick of her hand. Maryan smiled, remembering Stella doing the same whenever a handsome groom was around.

The senior tutors were on a table set at right angles to the Queen, Asti sat next to a man who looked like a street brawler forced into fine clothes. Five burly men sat with them. Each wore a crimson jacket showing a lace-trimmed shirt cuff peeping from their sleeves. Barely older than Maryan, two of them eagerly appraised the serving girls bustling between the tables.

As she made her way behind the top table, Etelan surprised Maryan by turning a gleaming smile upon her. "Ambassador Mordacai, may I point out this young lady."

The rumours in the kitchen said he was a magician, as well as being the most powerful noble of Garalandia. Bemused by the request, the Ambassador regarded Maryan with studied consideration. His well-trimmed beard jutted from his chin. Padded epaulets bulked his shoulders and dark gemstones embellished the front of his black velvet jacket.

The Queen rose, plunging the room into silence and dragging all attention toward them. "This young lady performing simple labour amongst us is none other than the sole daughter of Amara the Magnificent." She reached out to stroke Maryan's blushing cheek. "That woman was almost a sister to me. I swore I'd treat her child with the love I'd give my own daughter."

"Your daughter is also amongst the serving girls?" The Ambassador surveyed the room.

"That would be frowned upon. Some might think me to be showing favouritism to my own bloodline." She hugged Maryan before waving her back to her duties. "We are a proud people. The highest serve and must earn the right to do so."

"Isn't that true in most lands?" The Ambassador raised his stemmed glass toward the Queen. "My own prince, Chentene, works every day to improve the lot of his people."

"For example," the rough-faced man beside Asti interrupted. "He's just improved life for another thousand by pressing them into the army." He barked a laugh and wrapped his arm around Asti, squeezing her against his chest. "Of course we only send men to fight. The women stay at home to comfort those who remain." Another guffaw assaulted the room.

As if it was a dead rat, Asti lifted the man's hand from her shoulder. Maryan waited for the explosion, but the tutor allowed him a cold smile. "So men are expected to fight in Garalandia?"

"The only time a woman fights is in the bedroom!" He coughed red wine down his chin.

"Barag!" the Ambassador's face turned white. "You are a guest. Control your tongue." He addressed the room. "I apologise for my colleague. As Garalandian champion, custom affords him the right to uncontrolled and occasionally thoughtless speech."

"I understand it is the tradition in many royal households," Asti said. "Only such people are usually known as fool, or jester."

Barag's face briefly suffused red before he exploded in a horse-like laugh. He squeezed Asti to his chin. "Wench, you have the courage of a man."

Mesmerised, Maryan remained frozen until another girl nudged her into movement. She took the dirty dishes down to the kitchen and returned with a tray of pudding bowls. The Ambassador's gaze followed her, his fingers stroked his beard and she noticed his full lips buried within the dark bristle. Stella would ponder kissing such a mouth. The thought made Maryan glance away to cover her blush.

At the end of the table, she felt the eyes of one of the young guards burning into her. Framed with black curling hair, his square face wrinkled as he flashed a smile. Maryan walked straight into a servant coming through the door. She ran down the corridor, her heart pounding, thankful the meal was over.

After service and the tot of spirit, Madame Ferani laid her hand on Maryan's arm. "Girl, I must speak with you." She beckoned her into the small room the cook used as an office. Two brimming shot glasses appeared. Maryan couldn't refuse, but nursed it rather than throwing it back the way the cook suggested.

"You've been investigating the disused rooms," Madame Ferani said without preamble. "You mustn't stray in there, it's dangerous."

"Dangerous?"

"Odd things happen in that wing. People hear voices."

"The dead don't visit us, or my mother would have come to see me."

"Not if she isn't dead."

"Asti the Red says she is." Maryan paused remembering the picture. "Madame Ferani, what made her hate my mother so much?"

The cook refilled her glass and gestured for Maryan empty to hers. Dark shadows cloaked the woman's face. "She would. That scar." she ran her nail down her cheek. "Your mother almost cut her face off. Asti was supposed to go to the games in Bara. It was only a training session, but your mother sliced Asti so badly she took months to recover, by which time, Amara had won the honour."

"And vanished?"

"If Asti hadn't been lying in a hospital bed, all would have suspected her of revenge." The cook pressed her splayed hand across her heart. "Remember I'm from Bara. I know the chaos her vanishing caused. If some man had taken her, do you think he could refrain from boasting?" She shook her head. "Don't give up hope that she'll return."

What could inspire somebody to harm a blade-sister? Could she ever hurt Sami?

"Now remember, stay out of those rooms."

Half way along the corridor, Maryan glanced back. She wanted another look at the picture and nothing was going to stop her enjoying this secret. All she had was the recollection of her mother's crushing embrace. A fading memory filled with the smell of metal polish and leather, not even a voice remained.

After checking that the cook was no longer watching, she lifted a candle from a table, clicked open the doorway and crept into the servant passage. Wrapped in darkness, the candlelight threw weird shadows around her.

In the abandoned suite, moonlight spilled from the windows. It carved a shadow across the floor leaving much of the room cloaked in gloom. Maryan tiptoed quietly over the ragged carpet aware that if anybody saw her she'd be added to the tales of ghosts.

Voices filtered down from the apartments above. Surely, whispers working their way from other chambers weren't the long-feared phantoms?

The picture captured a private moment, two women enthralled with each other. Although easily visible in the moonlight, Maryan held the candle high, trying to fathom the meaning behind the devotion they shared. Could her mother truly have injured her friend deliberately?

The flame danced in a draught and the runes arching over their heads rippled, changing shape. Maryan spun, wondering if somebody was playing a trick on her. Nobody else was in the room. Scared she'd find the picture had come to life, she turned slowly back to the canvas.

Nothing had changed. The women remained frozen, staring into the distance above her head. She raised the candle and once more, the runes shifted, forming letters.

Now you are Queen – forgive me, A.

It felt like a voice had whispered from the grave. What debt of honour did either of them owe to Etelan?

A banshee screamed! Maryan whirled, extinguishing the flame. The sound died. Breathing - rasping breathing surrounded her. She held her breath and the noise stopped. It had been her own fear-filled panting.

Maryan crept on tiptoe back to the doorway. "Is somebody there?" she whispered. Her voice came out cracked and thin.

An awful, venomous howl echoed through the deserted rooms.

She hefted the candlestick and stepped in front of the open door. "Fleur, if that's you, I'm going to give you such a kicking."

Her moment of bravery failed. Wicked green eyes flashed close to the floor rushing towards her. The mad Queen was coming.

A desperate voice pleaded, not aloud, but inside her head, *'Help me.'* Something hit her leg, bounced off and scurried by. The glowing eyes blinked. The hissing phantom struck with tooth and claw ripping her skin before squeezing past.

"Jasper!" Maryan cursed. The voice in her head squealed a frantic call. *'Help me!'* Maryan chased the scrambling cat. If the Queen rode behind his eyes tonight, she'd get a shock.

In the end room, she saw Jasper bat a huge rat viciously into the corner. The rat darted to escape, but Jasper caught its leg. Maryan's head rang with the scream of agony. *'I'm doomed, help me.'* She tried to kick the cat away. He twisted, dropping his prize and spitting furiously.

"If you're in there my Queen, I'm sorry." She swung the candlestick and connected. Barely alive, the rat struggled to haul itself to freedom. Jasper dived for the fallen animal, but Maryan blocked him. Doubt flickered, fight or flee. Jasper decided. His scowl smoothed and with his tail held high, prowled out of the room.

Maryan knelt to inspect the rat, wondering how it had spoken to her. She gathered the near dead animal into a sling formed out of her blouse.

Back in their dormitory, Kait sat at the communal table with a ball of light glowing above her head. "What's happened now?" she said, aghast at the blood seeping through Maryan's clothes.

"Not me, this." Maryan let go of the makeshift sling tipping the bundle of fur and gore onto the table.

"Have a care!" Kait hissed. "These books are ancient. They shouldn't be here." She gathered them lovingly onto the end of her bed before squatting to study the rat. "Can I have it? I've never had a castle rat to dissect."

"Dissect? No, he's still breathing, at least I think it's a he."

Sliding a wooden stick from her loose bun of red hair, Kait moved the rat carefully. "Yes, it's male, but only just. What happened to him?"

"Jasper."

“In that case, I’m honour bound to save him, aren’t I. You know it’s kinder to kill him. He’s going to lose this leg and the other won’t work well.”

“But I can hear him.” Maryan dug her fingers into her temples. “He’s begging me to help him. I can’t simply let him die.”

“It’s true then, these rats *are* that powerful.” Kait cradled its tiny ribcage, shifting the rat gently from side to side. “Their telepathy is legendary. Half the people of Serenia can supposedly hear them. They’re extremely intelligent. Come on then, my little specimen, we won’t give up easily.”

Chapter 4

As the men emerged through the Tunnel of Heroes, their oiled, heavily muscled bodies glinted in the morning sun. Each wore a leather kilt and bore a sword in a back-mounted scabbard. They marched two abreast, followed by a craggy-faced, older guard. He nodded an acknowledgement to Asti, before directing his squad to the far side of the arena.

Asti's puckered socket swept the class, quelling the excitement rippling through the girls. "I thought you'd welcome the opportunity to observe other fighting techniques. Therefore, I've agreed with their force leader to share the arena." Her glare held them silent. "If I can be confident you won't embarrass Serenia with your inept style, I might arrange a couple of trial bouts later."

"I wouldn't object to a trial bout," Stella muttered.

"One of them appears more interested in somebody over here than in his training," Sami whispered and nudged Maryan.

The puppy-eyes of the shaggy-haired youth from the dining room were fixed on her. He beamed the moment she turned in his direction.

"Looks like an ape with a grin. Come on, raise your guard." Sami swung both blades into a high attack. Maryan's own swords flashed, dividing Sami's. She forced them wide and trapped Sami's neck between the training blades with a swooping flourish.

"Showing off for somebody?" Sami winked.

At the end of training, Asti spoke to the older guard before calling the class across the arena. She gestured for them to form a semi-circle facing the four men. The force leader had been working the soldiers hard, filling the air with the musk of sweat. When Maryan peeked at the young guard, something moved inside her.

"Force Leader Tolan, will allow me to use his protégés here to demonstrate our style differences. I think this should prove interesting. We've agreed first blood, but no penetration."

Maryan glanced at Stella who widened her eyes, feigning innocence.

"Justin, are you agreed?" Tolan, the rugged-faced force leader, asked. The taller, darker youth nodded. "Fredrick?" The shorter guard flicked a nervous smile at Maryan before nodding his response.

Justin wore his black hair cropped into a velvet cap. His body appeared assembled from slabs of muscle that slid easily under his tanned skin. Several long scars ran along his biceps. A dominant nose and brow framed eyes that matched the blue of the sky.

Fredrick had wide shoulders that made his neck run straight up into his head. In contrast to Justin's smooth skin, a triangle of hair covered his chest tapering into a line down his washboard stomach. His arms bulged with every movement.

"It is an ape!" Sami hissed. "I think he's hairier than Rose."

Maryan couldn't answer. Frogs she didn't remember swallowing were bouncing inside her stomach making it hard not to squirm.

The two young guards tipped their heads in rapid discussion before moving to either side of Asti.

Holding her attention focused in the distance, Asti's blades spun in slow circles. Justin ducked forward, his sword carving an arc just below knee height. She rose from the floor. One foot kicked the weapon from his hand, the other hit his ear, sprawling him sideways. Her sword sliced a neat line across his bicep drawing a trickle of blood.

"Justin, you're dead," Force Leader Tolan barked.

Fredrick, the shorter guard, unleashed a frenzied, two-handed assault, his heavy blade crashed Asti's defence aside. He spun, his sword slashing towards her scalp. The tutor blurred, moving her weight sideways guiding his attack into the sand. Her sword swept up, almost catching him, but his body snaked away easier than his bulk would suggest possible.

They circled, feint within feint, Asti's lightning-quick blades seeking an opening, but always rebuffed by Fredrick's powerful defence.

Following a lightning fast manoeuvre, Asti's ankle twisted and she stumbled, apparently out of control. Fredrick held back, only to find his chivalry rewarded when her trip turned into a roll. She drew her blade across his thigh. Mouth open, he threw his arms wide in appeal to the force leader.

"Good bout." Asti brushed the sand off her arms and slapped Fredrick on his shoulder.

Tolan turned his battered features to his own men and the class. "What did you learn?"

"You can't trust a woman," Justin, the taller, more poised youth grinned at the class of girls.

Asti's chilling stare wiped the smile off his face. She allowed an ominous silence to grow before a bark of laughter sprang from her lips. "Almost right. In battle, never hold back. See a thing through regardless of what you imagine is happening." Her sword flashed to his throat. "And never trust a woman."

She swept her cloak around her shoulders. "Force Leader Tolan, once young Fredrick has been tended to, we should schedule some more bouts." She searched along the class. "Rose, escort this guard to the infirmary."

Excited chatter bubbled amongst the girls. Maryan leant against the tiles, grateful for their cooling surface. She suspected the bathhouse would have steamed without flames in the boilers.

"I think Nasti is getting old. She almost took a beating then," Fleur said, her voice strident. "That hairy guard is their youngest ever blade-master, but he shouldn't be able to hold off a virgin that way."

"I agree," Stella purred. "Maybe if it had been one of the other 'virgins' he wouldn't have fought so hard." She leered wickedly at Maryan. "It looks like you have an admirer."

Sami crinkled her nose. "All that hair! Can you imagine that pressed against you?"

Maryan could and the thought set the frogs flip-flopping against her pelvic bone. She felt panic tightening her throat at the idea of having to serve on the tables. Maybe she could be ill.

Almost reading her mind, Stella threw a sponge to get Maryan's attention. "Do they eat with the Queen? Are you going to be seeing Justin and what was it?"

"Fredrick," two girls chimed.

Unable to speak, Maryan grimaced and threw the sponge back.

“Why did they choose you?” Stella shook her head. “I’m sure I could have done a better job.” She stood up, flicked her damp hair over her shoulder and pretended to spill a glass of wine onto Maryan. “Oops, oh, My Lord, let me clean the stain.” She ran the sponge between Maryan’s breasts. “But it seems to be down here.” She wiped across Maryan’s stomach, reaching lower.

Maryan laughed, put her toe against her friend’s shoulder and pushed her over.

Stella dropped inelegantly onto the wet floor. Naked, she pouted, resting with her arms behind her. “I bet his young lordship wouldn’t have rejected me like that.”

Making her way to the kitchens, Maryan studied herself in the mirror at the far end of the corridor. She hated her walk, the way her skirt hung and when she pushed her shoulders back, the lack of any curves beneath her white blouse.

“I hoped this was your route to the palace.”

As Fredrick uncurled out of the window seat, every muscle rippled along the length of his legs. The bandages on his thigh stood out as a line beneath the fabric of his tight hose. Maryan tried to avoid staring at the bulge a handbreadth above.

“Did they sort things?” she said.

“I insisted they leave a scar.” A rueful smile touched his lips as he ran his hand back through his hair.

“Why?”

“A memento of the day I faced Asti the Red. I’ve idolised her since I first lifted a blade.”

“She only won with a low trick.”

"She beat me and taught us all a lesson."

"I hoped you'd trounce her."

"If you knew how good she is." Fredrick's admiration glowed. "Each time I stepped up my attack, she just matched me. I'd never equal her. She's marvellous. You're so lucky to have her."

"She's ridden my back for as long as I can remember. You can have her, if you want."

The frogs in her stomach settled. "I've got work to do. We can't have your lordships waiting, can we?" His face was too square to be attractive and his arrogance annoyed her. "Besides, if you rush you might get to sit next to wonderful Asti the Red."

"What?" Fredrick grabbed her arm. "I've lingered here for an age in the hope of meeting you."

"Life is full of disappointments isn't it?" She pulled free, forcing herself to glide, rather than stomp the length of the corridor.

During service, she could sense Fredrick urging her to look in his direction. She averted her eyes only to meet the ambassador's dark stare. He appeared completely absorbed, studying her with the same piercing intensity as Kait examining a specimen. She found it difficult to keep her attention turned from both of them, but managed to avoid dropping any plates and welcomed the shot of spirit Madame Ferani offered.

Night shrouded the corridor and only a single candle illuminated each stretch. She ran her hand along the wall, deftly finding the concealed latch to click the door open. Even though it might be silly, she wanted to feel like a normal girl, telling her mother that she'd met a boy, fallen for him and made a fool of herself.

She slipped inside, turned and bumped into a broad-shouldered figure.

"I insist you speak to me," Fredrick said.

"I'm tired. Leave me alone."

He squeezed into the space and swung the door shut. The pitch black of the passage closed around them concealing everything. Maryan could hear him breathing.

"I've never met anybody like you," he said.

In the silence, she felt the growing pressure to say something. A different kind of tension grew. She'd heard about these moments, but hadn't imagined having to face them. She waited, hardly daring to breathe.

"You are still there, aren't you?" Fredrick asked.

"I'm here."

"Can I kiss you?"

"Why?"

"I know nothing of courtly ways, but isn't that what we're supposed to do?"

Did she want to? Her pounding heart threatened to break through her ribcage. She wondered if he could hear it. He took her in his arms. His mouth searched for hers. He tasted of wine. Caressing beneath her plait, he slipped his tongue between her lips. She explored his mouth with hers, relishing the sensations before breaking the kiss.

"I thought you knew nothing?" she said, trying to keep her voice calm.

"I said I knew nothing of courtly ways. I was raised on a farm and know enough about …"

Maryan relaxed against the slabs of his chest. "Fredrick, I'm a virgin, this was my first kiss with a man."

"Then we'll learn things together won't we." His mouth found hers again, his tongue probed and she moulded against him. Panic rose when his hand slipped from her waist to her breast. Why hadn't the gods granted her even half of the luscious flesh a woman should have? Once he sampled her flat chest he'd run a mile. She gripped his arm, but failed to stop his exploration. He touched her nipple, awakening a yearning that shot through her body.

The bulge pressing against her hip emphasised his excitement. Uncertain, she stroked the muscles beneath his jacket. She paused. He shifted to make a space between them. Her fingers skimmed across the tight fabric of his hose finding the length of his erection. It felt as thick as her wrist. Breathless with anticipation, she rested her head against his shoulder. His hand ran down her back fumbling to gather her skirt.

She grabbed his forearm, stopping him. "Not here. Not now, this isn't what I want." She heard the words, but wasn't sure she meant them. If he insisted, could she stop him? Would she? His breathing was ragged, hot on her neck. She could hear his heart pounding. His fingers dug into the skin beneath her skirt. "Please?" she whispered.

Fredrick sighed, releasing the fabric. "What is this place?" he asked. His voice sounded husky in the darkness.

"A servant passage. The palace is riddled with them."

"Where were you going?"

Maryan gripped his hand. "This is a secret part of me. Don't laugh." Running her fingers along the stonework, she opened the door leading into the abandoned suite. Moving stealthily, she guided him through the shadow-draped rooms until they reached the painting. "I found this."

"Who's the other woman?"

"My mother, Amara the Magnificent."

"Really! Amara, the vanishing hero, was you mother. What was she like?"

She shrugged. "In Serenia we go into an academy as young children. I knew her, but didn't."

"And your father, where's he?"

"We never know who that is. The handmaidens plan the bloodlines using visitors from other lands."

"What! They're led from woman to woman like prize bulls around a village?" Fredrick coughed. "That's awful. I thought women wanted romance, not sex with strangers."

"We don't … you know, have sex. The handmaidens collect the semen and gift it to a warrior.

Shaking his head, Fredrick grimaced. "I can't see how that works."

"Trust me, if a handmaiden is assigned to gather your seed, you'll not argue. They train from birth in seduction."

Standing behind her, he hugged around her waist. The warmth of masculine closeness felt good. She turned within his embrace to savour another kiss. His breathing quickened and his arms locked tight around her.

“I have to go,” she said and broke free.

When Maryan eased the door open, Sami’s snoring was the only sound in the dormitory. Stella would be in the town and Kait was working in the Infirmary. She slipped into her friend’s bed, burying her face into the sweet smelling curls filling the pillow. Sami rolled over to return her kiss.

“Have you …” Sami whispered.

Maryan didn’t want to talk, but slipped under the covers. She found her friend’s nipple and teased it with her tongue. Sami’s nails traced up her back, urging her to suck more roughly, drawing the hardening flesh into her mouth. She trailed her hand over Sami’s smooth body, sliding across the strip of trimmed hair.

Sami reached up to grip the top of the bed, surrendering herself completely to Maryan’s dominance. Driven by swirling passion and rapt in the scent of desire, she tasted Sami’s skin, skimming her tongue across her friend, sliding lower.

Her thoughts flared in a kaleidoscope of wild images. Visions of yielding to Fredrick’s lust collided with the tangle beneath the woollen blanket. Arousal beyond imagining demanded satisfaction. Memory of his wine-flavoured tongue and the bristle of his chin mixed with the soft moistness of Sami’s body. Wrapped around her friend, she urged Sami farther into wild abandon. She responded. Her hips rolled, forcing Maryan against her. Nothing existed outside their entwined limbs. The sensation of her friend’s climax beneath her exploded through her own body, drenching her with a wave of ecstasy.

Maryan lay sated for an age beneath the blankets, tracing her fingers languidly around Sami's enviable curves.

"A liaison with the gorilla?" Sami said. Maryan nodded. She had her head against Sami, listening to the pounding of her friend's heart. Sami drew her from beneath the covers to stare into her eyes. "Still blade-sisters?"

"Thrippas, yes."

Chapter 5

Blue sky arched over the arena walls and the bright, early morning sunlight carved shadows across the sand covered killing floor. The girls emerged to find a large training frame erected just beneath the royal box. Tiny coloured loops hung from the cross-members of the structure at various heights.

Asti gestured with her sword for them to line up. "The Amaran defence technique. Not actually created by, but used to great effect by the mother of our class member." Asti paced along the line of girls. Leaving her red cloak hung on the side of the wooden training frame, her breastplate and greaves gleamed in the sunlight. By midday, the arena would be warm, but Maryan couldn't decide if it was the chill in the air, or the way Asti spat her mother's name that raised the shiver along the fine blonde hair on her skin.

The tutor set her twin blades into a slow circular motion. They spun faster, a faint thrum betraying the speed. "The objective is not simply spinning the blade, but retaining control of the kill potential of each weapon. The swords froze with the tip of one a hairsbreadth from a girl's nose, the other resting on the throat of the girl alongside her. "Total control."

Asti entered the frame and swept her swords into a blur. "Give me a colour."

"Red," somebody said.

"Green," called another.

The blades stopped with their tips each through a loop, one red and the other green. Asti repeated the trick several times before stepping away from the frame. "Later, you shall try to achieve the same, however, first, rotation. Spread out around the arena." Drawing their swords, each member of the class moved to a clear area. Asti demonstrated the basic technique. "And then … strike!" She froze with her blades poised, one to the side and one directly ahead.

Maryan held her arms locked rigid, dreading what was coming when they moved to the next phase. Asti would choose her from the line, sneer at her awful attempts and force her to endure the laughter she coaxed from the class. At times like this, she hated her famous mother. Scuffing her feet in the arena floor, she whipped the swords back into rotation, freeing her mind to wonder what it felt like to stand in the arena amidst the cheers of a thousand people. She glanced at Fleur, imagining her lying in the sand, blood pumping from her throat. No, she changed the image. Begging for mercy, but not dead, Maryan felt better with that. The movement warmed her and sweat slicked her skin. Her forearms ached each time they jerked the momentum of the blades to an instant stop.

Finally, Asti signalled a halt. "And now for the frame. Who's first?" Asti retrieved her red cloak, swirling it around her shoulders. She settled her ebony fists on her hips. Her attention shifted to Maryan, then passed along the line. "Why not Fleur? Let's see what our budding blade-master can do."

The Queen's daughter stood in the centre of the frame, grinning confidently. Her twin swords moved, whistling and glittering in the sun.

"Blue, orange," Asti barked.

The swords lashed out, flicking two rings away. Fleur scowled at the tittering class before whipping her blades back into motion.

"Yellow, green."

The spinning rings danced away.

"If the best in class cannot penetrate, I shudder regarding the safety of Serenia."

A shout rang across the arena floor "Class Leader!" A young girl in a white dress hurried towards the group. Maryan recognised her as an apprentice healer.

Asti held her hand up and marched across the arena to meet the girl. The message the healer whispered changed the tutor into a stone-faced image of simmering fury.

"Sami, to me." Asti surveyed the class. "Fleur, you're in charge. Test each girl with the rings and make them work." She started to walk away and then stopped. "Maryan, to me also, don't dawdle, keep up." With her fists clenching and releasing and her red cloak flowing behind, Asti stormed through the Tunnel of Heroes. They marched into The Academy, along the corridor and into the Infirmary. The reek of cleaning fluid permeated everything. Doorways led off into small wards and staff in white robes moved quietly between the rooms.

Asti held out her hand. "Your blades." Her grim expression invited no discussion. Both girls presented their swords hilt first and she motioned for them to sit on a bench. "There has been a terrible incident. Sami, there's no easy way to say this, Arlaine is dead."

"How?" Sami said. Her words cut off in a choke. "I'm the one going into danger. She's safe. What could have happened?" She tore the leather tie from her hair and twisted it. He face contorted in sobbing grief, her streetwise composure evaporated, leaving her as vulnerable as a newborn. Maryan's emotions tumbled, aching for release. She grabbed Sami, hugging her, agonised by every retching sob wracking her friend.

Asti stood parade ground rigid in front of them, allowing them time before speaking. "I am going to take you to her and then we shall seek answers."

They went into a side room where a healer waited close to a body draped with a sheet. Asti motioned for Sami to approach the bed. "It is important that you see her, but don't let this taint your memory. Her spirit is now free and she's in no pain." Asti drew the cover back.

Lifeless, with her normally immaculate makeup wiped away, Arlaine's perfect figure lay on the table. Maryan felt her legs sag again. Her stomach heaved uncontrollably at the bruises covering the corpse.

Sheelan, the head of the Handmaidens uncurled from a chair in the corner. Even taller than Maryan, the woman wore a simple white robe cinched at her waist by a golden chain. Ash blonde hair tumbled either side of her slim, tear-streaked face. "She fought him fiercely, but he beat her into submission."

"Who?" Sami asked.

A nod passed between the handmaiden and Asti.

"The Garalandian champion, Barag."

"He's already dead." Sami leapt for the door. "Get off me!" she squealed. A male healer caught Sami in a controlling hold. "Let go, or you'll pay as well." She squirmed violently against the restraint, crashing her forehead into his face. Another male healer grabbed her from behind and clamped a cloth across her nose and mouth.

Maryan ran to help, but Asti blocked her, catching her in a steel-hard grip. "As selfish as your damned mother. Don't think, just act."

"You're mad. Everything that spills from you is about my mother. Sami's my friend and I'm with her. That man's dead." Maryan clenched her fists to beat Asti aside, but the dark-skinned tutor kept her strong arms around Maryan's subduing her against the unyielding breastplate.

"You're here to help, not hinder," she hissed into Maryan's ear. "Can we find somebody in your family who understands friendship?" The odours of the tutor's body filled Maryan's senses. She smelled the same as her mother had, leather and metal polish. Maryan calmed down.

Asti relaxed her grip. "If either of you go against Barag, you'll die. He's an honoured visitor and a champion. Help your friend."

Maryan slumped, unable to understand how to help. Every part of her cried out to seek revenge. She stared past Asti, yearning to hold her blade-sister and jealous of Sheelan cradling Sami in her distress.

"Tonight, Sami will be taken from The Academy and put into a safe location. It could be some weeks before she can return. You will act as if nothing has changed. This is important. Be with your friend, love her, let her ramble. It's what she needs." Maryan felt numb, unable to speak. The idea of serving in the same room as the animal who had done this to Arlaine filled her with dread.

The frosty atmosphere in the dining room sent a shiver through Maryan. Wine flowed and Barag sat next to Asti proudly displaying the scoring on his forearms.

"She came at me like a wild cat. I had no choice." He rolled the linen shirt back over his muscled arms as he addressed the room. "That's the trouble with you women. You fight with your hearts, not with strategy. A man thinks things through and then uses overwhelming strength. A woman will always lose when she attacks a man."

Fredrick risked a downcast peek at Maryan. The Queen had banned the guard from leaving their accommodation until the matter became fully resolved. Fully resolved? Maryan kept herself focused on the serving dish in her shaking hands. So many tales of how women suffered at the whim of men and now, Arlaine, better the path of the legion than torture.

"Possibly your fighting style is different to ours," Asti's strident voice filled the silence. "Why don't we perform a demonstration match? You and I should meet in the arena to show how our styles differ."

Barag glanced to the top table, where the Ambassador wore an unreadable expression. His wide, padded shoulders twisted as he spoke to the Queen. "Of course, it must be controlled. We cannot risk any chance of injury."

"Of course not." Etelan tossed her unbound hair back over her shoulder. "We shall have a demonstration showing that our nations can work together. Such a bout might wash away the taint of this unfortunate incident."

Flicking the hilts of Asti's twin blades, Barag sneered. "Will you use these toys, or bring a proper sized weapon to the bout?" His laugh shook the room. "Maybe you women should stick to sewing, you know, needles, pins and scissors." He coughed red wine down his chin and wiped his mouth on the tablecloth.

When she entered the hidden rooms, Maryan's heart fluttered like a trapped bird. With his curfew, she wouldn't meet Fredrick tonight, but she sneaked into the shadowed room anyway, hoping to find peace by sitting with the picture.

A wine-fuelled bellow hammered through from the floor above. "Of course I can beat her. I'm going to put another set of scars onto the gruesome witch. Somebody has to teach her obedience. Thrippas, the men of this land need a good kicking for allowing their women to get so out of line."

"This is intolerable," The Ambassador's deep tones rumbled. "Once again, Asti the Red blocks my plans."

"What do you mean … again?"

"She's got in the way before, not that she knows it. It must look like an accident, but she mustn't come out of the arena. Make a show of things, before I bind her defenceless. What were you thinking when you beat that woman to death?"

"It was the Queen's own daughter who tricked me. The darling princess got me in a clinch, but refused to go farther. She had me pumped up, not thinking straight. She said the handmaidens would do anything I asked. The little ferret even pointed out the girl." He paused and when he finally spoke, he had a proud tone to his words. “Gorath, she fought, almost frightened the life out of me.”

Stunned with grief, Maryan sat in silence. Fleur had instigated the attack. It couldn’t be possible. More than that, the Ambassador would use magic to help his champion. Regardless of her feelings about the tutor, Nasti had to be warned. She hurried to the dormitories to find Steppis.

“You can’t see her. She will be away all night with Sami’s mother. She needs to focus before the match.”

“But the things I heard, what can I …”

“You can do nothing,” Steppis said. “You are to tend the royal box during the bout. You will be there to support the Queen.” The old tutor ran the flat of her hand across her short grey hair. “Now, will you help to gather your friend’s belongings? She’ll be shipping out of here before morning.”

Working in a trance, Maryan loaded Sami’s clothes into a crate that had appeared in the centre of their dorm. Kait helped, but Maryan couldn’t bring herself to talk.

Finally, Kait exploded and kicked the wooden box. “Speak to me. None of this is my fault.”

“I just wonder if I should be helping Sami. I feel helpless.” Maryan pressed Sami’s perfumed vest to her nose before folding it neatly. “Why didn’t you come to calm Sami? You weren’t even there for us.”

“Why didn’t I help?” Kait’s tone stayed low, devoid of emotion. “You haven’t asked, but you judge me. I drove myself into the ground for her. I made Arlaine’s body look presentable and I did it on my own. I could have used some support then.

Instead, I worked until I passed out. By the time I'd recovered, you'd been and gone." Her voice rose in fury as she pounded her chest with her tiny fist. "I healed dead flesh. I straightened her broken limbs. I repaired the gash ripping her mouth up to her cheekbone. They all said it couldn't be done, but I did it, for Sami. So don't say I didn't do anything."

Maryan crushed Kait in a hug. "I'm sorry, I want to lash out at somebody and I'm forbidden to do it."

"I think Asti has that in hand, don't you?"

"She's in danger, the Ambassador is going to hold her with magic and let Barag carve her into pieces."

"Then I'll be close by, and if that happens, I'll stop him."

"He's a master magician. Could you do it?"

The aura that flared around Kait made Maryan step back. "I've been studying. Learning things the feeble-minded healers here think are dangerous. Oh yes, I can stop him, that I promise."

"**Could** you give me a hand with these?" Maryan shouted to the guard standing by the entrance to the arena.

"You girls are getting too cheeky, by far," the guard called back. "It's going to be a busy one today. I've already stopped three people from sneaking in."

Maryan shrugged. "I get enough of Nasti during school-time without being forced to watch her on a day off."

The guard took one of the cushions from the pile in Kait's arms to feel the softness. "We don't want those poor rugged men to get numb bums sitting with Etelan, do we?" She winked at Maryan. "I hear they have quite nice little peaches."

Maryan felt herself flush. "I wouldn't know …"

The guard laughed and waved them through.

Once inside the arena, Maryan started to put the cushions out on the chairs.

Kait peered over the edge of the box. "I'm going to claim this seat here." She squeezed Maryan in a warm embrace. "Don't worry so much. Nobody will see me until the crowds start to arrive. You get back to arranging things up here."

Word of the bout had spread and the arena soon started to buzz with chatter as the people of the town scurried to find seats. As the arena filled, those standing around the top tier looked in danger of tumbling onto the lower levels and attendants had to force people to leave.

The five guards from Garalandia sat behind the Queen and the Ambassador. Fredrick's wide shoulders twisted as he tried to get Maryan's attention. Beside him, bobbing and agitated, Justin searched the crowd until he fixed on a flash of colour in the public gallery. Stella grinned up from the seats and blew a kiss.

The Ambassador shifted around in his seat to admonish the two young guards, but Fredrick was too absorbed to notice. Mordacai's expression darkened when he realised Maryan was the subject of his attention.

Oblivious to the exchange, Etelan craned her neck to look out across the crowd. "I don't know why there is such interest. Surely the people appreciate that we couldn't allow anything too serious to occur." She straightened the cloak trimmed with white fur on her shoulders.

A murmur rippled around the arena when Asti emerged from the tunnel. Her back-mounted scabbards were empty and she carried a small table with a delicate wicker basket balanced on top. She placed it in the sand beneath the Queen's box and bowed.

Barag burst from the shadow of the tunnel into the grey Serenian morning. He brandished a large sword in his fist and upon his left arm wore a round, buckler-style shield. He waved to the crowd, but an abusive silence greeted him. Unperturbed, he crossed the killing floor to stand alongside Asti. His smile slipped into a puzzled frown. "What's going on here, I thought we came to fight."

Asti curled her hand to cup her face, raising her voice theatrically. "Why Barag, all I'm doing is what you suggested." She flipped the wicker lid open and delved amongst the rags. "Needles, pins …" She waved a strip of cloth with a dozen tiny slivers twinkling along its length. She rummaged again, "and scissors!" A small pair of sowing scissors flashed in her hand. They spun above her head, until she opened her palm letting them click shut. A thumb-long point glinted from her fist.

The arena erupted in laughter. Barag whirled, growling up at the people staring at him. His massive sword crashed onto the table, shattering it into spinning shards. "You mock me, you all mock me."

Dropping her voice, Asti spat her next words. "She fought like a wildcat to protect her honour. Was she any better armed than I?" Her hand flashed and the scissors ripped Barag's cheek.

“Bitch,” Barag swung for Asti’s throat, but she ducked the blow. The tiny blades lashed out, gouging his arm.

The Ambassador impassively watched his comrade on the arena floor. “Etelan, you said nothing dangerous. What tricks will the woman pull next?”

“Surely, you don’t fear for your champion?”

“He’s an animal. Once he starts to fight, he loses all inhibition. I hope she can handle that.”

Barag attempted to slice Asti’s legs from beneath her. She leapt, kicking in a high arc over the blade. She feinted with a jab, making him duck, then slapped him sideways, leaving a line of needles sticking out of his cheek. He brushed them away. Crouching, Asti stalked forward, head low and arms wide, her small pair of scissors red with Garalandian blood.

Lashing out clumsily, Barag attacked again. Asti slipped beneath the sword, caught his wrist and struck his elbow with her opposite palm. The huge blade dropped to the floor as the joint snapped.

Fear-filled, Barag threw an imploring look to the Ambassador in the box. Mordacai’s fingers bent in a wave of dismissal. He tried to run, but Asti crashed him against the arena wall. Her feet left the floor and both heels hit his face. Blood poured from his eyes, nose and ears. She dragged the near unconscious champion across the arena by his hair until they stood before the Queen.

Etelan sprang from her seat and gripped the balustrade. “No serious harm! Asti the Red, I command you to cease the bout.”

Asti's skin glistened with her opponent's blood. Her gaze settled, bringing her puckered socket to regard the Queen. She stood with one hand pointed to the man on the ground. "This animal murdered a citizen of Serenia. By ancient law, any Serenian is bound to execute him."

"Times change!" The Queen pounded on the edge of the arena.

Asti dropped to one knee and stabbed twice, picking out Barag's eyes with the scissor blades. He writhed and screamed. She kicked his jaw to straighten him out before raising her hands high above her head.

"Stop her!" Etelan pleaded with the Garalandian guard. Tolan and his men remained stone-faced and motionless.

On the arena floor, Asti dropped her full weight through her knee on Barag's windpipe. A short stab wedged her tiny scissors deep into the man's left eye. She stood up and pounded them into his brain with her heel.

In the silence that followed, she pointed at the Queen. "If you won't honour our traditions, maybe it's time for us to change the leader of our nation." Keeping her back rigidly straight, she marched purposefully across to the shadow of the tunnel.

Nobody moved and nobody cheered. The body of the fallen man twitched in a growing pool of blood.

Chapter 6

The kitchen felt gloomy with less than half of the lamps burning to illuminate it. A lone figure worked at the far end of the kitchen preparing a meal. Madame Ferani brushed a dusting of flour off her face with the back of her hand and frowned. "Didn't they pass the message?"

Maryan shook her head.

"There's no service for our guests, the Queen is dining in private."

Lost and unable to react, Maryan stared at the cook.

"Get away with you." She flapped her hands to chase Maryan from the kitchen. "We will require your indispensible services tomorrow, but get back to whatever a girl of your age does at this time of night."

Sometime later, Maryan found herself perched on the windowsill in the hidden rooms, her knees tucked under her chin and her arms clenched around them. She studied the women in the picture and wondered at the brutal arrogance Asti had displayed in the arena. Is that how her mother had been?

"Maryan," Fredrick whispered.

She jumped. Her first urge was to run into his arms, her second was simply to run. Instead, she slipped from the windowsill and folded her arms.

"I'm glad you came. We're returning to Garalandia in the morning. Mordacai has completed his task." He ran his hand back across his hair. "Did you know that your friend, Stella, is coming with us? She's betrothed to Justin."

"I hope she knows what she's getting."

“I think she does. He’s the heir to one of the largest estates in Garalandia.”

“Then I’ll come with you.” She rushed to embrace him, but he cowered as if she brandished a sword.

“I’m to stay away from you.”

“Why?”

“A guard doesn’t ask questions when an ambassador shouts.” He shuffled his feet, avoiding Maryan’s stare.

“What are you not telling me?”

“Tolan says …” His hands twitched, reaching, before dropping to his side. “He said somebody of a higher rank had an interest in you. If I wanted to keep my head on my shoulders, I’d better stay away.”

“What? Who?” She felt herself blanch at the memory of a gaze following her around the banquet room. “Gorath, you don’t mean the Ambassador?” She grimaced. “He’s at least a hundred years old. That’s disgusting.”

Fredrick shrugged. “We do things differently in Garalandia.” He glanced over his shoulder. “I’ve got to go. I’m taking a risk just being here.” He studied her, drinking every feature, before vanishing back through the servant doorway.

The next day, storm clouds hung low across the darkening sky. Maryan waited above the gate to watch the Garalandian party depart. The slow clatter of hooves echoed in the drab morning. Head down and with his broad shoulders slumped under his cloak, Fredrick rode beneath without a glance upward. Maryan felt as if a piece of her was leaving with him. Stella twisted in her saddle to search the crenelated wall, Maryan lifted her hand to wave, but Stella raised her hood and turned away.

Not caring that she was late, Maryan trudged down the stone staircase and slipped into class taking a seat close to the door. The schoolrooms all followed a similar style, rows of individual wooden desks with matching chairs facing a teaching wall and table. She ran her hand across the surface. Her mother, Nasti and even Steppis had possibly sat in the same place. Eons of students had scratched initials and tags into the dark wood, the intertwined scars were rendered most unreadable.

"Will you girls settle?" Steppis slammed her hand flat on her desk, silencing the babbling chatter.

"Please, class leader, what's going to happen to happen to Asti?" a girl asked from the back of the room.

"She's going to be executed," Fleur said. She twisted in her seat and searched the class for approval. "She's too much trouble, always has been. She's an example of all that's wrong with the Serenia."

"That's enough," Steppis barked. "The council will decide what will happen."

"She was right though, wasn't she? We should execute foreigners who break our laws," a girl called Nadine said.

Steppis shook her head. "I don't believe it's a secret Serenia is a dot on this world." She tapped a long cane on the top left corner of the map on the wall. "See us here. This tiny region tucked away riseward of almost everything." She tapped across the map. "To fallward, Garalandia." She indicated the lands on the far right. "Even Walsholm is many times our size."

"But we're the most respected nation," Nadine said.

"Don't be stupid, girl. Use your eyes," Steppis snapped. "Nations like Garalandia and Sudaland could swallow us without a thought." She rapped the cane against the huge expanse to the darkward covering half of the map. "Thrippas help us if Bara decided it wanted our lands. The Emperor has more servants than we have warriors."

"We have the Virgin Legion." Nadine thrust her chin forward.

"Their armies outnumber us. We survive their avarice by negotiation, not by strength."

The door opened and three guards entered. One approached Steppis to hand her a note, the other two surveyed the class.

After folding the note, Steppis nodded once before focusing on Fleur. "These guards will escort you to attend the council."

Fleur's face went white. She started to speak, but paused before straightening her back and marching out of the door as though the guards were her personal escort.

Steppis waited until the door closed before speaking again. "Tomorrow, the civic leaders have called a meeting of the town. There are to be announcements that affect us all." Her attention settled on Maryan. "See me when the others leave. Class dismissed."

All of the girls burst into chatter. Surrounded in the hubbub, Maryan watched her friends filter from the room before making her way to the tutor's desk.

Twisting the note in her stubby fingers, the old warrior studied Maryan. "In the morning, you will return all clothes and equipment to housekeeping. From there, you will follow the instructions Dorrat shall provide. I hope you feel confident of the accusations you made, because both of our futures depend upon it. Dismissed."

After leaving the room, Maryan slumped against the wall, wondering why she had to return her uniform. She hadn't damaged that much. More likely, Fleur had manoeuvred her mother into throwing her out of school completely.

The effect of the oddly tidy dormitory hit her. Kait sat on the edge of her bed, sorting through a pile of books. She used her thumbs to divide her red hair to either side of her face. "What's happened?"

"Something's going on. I think I'm going to be punished for what I heard about Fleur." She lifted Carl, the crippled rat, and snuggled him against her chest. His warm, thumb-thick tail wrapped around her forearm. Avoiding the ruined rear limbs, she eased him to her shoulder. "I've been told to report to Housekeeper Dorrat tomorrow. I wish I knew what was happening."

Knowing how much Kait hated studying her with magic, she hesitated to ask. "The evil that hangs over me, has it diminished now that Asti is imprisoned?"

Kait squinted and immediately rumpled her face. "It's awful, a seething madness swirling ever closer,

I'm surprised you can't feel it. Maybe I shouldn't go."

"No, you must. To study at Idrahail has been your dream."

"There are other paths to wisdom." Kait glanced to the door, cautious of eavesdroppers. "There are great powers hidden in dark places. Perhaps I should be seeking guidance from those, rather than the stuffy traditionalists."

Maryan coughed a laugh and dropped onto the bed. "And when are you leaving?"

"Tonight." Kait tugged her hair back. "I never claimed I could plan."

The empty bunks emphasised how events had suddenly stripped away her friends. She sat opposite Kait, their legs crossed, knees pressed close and their fingers intertwined.

"This should be a time of happiness." Kait shook her head in frustration. "Me heading for Idrahail, Stella getting married, Sami and you off to become heroes. Instead, life feels so chaotic. We're all abandoning you to face whatever Fleur and her mother are planning."

"Don't worry. I'm used to being alone." Maryan gripped her friend's hands tighter.

The long tail tickled, reminding her that Carl sat on her shoulder. His thoughts pushed into hers. *'Alone? I wonder what that feels like.'*

"He's talking to you isn't he. I'm glad I didn't dissect him."

"He wonders what it's like to be alone. A telepathic rat is always chattering with their family."

Kait wriggled close enough to wrap her arms around Maryan. “We are family and we always shall be. I wish I knew what Etelan will announce tomorrow.”

The wagoner collected Kait in the early morning. Once she’d left, Maryan wept in solitude. She doubted ever falling back to sleep, but tumbled into a deep slumber. The room felt cold and empty when she jerked awake. The noise in the corridor meant that people were already heading to the arena.

“Gorath! Of all days.” Maryan dragged a robe over her head, barely taking time to check her hair. She gathered her uniforms and headed for the palace corridor. Outside Dorrat’s office, she calmed herself, remembering the first time she had been here, before tapping on the door.

“Come.”

Maryan heard a scuffle and the door whipped open, dragging her inside still holding the handle. Her stack of uniforms toppled and scattered on the floor.

“Get in here.”

Scrambling on her knees trying to refold her clothes, she found her nose pressed against a silk-clad thigh. Maryan’s previous encounters with, Janice, the Queen’s dressmaker, had been in the palace corridors where the tiny woman bustled along, always in a hurry and usually with her brow creased in anger.

The deep blue dress Janice wore today emphasised her doll-like stature. Darts shaped the bodice from her pinched waist and the fabric flowed in pleats over her hips. The complex lace at the hem swished against the floor when she moved.

“How long have I got?” Janice said, squinting through the window to check the height of the sun. Pursing her lips, she appraised Maryan the way a farmer considered ropey stock.

“Less than three candle bands,” Dorrat said. “This secrecy is driving me mad, I’ve no idea what is being planned. I tell you, these warrior types are going to put me in an early grave.” She crushed a single sheet of paper in her fist. “You are to be prepared as a member of the Queen’s party wearing appropriate attire.”

Using finger and thumb, Janice lifted her thick honey-blonde hair back from her forehead, tossing back over her shoulder. “Follow me.” She guided Maryan through the long storeroom attached to Dorrat’s office. At the far end, they went into a small room surrounded by mirrors. She snapped her fingers and pointed to a chair. “Strip and leave your things there,” she said before vanishing through another doorway.

Confused, Maryan struggled to tug her robe off over her head and waited.

Janice returned clutching a bodice. She tugged it tight around Maryan’s chest. “I’m going to have to piece it,” she muttered and ran from the room.

Whichever way Maryan turned, she found her reflection, naked and repeating into the distance. She hated her body, wide shoulders, slim hips and no breasts. Goose pimples prickled and she gripped her shoulder, hanging her arm across her chest to cover herself.

Wielding a dress and armful of fabric, Janice bustled back into the room. She clucked and mumbled the whole time, but eventually stepped back to indicate she'd finished. Maryan ran her hands over the bodice, admiring the way the makeshift gown fitted. "It's beautiful."

"It'll do for now." Janice sniffed, but her smile showed she appreciated Maryan's pleasure. "Now it's time for you to join the Queen's group at the arena." She nudged Maryan toward the door. "Go girl, the town is waiting."

Maryan tried to hurry, but the full-length dress made running impossible. The ridiculous shoes Janice had forced her to wear caught on every crack in the pavement. She toyed with the idea of prising them off, but knew that she'd never manage to fasten the row of tiny buttons without help. At the arena, she crept into the back of the royal platform. The Queen's head jerked up and down to assess the work of the dressmaker before her eyes creased into a smile. She nodded once and then turned to face out into the crowds.

On the wooden platform in the centre of the floor stood a masked warrior dressed in black. Stripped of her red cloak and draped in a simple white gown, Asti glared around the arena. Alongside Asti, wearing a similar gown Fleur trembled, her downcast face livid white.

Etelan rose, her authority silently commanding the commotion to die down. Only the faint sound of the wind cresting the top wall remained. "My people." She paused, searching, apparently determined to gaze into each face around the stadium, "My people, today I will change lives forever. It is not a decision I take lightly. If I could have avoided much of this, I would have."

"Firstly, for the crimes of sedition and treason, I pronounce the following sentence upon the vagabond who previously walked amongst us using the name, Asti the Red. I banish her from Serenia, exiled without hope of pardon. All lands, chattels and property above personal clothing are relinquished, to be dispersed as I see fit."

The queen gripped the edge of the royal box bleaching her knuckles white with the tension. "For your crime of murder, I sentence you to flogging and humiliation, stripped here before the eyes of any who care to watch and thirty lashes applied to your back."

Around the arena, people gasped. The agony of twenty lashes could kill a person. Thirty may prove a death sentence.

In a single movement, the black-clad warrior tore Asti's gown from her shoulders revealing her long-muscled body. The naked warrior gazed around the arena before turning to grip the cross rail of the platform. After fifteen lashes, her legs shook, at twenty-five, she sagged and the flogging stopped until she hauled herself erect. Each of the last five lashes echoed around the silent arena, the sound of the final wet crack hung on the air long after it fell.

Asti staggered and a guard attempted to assist her from the platform. She accepted the proffered cloak, but refused any assistance.

Etelan, who had stood in silence to watch the punishment spoke again. "My daughter, Fleur, for reasons known only to her, tricked the Garalandian champion with misleading words. This act led to the death of Arlaine, the flower of the handmaidens. More than this, she has wrongly assumed that kinship to the queen grants privilege. This is not so. To her, I hand the sentence of flogging and humiliation. She shall be stripped here before any who care to watch and ten lashes applied."

Fleur's gown was torn away leaving her pale skin glowing in the gloomy daylight. She turned to run, but the attendants wrestled her against the cross-rail of the platform. Two powerful guards gripped her arms, forcing her upright. Each lash ripped a heart-rending scream from her throat. Etelan watched without shedding a tear as the guards dragged the barely conscious Fleur from the scaffold.

The crowd turned in silent expectation when Etelan once more gripped the balustrade. "Friends, people who chose me to lead. I promised to serve without prejudice and favour, but I beg a concession. It is over five years since my close friend, Amara, vanished. No trace of her has ever been established. I ask the people of Serenia to grant me the right to name her my sister. In doing so, I assume familial responsibility for her daughter. If you allow this, I claim Maryan as a child of my line."

Following so soon after the horror they had witnessed, the people of Serenia revelled at the good news. Their cheers filled the stadium.

The Queen proposed to adopt her as a daughter. Maryan sagged almost as Fleur had done. Her vision narrowed into a tunnel of hands beckoning her to the front of the royal box. Etelan wrapped her long fingers around Maryan's biceps before kissing her forehead. She hugged Maryan fiercely and waved to the wildly cheering crowd. Etelan picked out favoured friends for a special wave before turning. "Daughter, come with me," she said over her shoulder.

Maryan followed her to the doorway leading to the private rooms of The Residence. The door opened into a corridor lined with ancient busts perched on white columns. Her fear of clumsiness rose and she wondered how irreplaceable these items might be. Even though a thousand questions pestered to be asked, she remained silent until they reached a large room furnished with low seats. Etelan sat in one and gestured for Maryan to sit opposite.

"I suppose this seems strange to you?" Etelan said.

"I'm speechless. What does it mean? What am I supposed to call you?" Maryan knew she was babbling and breathed to calm her simmering emotions.

"Why not try Auntie when we're alone and Queen Etelan in public." Etelan touched Maryan's knee relieving some of the tension.

"I'm sorry, I didn't realise that you knew my mother. What can you tell me of her?"

"Of course I was never as close as Asti. They grew up together and were blade-sisters until the incident in the arena. Even so, we were close. I should have been part of the escort, but I had to remain due to the trouble at home. It was the time of succession and I had been named a candidate."

Maryan thought of the inscription on the picture and was about to mention it when something stopped her. Instead, she changed her question, "What will happen to Asti now?"

“That woman has been a thorn since birth. She’ll be escorted to the border and cast out. Part of me hopes that she does try to return; then I will do more than flogging.” Etelan’s venom was frightening, but the frown marring her beauty smoothed and a smile filled with sunshine lit up the room. “Of course, Fleur always resented not living in The Residence, but I think I shall move you into a room here. Do you mind leaving your dormitory?”

The idea of returning to the empty dormitory, or getting new roommates so close to graduation frightened Maryan more than she could admit. “But what of Fleur?”

“Evil isn’t she? A total pain,” Etelan stated without a smile. “She’s being sent to a different training academy, a tougher one that will beat the stupid ideas out of her. I hope she’ll return as a daughter to be proud of.” She clapped her hands to summon the housekeeper.

“We’ll be moving my daughter into the rooms close to mine. Please arrange whatever needs to be sorted out with Steppis,” Etelan instructed Dorrat. She leapt to her feet. “Come, I’ll show you around your new home.”

Chapter 7

Maryan cannoned into the solid frame of the Garalandian Ambassador. He staggered under the impact, his face twisting angrily, only smoothing when he recognised her.

"Ambassador! Gorath, I'm so sorry, I just …"

He touched his finger across her lips, forcing her to silence. The corners of his mouth twitched beneath his trimmed beard. "No need. I'm sure it was my fault."

"Sir, it's good to see you again. I'm sorry … I'm late, the Queen has arranged dancing lessons for me in the belief I'll become more graceful."

"If that's the case, I hope that I may soon sample the results." He smiled again, before gripping both her shoulders to move her firmly to one side, stepping the other way in an awkward parody of a dance step.

She watched him continue along the corridor. If the Ambassador was here, did that mean Fredrick had returned? When he'd first left, she'd thought he might write to her. Days had flowed into months before her hopes had faded. Her longing had vanished and she often imagined how she would treat him if he dared to show up again. Had the Ambassador really made Fredrick stay away? Memories of their liaisons in the hidden room still warmed her.

Realising what the Ambassador had just suggested froze her blood faster than a dip in the cold plunge. Stella had always claimed that older men were more fun, but Maryan knew she needed an excuse to get away from for a time. As she ran to the dancing lesson, she prayed to Deepala, the deity of the handmaidens, to preserve her from lustful attention.

Two days later, the goddess of love despatched a dragon to answer Maryan's prayers. The huge beasts travelled starward on their mating migration from the warmer lands. Usually, they moved on, but one had decided to settle and had started taking livestock. Sheep for wool and meat gave a rich income and the farmers bitterly resented anything as mundane as a dragon disrupting business. When this happened, the schools provided teams to support the warriors and help to either frighten the dragon off or kill it.

The wagon ride out onto the farmlands took much of the morning. A cold wind blasted down the ravine leading to the borderland. It whipped Maryan's skin and forced the girls to huddle on the wagon floor.

"My mother says these hunts are the best way to get noticed for your legion of choice," Nadine said. She glanced across at Maryan. "Are you okay?"

Although Maryan nodded, she'd not joined the wagon of volunteers to enhance any selection ambitions she might harbour, but to escape the perils of meeting the Ambassador.

When they arrived at the farm, it was already bustling with soldiers of the various legions preparing for the hunt. The swaggering team members shouted obscenities at anybody who crossed their path. Serenia provided mercenaries to foreign lands to undertake specialist tasks. Some of these women might have worked in the far reaches of Bara or on the other side of Garalandia, along the border with Walsholm. Such postings were often dangerous and those on leave used the hunt as light entertainment.

Where the virgins wore a single plait, other legions had their own tags. Shaved heads, hair worn in snake-like tangles or wild crests dyed in lurid colours. Instead of polished metal, some wore stained leather, where others opted for linked mail. Each legion felt it had the greatest honour to protect and any opportunity to compete with the others provoked fierce loyalty.

The delicious fragrance of cooking wafted on the air. "Spit roast lamb," Nadine said, leaping off the tail of the wagon. Long counters piled with food formed a corridor leading them through to the barn, where they could eat and be briefed.

Despite misgivings about being on the hunt, Maryan's mouth watered at the smell. "Who's providing this?"

"The farmers pay. Let's face it, we can't eat anything like the number of sheep a full sized dragon does. It's good sense for them to encourage us to come back."

One of the farm labourers helping to serve tossed a lick of brown hair back off his forehead and risked a shy smile as he held out a ladle of gravy for Maryan.

"I believe some of these farmers have quite large holdings," a voice behind her said. The rest of the line laughed. "Is yours worth seeing?" The girl stretched across the table to pat the young helper's cheek. Neck red, he dropped his stare. Maryan tried to smile warmly. He flushed even redder, stirring the whole line into a jeer.

"Don't be shy, love. We're not all virgin legion," an anonymous voice shouted.

Clutching her brimming platter, Maryan wound through the crowd into the briefing area. A warrior with a scar running across the top of her shaved head stood at the end of the table.

"Have any of you been on a hunt before?" Silence greeted her words and she held aloft a child's toy dragon. "A dragon is almost the perfect fighting machine." She used a short baton to point to the side of the dragon. "Each flank is armoured. These scales can deflect any shaft or spear." She turned the toy so that the model pointed at them. "They really do breathe fire. Great gouts, hot enough to melt stone. If it hits you, you're not even cooked meat, you're barely a cinder. The only weakness is here." She jammed the baton half way into the toy through the stitching under the dragon's tail. "A dragon has a stomach full of exploding gas and a short passageway up here that leads to it." She grinned at the girls. "Our task is to push a burning spear right up its arse."

"What happens then?" a girl asked.

"If things go right, the dragon explodes. If things go wrong ..." She rubbed her hands together signalling this was all the training they were going to get. "You will work in teams." She gestured at a line of warriors. "Your leader will allocate you a role as either a beater or a baiter. Good luck."

A stocky, bad-tempered looking woman pointed at Maryan "You, you're mine. Get over here." She jerked her thumb to indicate the exit and marched out onto the rolling fields.

Maryan hurried to keep up, following her to join a group of warriors. The woman had short, crimson hair, her tanned shoulders bulked wide beneath a leather jerkin. She wore heavy sandals laced around tree trunk calves bound over the top of woollen leggings. “We’re the Boustan girls, tough academy, tough legion,” she called without glancing back.

The team were already sweating as they unloaded a huge crossbow from a wagon. Maryan gasped at the size of the beams the women hefted with apparent ease.

“Catch,” a warrior said.

Maryan barely had time to react before a quarrel the thickness of a sapling dropped straight at her. She caught the bolt with both arms and staggered under the weight.

“Don’t dither. Bring it over here,” somebody shouted. An angry faced woman with bright yellow hair had wrapped cloth around a similar quarrel. She held it on end, soaking it in oil from a jug.

“I’m Maryan, Serenian Academy.”

“We know who you are,” the warrior interrupted.

“Hello, sister dear.” Fleur slipped from behind the wagon. She’d cut her hair into short spikes and dyed it purple. “Boustan is my new home. I came up with our plan to get the dragon. The other teams will be using sheep or goats for bait, but we’re going to stake *you* out. Nothing attracts a dragon more than a writhing female. Once it’s bent over, we skewer it and win.”

“And what happens to me?” Maryan said, fearing the answer.

Fleur shrugged. A rope looped over her from behind, trapping her arms. An evil smelling cloth was rammed into her mouth. She tried to squirm, but the battle-hardened warriors easily bundled her into the undergrowth.

The Boustan girls had earmarked a corner of the field with a clearing flanked by thick bushes. Four of the team wrestled their monster crossbow into the position, draping it in netting covered with leaves. Two of them hammered stakes into the ground, fixing Maryan spread-eagle, gagged and helpless. She tried to pull free, but the bindings held firm. The crimson-haired leader shouted. “Hey Dogface, you want to make love?”

A broad-backed woman shambled toward them. Her upper lip had a thick shadow of black hair. Her face was a ruined maze of violet scars. A flaccid roll of pale flesh oozed over the waistband of her woollen leggings.

The team-leader smirked. “Since her injury, she doesn’t get enough affection. We tend to have to tie her conquests down for her.”

Dogface dropped on her knees, tore Maryan’s robe open and forced a probing hand between her thighs. The woman’s gurgling chortle sounded both childlike and cruel, a line of drool trickled from her lips.

The mournful wail of a dragon’s call hung on the air.

“Get clear, get under cover!” somebody shouted. Dogface licked Maryan’s cheek before running for the bushes.

A giant shadow swept across the clearing. Gliding on leather wings, the dragon circled. The ground shook as the beast landed close by.

If Fleur wanted her to writhe, Maryan knew she needed to stay motionless. She remained frozen, fighting the urge to struggle against her bindings. At the far side of the clearing, a staked goat bleated. The dragon craned around, drawn in that direction. One set of claws lifted and then the other. Just as the beast squatted to launch, Maryan felt something gouge into her side. She coughed around the gag and squirmed.

Smeared in mud, Fleur grinned from under the bushes nearby. She prodded again using a long branch and then whistled an ear-piercing screech. Once the dragon swung to regard Maryan, Fleur shuffled away into the surrounding undergrowth.

Another team's flaming bolt arced across the field, bouncing off the dragon's side. With a deafening roar, it threw back its head. A voice of pure evil echoed inside Maryan's thoughts. *'Attack? These fleas would attack Tamaar, queen of the dragons, in her brooding ground?'* The beast glided the short distance to where the bolt had launched. Flames raked the bushes, scouring the area down to smouldering earth.

Maryan flinched, hoping the dragon had forgotten her. It wheeled, filling the air, with its fearsome call. The ground shook as Tamaar landed. Eyes glittering with a thousand facets, she stalked closer. *'A girl? For me? Oh, what a treat.'* The dragon's dripping nostrils examined Maryan, choking her with chemical breath. *'Do you feel fear my pretty ...'*

Whether something betrayed the Boustan girls, or Tamaar already knew of their presence, she whirled with unbelievable speed, bathing the concealed crossbow in a wash of flame. She pounced amongst the smouldering bushes. An agonised yell proved that at least one had managed to escape the furnace. Like a dog searching for a lost bone, Tamaar dug furiously, shovelling mounds of earth onto Maryan. A scream pierced the air. The dragon reared, shaking its victim before silencing her with an awful crunch. A severed arm hit the ground close to Maryan with a wet slap.

Tamaar's tail curled high as her head crashed back into the bushes. Another bolt flew across the field. It struck true, burying deep inside the dragon. The earth heaved, pounding Maryan unconscious.

Maryan came round to an ominous silence. Through the debris covering her, she could see thick clouds rolling away to unveil a clear sky. She'd survived the dragon, but unless she pulled free, the cruel elements of the Serenian autumn would kill her. The cold earth sapped heat from her body. The sweat drying on her skin already felt chilled. Whether Fleur was alive or not, Maryan couldn't expect any help.

The bushes trembled. Large, feral cats roamed these parts searching for prey. A staked out girl would prove an easier kill than a guarded sheep. The dead hand moved, a finger curled, beckoning to her from beyond the grave. Maryan lay hypnotised. The hand twitched violently. It rolled sideways revealing a dragon not much larger than her fist tugging on the raw tendons. The small creature ripped the flesh, rolling to tear mouthfuls free. Its glittering eyes regarded her between each mouthful.

After feeding, the dragon attempted a bugle call. Instead of a mournful wail, it coughed a brilliant flame, leaving a purple blur on Maryan's vision. Tamaar had claimed this area to be her brooding ground. Her egg must have hatched.

The dragon stalked close, its chemical breath swept Maryan's face before it squirmed beneath her torn robe. Its sharp claws tugged at her skin as it burrowed farther into her clothes. It reached her flat stomach where it curled and stopped.

Chapter 8

'Mistress?'

A distant voice forced into Maryan's thoughts. She snuggled deeper under her blankets, wishing the stupid rat would shut up and let her sleep. Wrapped gloriously warm against Sami, she thought about glancing across to see if Stella had come in, but decided it was too cold to raise her head out of the warmth.

'Wake up. I need help.'

'Carl, what do you want? It's dark and I need to sleep.'

'Open your eyes and think what you can see.'

Silently cursing the animal, she thought about the room, Stella's painting and Kait sleeping in the other bed.

'No, that's not right. What can you see now?'

The rat kept nagging, forcing her to open her eyes, darkness, brambles and a dead hand. *'I can see bushes. I'm close to where they killed the dragon.'* She tried to call out, but her mouth wouldn't work. Her jaw ached, locked in place by the gag. Every movement grated. *'I'm buried under earth and bushes.'* She formed a picture of her location, a tree, a fold in the land. Voices sounded in the darkness.

The earth covering her had turned into mud. Her arms, held too long in a single position, felt dead. The only warmth came from the ball of heat nestled beneath her tattered robe.

'Why have you buried yourself like this?' The rat nuzzled up to her face. 'It's too cold out here. If you need a burrow, you should be much deeper. This is no use, no use at all.'

Despite the grating pain, Maryan forced her head to one side to touch the rat's twitching nose. *'Get help.'*

'Your nestmates are close by, they brought me with them. It's too cold. I'll find them.'

"There! Did you see it?" Etelan's voice sounded somewhere in the night. "Follow that rat and don't lose sight of him again."

The bushes rustled. "My Queen, I've found her!" Shapes moved and a shadow loomed. "Get a torch over here, I think she's alive, thank Friggit. Get her out of this." Steppis appeared. A blade flashed, cutting the gag away. She wanted to speak, but only sobs would come.

"Easy child." The old warrior stroked her face. Farm workers tore into the dirt with their hands. Steppis cut the ropes on the stakes, carefully folding Maryan's arms close to her body.

Etelan slipped a thick fur from her shoulders and passed it to Steppis. The old tutor tugged it beneath Maryan, wrapping her limbs within the warmth. She lay free of the earth, but when she tried to move, nothing obeyed. Paralysed, they slid her onto a stretcher.

"Dragon," she mumbled, trying to tell them about the pup nestled on her stomach.

"It's dead," Steppis shushed her to silence.

The next thing Maryan knew, she could feel the warmth from an open fire and smell the lingering odour of home cooking. Dark wooden benches and battered chairs formed a horseshoe around the grate.

The walls hung with small pictures of farm animals. Gnarled beams, tar-black with smoke, crossed the ceiling, each one studded with horse tack.

Etelan appraised the room with a nod. “Quite adequate, lift her on there.” The farmer’s wife rushed to claim the candlestick from the centre of the ancient table before the two farm hands put the litter on it. Etelan waited. “Thank you for your assistance,” she said.

Recognising the dismissal in her tone, the farmer ushered the others out before he and his wife left, closing the rugged wooden door behind them.

The tall healer who had tutored Kait pressed his head against Maryan’s chest. “We need to strip her,” he said. “Fetch light.” Because of his lack of magic, Kait had always been scornful of this arrogant old man.

Maryan tried to warn them again, “Dragon,” she slurred, frustrated that her mouth wouldn’t function.

“Yes dear, it’s gone now,” the healer said, his attention fixed on the implements in his bag. He produced a heavy set of scissors and started to cut.

She tried to squirm, “No! Dragon, inside …”

“Get something to calm her,” Etelan snapped. Barely restrained fury pinched her features.

As the scissors bit through Maryan’s ruined clothes, a high-pitched squeal burst from her tattered robe. A severed length of tail flopped onto the table. The furious dragon pup sprang from its slumber on her stomach, spitting flames at the healer’s face.

“Gorath! Kill it, get it!” he shouted, batting his arms frantically.

Steppis slapped the dragon to the ground with the palm of her hand. It bounced off the floor, rolling in a daze on the stone tiles. She raised her foot.

"No!" Maryan forced her voice into action. Her scream froze the grey haired warrior. "It saved me, don't kill it."

Steppis crashed a bucket from the fire grate over the furious little beast. It clattered across the floor until she jammed one foot on it to hold it still.

"This is becoming a circus. Can we get on?" Etelan glared at the flustered healer. "Care for her as needed, then bring her to my rooms the moment you can move her." The Queen swirled the cloak around her shoulders, scowling at the mud smeared on the fur. She cradled Maryan's cheek with her palm. "Come home soon," she said and swept out into the night.

Maryan loved her rooms. Designed to pamper royalty, she had her own steam room. Scented water dripped onto hot coals, filling the air with a glorious fog. Condensation ran down the austere white tiles and she finally felt warm.

Wiping sweat from her skin with her palm, she admired the tiny dragon. Born to live in hot climates, he now preened in the warmth, his head swayed as he warbled a bubbling song. He'd given the healer the fright of his life. She chuckled at the memory of the silly man dancing around with the small creature trying to singe his eyebrows. The pup had squealed inside the bucket and the warriors had wanted to kill it, but Maryan had managed to stop them. Instead, they'd allowed it to nestle back onto her so that they'd both be quiet.

His injured tail looked pitiful, immediately earning him the name 'Stump.' She'd insisted the healer bandage it before they'd left the farmhouse. She would have frozen without the heat of his body.

"My Lady?" A voice called through the door. "The Queen insists that you dress suitably to attend her in the interview chamber. Do you need any help to get ready?"

"No, I'm fine." She raised her leg to rub her hand across her glowing, pink skin. "I'll be dressed in a moment."

Even the vertical cold plunge seemed inviting. She definitely preferred dropping into a narrow, deep bath, rather than swimming the length of the stream-fed, communal pool. She stepped off the edge, hitting the surface with a gasp. The cold water hammered shut over her head, squeezing the breath from her lungs. Shivering, but delightfully refreshed, she hauled herself out to get dressed.

Before leaving her room, she cuddled Carl against her face. *'We're equal now, you saved me.'*

'Nestmates do that.'

After a final hug, she put him into his cage. Stump hissed when she pushed him into a metal box hanging from a hook on the wall. His nose snuffled against the air holes the moment she closed the flap. "No. You stay locked in there."

If Fleur had survived, she would be in serious trouble with Etelan. That thought felt warm. It had been too long since she had felt any safety under the protection of an adult.

The Queen waited in the room full of low seats she used as a semi-formal meeting place. "Sit down.

We've a lot to talk about." Etelan smiled with the warmth of sunshine, handing Maryan a goblet. "I have to discuss some matters of state and parts of what we say must remain secret."

The hint of intrigue drew Maryan forward. Etelan nodded, signalling for Maryan to drink. The unusual taste of thick, red wine ran down her throat.

"Your history lessons will have told you that real alliances between nations are formed by marriage, not treaty."

A smug feeling of revenge surfaced. The Queen planned to marry Fleur off to somebody, probably to an old man. Maryan could almost pity whichever poor fool ended up with her on their arm.

"Luckily, fate has granted me two daughters."

Maryan puzzled over the words. She didn't know Etelan had another child. She searched her memory, trying to find any mention of the girl. The truth dawned. "Me! No, forget it. I'm not …" Maryan drained the wine before her fingers loosened on the goblet. She tried to flee, but her legs gave way, dropping her back into the chair.

Etelan's mouth tightened into a thin smile. "You've been drugged to make you more compliant. I couldn't take the whining if you could speak." A cold faced, older version of Fleur loomed over her.

Opening the door without a sound, the Garalandian Ambassador entered. His thick fingers wrapped around Etelan's shoulder "Is our little princess ready?" He nuzzled into her neck, his white teeth nipping her ear.

She ran her nails into his beard. "Maybe not willing, but she is, as you promised, unable to object." Pulling free of the Ambassador's embrace, Etelan grabbed a handful of Maryan's hair and yanked her head back. "Understand. If you try to escape, that boy you were so fond of, Fredrick, and all of your sad little playmates will die." She settled by Maryan and held her hand. "Fleur almost messed up the plan with her last stunt. She's too high-spirited, but she will succeed me to this throne." Etelan's expression feigned contrition. "I'll explain to the council that you have replaced her in this vital role and I'll punish her with such venom, all will shake at my anger.

"Eventually, the people will recognise how cruelly I have treated poor Fleur. She, of course, will respond nobly. When the time comes, they'll vote for her. Not because I corrupted their precious traditions, but because they want to."

She smiled at the Ambassador. "Mordacai, you can send for your team. I'm finished here. After supervising the collection of her things, I must prepare to celebrate the imminent wedding of my daughter."

Chapter 9

The Ambassador's men handled Maryan roughly. One threw her over his shoulder, leaving her head dangling down his back. The coarse fabric of his jacket reeked of sweat and worse. She tried to shout for help, but couldn't move. Not even a tear would form in her eye.

He carried her along a passageway and down a narrow flight of stairs leading to a private courtyard. The cold air pinched her skin. The full depth of night draped everything with shadow. The only light came from lanterns mounted on either side of a magnificent, black coach. Garalandian servants bustled, making ready to leave. One held the coach door open whilst the other grunted in his struggle to manoeuvre Maryan through the tiny opening onto the seat.

The scent of a wood-burning heater combined with the smell of leather to give the interior a masculine feel. A rigid-backed Garalandian woman sat opposite. In contrast to her severe black dress, her white face gleamed against the dark upholstery. She pressed a handkerchief to her nose when the cages containing Carl and Stump were stacked on the seat next to Maryan.

The door closed with a solid clunk and the carriage rolled out of the courtyard. Maryan sat propped between the packs and crates. Sometime before dawn, the tingling running through every limb announced movement returning to her body. "Who are you?" she slurred.

“Patricia.” The woman allowed the corners of her mouth to tilt into the shape of a smile. “I’ll be your personal attendant.”

“You approve of kidnap?”

“Approve?” The woman said. “I’m Mordacai’s sister and he needs a bride.”

“Marry him?” Bile rose at the thought. “He’s too old. I’ll kill him the first chance I get.”

Patricia’s sour features creased. “Too old? What are you …”

“He’s older than my mother and I saw the way he pawed Etelan, I’m not going to marry an old lecher.”

“You stupid girl. It isn’t Mordacai you’re to wed. Prince Chentene, needs a wife and my brother needs you to produce a daughter to wed his son. The plan fits. You’ll not come to any harm. In fact your life away from these savages will prove more delightful than your pitiful imagination could ever conjure.”

“I’ll not succumb. Your prince had better watch out if he wants to keep his life.”

Patricia sighed, a stiletto blade slipped from her sleeve. She lifted Carl trapped in his cage. “If you give any trouble, if you show anything other than pure joy, everything and everybody you hold dear will die. Shall I demonstrate?” She peered through the bars at the animal staring back at her.

They rested at way-stations along the route, stopping at taverns suitable for a royal party. Providing Maryan spoke politely, Patricia appeared to be an attentive personal maid.

Early on the fourth day of travel, the coach pulled off the main road to make its way through the well-tended meadows of a wealthy estate. The fields ended at a high hedgerow opening onto a sand coloured forecourt in front of an impressive mansion. The iron-shod wheels clattered over a wooden bridge and through a narrow gateway in the wall.

"Is this Manda Torre?" Maryan asked, peering at the looming towers of the mansion.

"No, this is Mordacai's home." Patricia replied. "We're not far from the capital. We're stopping here to make you presentable."

Since leaving Serenia, Maryan had ceased plaiting her hair, leaving it hanging in rattails. When she raised her arm to sweep the tangle away from her face, the rancid stench of her body odour nauseated her.

"Hardly appropriate," Patricia muttered.

The coach stopped in a central courtyard, where the surrounding building soared over three stories high. Narrow windows looked down from the higher floors, but the only break in the lower walls was a black wooden door studded with square-headed bolts.

Inside, four steps led up into a narrow passage. A wide opening on their right led through to a large hall. A long polished table ran the length of the room. At the far end, a fire roared, logs the size of a man's leg crackled and spat heat into the room.

Patricia guided Maryan along the corridor, through a door, and up a flight of stairs to the next floor. Crinkled paintings of stern faced men and women glared down. The corridors whispered with servants gliding about their duties.

Walking ahead, Patricia entered a bedroom and crossed to where a gown embellished with precious stones hung from a hook on the wall. "You'll be wearing this when we arrive. Chentene will be eager to greet his bride." Her face crumpled into a sour expression. "You do know what is expected of you don't you?"

"Will you drug me again?"

"I suspect he'd notice."

"He doesn't know?"

"Chentene is a good man." Genuine adoration filled Patricia's face. "Too good for our nation. No, he thinks you're the royal daughter of Etelan, come of your own free will." She slipped the hilt of her dagger from her sleeve. "What will you gain if he finds this not to be true?"

A hot bath steamed in the middle of an attached room. Patricia stood with her arms folded, waiting for Maryan to undress. The clothes she peeled from her skin stank and the older woman kept her nose wrinkled until she handed them to a servant outside the door.

"You do know how to use a bath, don't you?"

"I've never seen one before. We usually roll in the snow once a year. Do I sit in it?" Maryan dropped beneath the steaming surface, holding her breath until Patricia tugged her upright by her hair. "Of course I can use a bath," she said, wiping her face.

A bustle of maids waited in the outer chamber. They sat her in front of a broad dressing table arrayed with bottles, paints and brushes. A round faced servant immediately started to comb the tangled knots out of Maryan's wet hair. Another used a contraption to fan heat from the fire to blow across her head, making her feel too hot. She squirmed under the attention. The moment her hair was dry, a tall, thin girl produced a mountain of what looked like horsehair and started to pin it onto her head.

"Get off me. That hurt!" Maryan squealed when a pin dug into her scalp. "Tell them to go away." She batted the mound from her head.

Patricia scowled, but shooed the maid away and slid behind Maryan. "One of those ridiculous plaits?" Her thin hands nimbly scraped Maryan's hair into a tight weave. Catching Maryan's attention reflected in the mirror, she nodded to the discarded wig. "They are the fashion. I'm sure you'll be wearing them by the end of the year." She sniffed as a thought amused her. "Unless, of course, the fools at court decide to mimic our savage princess and start to dress in metal and braids."

When the plait was finished, another servant opened a box of paints and dipped a small brush into a thick black fluid. Maryan squirmed away. "No, I'm not having my face painted." She slapped the box out of the maid's hand. The flustered girl squealed and dived to the floor desperate to stop the ink spreading into the carpet. Masked by the chaos, Maryan took the opportunity to slip a small pair of scissors off the table and conceal them in her bodice. They might not be much, but they could be a weapon.

"I really think a dab of rouge would improve things." Patricia tapped Maryan's cheeks. "Are you certain you won't try some?"

"Never." Maryan tugged away from the servants. "Make them leave. I've had enough of all of this."

A nod from Patricia dismissed the maids. She wrung her hands, raising her shoulders to her ears. "You should allow me to guide you, but for now …"

A tightening around her eyes indicated acceptance. “For now, I’m sure I could show the prince a scarecrow and he’d be happy.”

Patricia escorted Maryan back to the courtyard where a team of servants had restored a mirror-like sheen to the lacquered panels of the coach. Filled with a sense of impending doom, Maryan climbed aboard for the last stage of the journey. Her worst fears gnawed at her every thought. The Ambassador had ridden ahead to announce to the Prince that his bride would arrive shortly.

Fields rolled in all directions emphasising the vastness of the countryside. Maryan idly traced a finger across the veins in her wrist and wondered about opening one. Instead, she leant against the plush velvet cushion. A thought struck her. “If I’m to marry the Prince, I’ll have to meet the King. What’s he like?”

“What are you babbling about?” Patricia jerked her attention back to Maryan.

“If Chentene is a prince, there must be a king.”

Patricia sighed. “Many years ago we had a king, Calamore, a black magician of dreadful power. Using wizardry, he extended his existence beyond imagination. Surviving as a terrible wraith, he ruled through his descendants, allowing each the title of prince before robbing them of life.”

“Robbed them of life? You mean he killed them.”

“No, drained them of all of their life-essence to make a dark rider. An extension of his will, forever waiting to be recalled from the grave whenever he chose.”

“Where is he now, him and his dark riders?”

“The nations of Shudalandia rose up to give battle. After a terrible struggle, they finally dragged him to imprisonment. He vanished and the riders faded from memory. We don’t know if he’ll return, but after living through seven generations of princes, the title stuck. There isn’t a king and unless Calamore returns, Chentene is the absolute ruler of Garalandia. You’ll be an extremely important woman.”

The coach slowed to a stop and the Ambassador’s voice came from outside. “Patricia, the Prince couldn’t wait to meet his bride. He’s ridden out to greet her. Is our Princess ready?”

Until this point, it had felt unreal, like playing out a game. Only in tales were people dragged to foreign lands and forced into loveless marriages. Maryan felt life drain from her limbs as the true horror of her situation hit home.

Patricia brushed Maryan’s cheek with her cold hand. “Easy child, sacrifice is a woman’s duty.” After picking an imagined fleck of dust from Maryan’s shoulder, she opened the door of the carriage and executed an awkward curtsey in the tiny space. “My Prince, your bride is here. Is it your wish to come within?”

“It is my wish. Coming within is all I can think about!”

Laughter brayed through the dreadful band of over-dressed fops accompanying the prince.

Patricia briefly glanced back before climbing out. The coach tipped sideways on its springs, as a broad-shouldered man with a feather in his wide-brimmed hat squeezed aboard. He latched the door and pulled the blind.

"Hello, I'm Chentene."

Garalandia stretched from the farthest point Starward down to the border with Sudaland thousands of leagues toward the dark. Feudal territories, all sworn to the Prince, surrounded them, leaving her alone and defenceless. Maryan jumped when Chentene suddenly banged on the ceiling of the coach behind the driver. "Move on, my man!"

The coach lurched into motion and they swayed in time to the trot of the horses. She watched his every movement, her fist gripping the tiny pair of scissors ready to fight to the death. After all, Asti had destroyed the Garalandian champion with a similar set. The briefest glimpse had confirmed that men ruled in Garalandia. Women served only as decoration or servants. The arrogant spectres of the Ambassador and Barag lingered in her thoughts as she studied the man in front of her.

The brim of his ridiculous hat lifted revealing a strong face dominated by a too-large nose above plump lips. His coat appeared woven from golden thread. His legs were clad in tight stockings that moulded to the muscles of his thighs. His boots gleamed. The air had become fragrant. She'd never met a man who wore perfume before.

One corner of his mouth twitched a conspiratorial smile as he raised a finger to signal for her to remain silent. "My dear, I'm sure you are probably more scared than I, but I do assure you that I am filled with fear." He waited, rocking slightly with the motion of the carriage. "I have a role to play. My words in public might show me to be a supercilious bore, but I tell you now, I will not lay a finger upon you unless you wish, nay, *demand* that I do."

Maryan fingered the scissors, suspecting a trick.

He threw his hat on the seat, relaxing back into the sumptuous leather. "I know something of Mordacai. He's a good man, but he seeks influence and power for his family. That is the Garalandian way."

Her thoughts spun. His open-faced honesty invited trust. She wondered if he'd allow her to escape if she told him the truth. She hesitated. A wrong decision condemned her friends to death. "I'm not a princess." Her voice came out as a thin croak.

"Thank Gorath for that!" His laugh shook the carriage. "Have you ever met a princess? They're usually so inbred they look like a caricature of a horse. Mordacai described you as a princess by right, rather than birth. The daughter of a great hero worshipped by all and raised to royalty by a vote of the people."

The rumble of the wheels indicated they were running on paving. Chentene released the blind and with an exaggerated flourish, gestured out of the window. "Your new home."

She caught a glimpse of magnificent city walls sweeping in either direction. The light dimmed as the coach clattered into a short tunnel. Inside the citadel, the coach progressed through the sprawling market of the lower keep.

Uncertain of what she'd expected, Maryan studied the people. They looked similar to the townsfolk of Serenia, merchants in serviceable cloth and working folk in rougher, harder-wearing material. Stalls selling fruit and vegetables surrounded the edges of the square. Shouting street-hawkers balancing trays of steaming food wound through the chaotic throng. Good wives and soldiers rubbed against servants searching for provisions.

The coach rushed across to an exit from the square where the buildings were closer together. The commercial frontages gave way to wider, tree-lined boulevards. Their route wound in a circle climbing towards a palace set high in the centre of the town. The quality of the surroundings changed, becoming richer, primarily residencies. She did spot a couple of discrete shops displaying bolts of frivolous cloth and gaudy jewellery. A laugh escaped her. “Is nothing practical ever required this close to the palace?”

“Utterly forbidden,” Chentene said.

The coach stopped and Chentene sprang out to help her from the carriage. She gazed into his smiling face. The idea of snubbing the offer was tempting. Trained to move silently across any terrain, she should be able to exit a coach without stumbling. Uncertain of how refusal would offend and aware of the courtiers pressing close to windows, she allowed him to assist her descent.

At the front of the coach, the coachman drowned beneath a deluge of grumbling as he helped Patricia down from her seat. She looked terribly windswept, but immediately started to bark orders at the staff already milling around the coach.

“Dear Patricia, how would we cope without you?” Chentene said.

“Badly, Chentene, extremely badly.” Patricia’s face filled with affection.

Maryan wondered about the hold her brother, Mordacai, wielded to make her take part in this deceit. The woman obviously adored the Prince.

The suite assigned to Maryan rambled along an upper floor of the inner keep. In the reception room, the walls were panelled with light brown wood. Complex carvings ran around every edge. Carved wooden flowers and vines intertwined, climbing to meet in the centre of the ceiling to create a tent-like effect. Large windows assembled from small panes held together with criss-cross lead gave a view across the castle rooftops out to the far mountains.

A panelled door led to a boudoir arrayed with soft furniture, mirrors and closets. Another door revealed a bathroom, pink tiled with gold fittings. A tiny waterfall rippled the surface of a bath large enough to fit several guests.

Chentene opened the door into the bedchamber. The room had sofas and soft chairs positioned around the fire-grate. The heat from the burning logs felt oppressive after the long ride outdoors.

A bed stood against one wall, flanked by tables supporting entwined alabaster nude figures. Heavy tapestry curtains swept down from the ceiling, tied back to reveal a wide mattress covered with silk sheets.

Chentene edged closer to her, not touching, but too close in a bedchamber. "I'm not sure what you're used to. I hope these rooms will suffice. They were my mother's. They're large enough aren't they?"

She thought of the dormitory she had shared with Kait, Stella and Sami. The image of Sami melted into a grotesque mask of Arlaine as she'd looked in the

Infirmary. This man might seem pleasant, but she was here against her will. Because of him, her friend's beautiful sister had been beaten to death and Sami forced into exile on the far border.

Despite the heat from the fireplace, ice spread into her veins. "Can you leave now?" Maryan said.

Chentene's face dropped, his hands rose to embrace, but hovered without touching. "I suppose you've had a long journey." He shrugged, spun on his heel and walked to the door. "I'll let you rest," he said and disappeared.

She held her back straight, waiting until the door closed, before dropping into an overstuffed armchair. Curling into a ball, she hugged her arms around her knees and sobbed. Her life had been a series of scrambles, brief glimpses of happiness always dashed into the valleys of despair. A hand touched her back tilting her face into a bony shoulder. Patricia knelt to comfort her. Is this to be her life, her only friend, a killer working for the enemy? She pulled away from the woman and stood up.

Patricia's cold veneer slid back into place. "My Lady?" she said, her jaw moving as if she'd swallowed a midge. "Can we dispose of the menagerie? It's unseemly for a woman of your standing to have such things."

"Carl and Stump?" Maryan squealed, realising how selfish she'd been. "You must send to the kitchen immediately. I need grain and meat. About a fistful of each should do." She waited for Patricia to leave before bringing her pets to her bed. Carl scurried out of his cage and sat on his haunches.

‘Strange place, a lot of nests here, I can feel local rats coming to investigate.’ Carl’s whiskers twitched.

She picked him up and ran her face into his fur. ‘*You take care, you can’t fight that well anymore.*’

Squirming from her grip, he flipped over on the bed. *‘Back legs are overrated.’*

His optimism stung Maryan. In strange surroundings, Carl, a crippled rat, handled it better than an almost fully trained warrior of the Serenian legions did. She opened the lid of Stump’s box to release the tiny dragon.

“Oh, My Lady!” a surprised voice came from behind Maryan. A servant had quietly entered the room. She wore a pristine, white-bibbed apron covering the front of a simple, grey dress that swept the ground. In one hand, she carried a gleaming tray with two gold-glazed bowls.

Stump struggled out of Maryan’s grip, his fledgling wings blurring in the effort to support his weight. Flame lit the room and the poor girl screamed. The golden dishes shattered on the floor, scattering meat and grain. Stump dropped like a stone and sat on the largest golden shard. A single word echoed inside Maryan’s head. *‘Gold!’* His needle-sharp, front claws scrambled to gather the pieces within reach. A smug expression filled his face. *‘Gold.’*

“Not gold, silly dragon.” Maryan waved a piece of meat in front of his nose. He coughed a bright flame, driving her back.

The serving girl knelt to pick up the fallen grains. She managed to stop shaking. Her face filled with pleasure. “My lady, that’s wonderful. How big will it grow?”

“His name’s Stump.” Maryan struggled to remember how enormous Tamaar had seemed. She pointed out of the window, “Probably about from this wall, to that chimney there on the right.”

Once again, she tried to grab him, but he coughed a spurt of smoke-filled flame. Maryan frowned at the remains of fragile pottery. “Why did you bring such expensive bowls?”

“We thought these were for you. The Lady Patricia demanded raw meat and grain for the Serenian Princess.”

Maryan used the meat trying to entice Stump to come closer, but he remained glued to the broken pottery. Finally, he started to tear at the food she offered. “Would you feed Carl for me?”

“Carl?” the girl looked around then gasped when what might have been a fur hat on the bed opened its eyes. Her scream shook the windows and the handful of grain she’d gathered flew into the air. “It’s a rat! A monster rat, it’ll eat us alive.”

“These animals are my friends. They won’t harm you and I don’t expect any in the castle to harm them. Do you understand?”

Wild-eyed, the girl remained frozen, gawping around, obviously expecting more monsters to come out of hiding. “Y-yes, My Lady.”

“You may go.”

The maid backed out of the room, keeping her attention riveted on the animals. Carl started to gather the spilled grains and sat back on his haunches with his nose twitching.

"The exercise will do you good," Maryan said. "In fact, I might scatter your food around from now on. You're getting fat." She rolled her head in a circle, feeling the tension in her neck. "Thinking about it, I believe we could all do with some exercise. I wonder where the training ground is."

Chapter 10

The noise of a maid dragging open the heavy curtains woke Maryan. A crackling fire already blazed in the grate, warming the air and adding a fragrance of burning wood.

"Friggit! Are you trying to cook me?" Maryan shouted. She kicked the covers off and flung the windows open, grateful to gasp the cooler air. She pointed at the fire. "Don't light one of those things in my room again. Please send for Patricia." Although she hated being so dependent on the woman, she didn't have any choice until she knew her way around.

Faster than Maryan would have believed possible, Patricia bustled into the room. "You really should try to adopt more genteel ways. A lady should be cosseted … cared for." She wrung her hands.

"Trapped and subdued more like. I need some freedom. Now, where can I go for weapons training?"

Patricia's face crumpled. "A lady should never handle a weapon."

"Having seen those awful men surrounding the Prince, I can imagine why. Any decent woman would take it upon herself to rid the lands of such wastrels. I've trained every day since I could hold a sword. Take me to the exercise grounds … please."

Although her shoulders tightened, Patricia finally nodded. "I think you should get dressed though, don't you?"

Maryan started to rummage through the trunks of clothes Etelan had sent with her. "Am I supposed to train naked?"

"The Queen knew you were coming as a bride. She wouldn't expect you to want to train." Patricia came across to help. "What about this?" She held up a full-length suit made of brown wool the consistency of wire. "I believe this could be worn for outdoor pursuits." After delving in a drawer, Patricia unfolded a white linen blouse. "I'm certain this is the best you shall find. Ladies don't exercise in Garalandia."

"They do now." Maryan grabbed the outfit and started to tug it on. She hoisted the skirt around trying to make sense of the fastenings, struggling until Patricia came to assist.

"A lady should always be tended when she is dressing." Patricia straightened the seams and smoothed the fabric. The skirt touched the floor and the linen blouse blossomed from the shoulders of the outfit's trim waistcoat.

Maryan rolled her arms trying to loosen the fabric before turning to the older woman. "Ready."

Although she ignored the delicate treasures lining the passages as they made their way through the palace leading to the walled keep, Maryan sighed with pleasure when Patricia opened the door leading to the training facilities. In the centre of the courtyard, a line of wooden posts had been set into the ground for sword practice. On one side, a dummy hung from a gallows for spear throwing. On the other, an archery range. She nodded approvingly and went to pick up a training sword.

"What do you think you are doing, my dear?" a voice drawled from a doorway. A tall, elegantly dressed man emerged from the shadows. His strawberry-blonde hair lay in perfect waves sweeping back from his forehead. Bands of thick muscle peeped from the gaping white shirt tucked into his waistband. He wore soft, black leather boots laced to his calves, which moulded against his legs and matched his tight black breeches.

"You are addressing the Prince's bride," Patricia said, skewering the man with her fearsome stare.

"Am I? And what does the Prince's bride think she could do with a sword?" The man sauntered closer.

Maryan tucked the sword tip under the hilt of another training blade and flicked it at his face. He plucked the sword from the air and holding his easy pose, waited to see what she would do next. She lunged. His blade caught her thrust with a lightning fast parry, forcing her to change it into a high attack.

"Oh dear, has she been practicing with the boys?" He wove a complex guard, easily holding her away.

"Where I come from, the boys aren't allowed to train with us." She lunged again, determined to wipe the smile off his face. His sword blurred to counter, but at least she forced him into a defensive stance.

"And pray, where would that be?"

"Serenia."

"So, I have a true Serenian." The man grinned. "Chentene had to go that far to find a virgin bride, did he? This place is looking up." He flowed into his own attack, forcing Maryan to defend. Her long dress tangled on her legs causing her to stumble. She ducked to one side and attacked again.

"I'm convinced." The man held his arms wide. "I'm Harlon, the weapon master of Manda Torre."

Maryan put up her own sword, grinning in response. “And I’m Maryan, almost virgin warrior of the Serenian legion.”

“Almost?” Harlon allowed a leer to fill his face.

“Almost trained, not almost a …” she felt herself flushing.

“My Lady!” Patricia pressed on Maryan’s forearm to bend her down to her own height. “This man has a terrible reputation, you must be careful.”

“A reputation?” Harlon drawled, once more affecting his annoying tones. He picked up a small golden medallion he wore around his neck and squinted through the keyhole in the middle of it.

“What are you doing?” Maryan asked.

“I find that a woman doesn’t look right unless she’s framed within a keyhole shape.” He barked a short laugh, “A foible I picked up as a child.”

Even Patricia smiled. “And carried on into adult life I think.” She pulled forcefully on Maryan’s sleeve. “We must return to your rooms.”

“But first, when may I come to train?” Maryan asked.

“Come this afternoon. The Prince will be riding and most of the courtiers will be with him. Come alone …” He let the words hang.

“She most certainly will not.” Patricia held Maryan’s sleeve to lead her across the courtyard. “If you come down here, you must always have a chaperone in attendance. I can’t begin to tell you the things the ladies of the court claim regarding our weapons master.”

Back in her rooms, Maryan ransacked all of the chests that had accompanied her from home in the hope somebody had packed training gear for her. "Why didn't that woman send me anything practical to wear?"

Patricia's cough pulled Maryan's head out of the trunk she was searching. She stood up and bumped into Chentene attempting to peer over her shoulder. She tried to avoid him, but ended up pressing all of her weight on his toe.

"My dear Maryan, I hear you're planning a bit of an exhibition," he said, standing on one leg, trying to ease the pain in his foot.

"If you think you can stop …"

Chentene held out his hand to silence her. "Nothing of the kind. I merely thought you'd need some appropriate clothes." He rubbed his hand across his midriff. "We have some hunting apparel I've spread out of. I'm sure we can figure something out." He narrowed his eyes slightly as he studied her through his lowered lashes. "Would you join me in my rooms?"

Linking her arm, he guided her out of her suite. Just outside her rooms, he paused and held up his arm. "This is a picture of mother." The canvas portrayed a slim woman with a hawk-like nose. Chentene's face softened. "She died when I was quite young. Father never recovered."

She pretended not to notice that his eye glinted with an unformed tear. His display of emotion was so incongruous to her expectations. "Are all of these pictures of your family?"

"Yes, all of them." He waved his hand to indicate the length of the corridor. "So many generations frowning down on a young boy creates the pressure of the ages. It emphasises one's responsibility and quite twists the mind."

They entered a corridor flanked either side with treasures vanishing into the distance. Between the doorways, short columns supported white, carved busts, interspersed with tables displaying fragile ornaments.

He chuckled. "So much clutter. A royal family collects so many trinkets over the years." He stopped to run his hand over a huge vase. "A gift from Bara over a hundred years ago."

"If it serves no purpose, why not throw it out?"

"And offend a nation?"

The reception room of the prince's apartment could have served as a ballroom. Pale blue plaster covered the walls and delicate white beading formed geometric shapes around the tall mirrors reaching up to the ceiling. The sparse arrangement of furniture appeared lost in the wide space. He marched through to a smaller, more intimate room with soft chairs, a fireplace and a writing desk.

In the adjoining chamber, the royal bed loomed, growing, until it dwarfed them both. The waist high mattress was covered in a sky-blue satin quilt drawn as smooth as a lake. The headboard met a mountain of cushions. White and gold hangings draped from the ceiling gathered to each corner.

Maryan felt her skin flush and she spun around, desperate to gaze anywhere, but at the bed. Above the fireplace, a large hunting scene showed a deer leaping ahead of the chasing pack. She felt sympathy for the animal and loitered before following him into his dressing room.

Unaware of her anxiety, he flung open a wardrobe and walked inside, running his hand along the double rails of clothes. "Somewhere … yes here it is." He swirled a white linen shirt down from the rail and grabbed a pair of suede breeches. "Try these." He waved his hand to the door back into the bedroom. "Go on, I won't peep."

In his bedchamber, she removed her waistcoat and blouse. Reaching around to the fastenings at the base of her spine, she started to panic. There was no way she could manage them without help. She struggled, almost falling over in her efforts to undo the infernal skirt.

"Careful," Chentene said, emerging from the closet. His attention seemed fixed on polishing the dust off a pair of lace-up boots with his palm.

The squeak from Maryan stopped him in his tracks. She struggled to clutch the unbuttoned shirt to her chest.

"What?" he said, holding the boots out to either side.

"You said no peeking and then walk in."

"I'm sure that doesn't count. Need help with that? I've no idea how you women manage." He dropped his head to his chest as he unpicked the wired hooks. The speed it fell loose hinted he'd undone many such fastenings. She grabbed the waistband to stop the skirt dropping to the floor.

"See, I'll turn my back," he said.

When her skirt fell away, Chentene sighed and she realised he faced a mirror on the far wall. She hauled the breeches up as quickly as she could. "You cheated."

Chagrined, his hawkish smile reflected back to her. "And you wouldn't?"

She sat on an ornate, high-backed armchair and allowed him to fasten the boots along her leg. She watched his fingers work, threading the laces before using the flat of his hands to smooth the soft leather to her calves. Caressing her foot, he ran his hand up the length of her leg. His eyes slowly followed the line of her body until they stared straight into hers. A question hung in his gaze.

"Not yet," she said, feeling her heart pound.

"Not yet, is progress." He smiled at her. "Now, would my bride please go and enjoy herself in the training ground."

Filled with excitement, she rushed headlong from Chentene's apartments. Patricia waited outside and had to run a few steps to catch up. One of the ladies of the court approached from the opposite direction. Small framed, the tight bodice of her silver brocade dress pressed her breasts into a tight cleavage of perfect white flesh. She lowered her gaze as she dipped a polite curtsey, barely breaking stride.

Maryan stopped to watch the woman's hip-swaying walk. Her skirts rolled like a boat at harbour, gently swishing on the floor. "Does this passageway lead anywhere else beside the royal chambers?"

"No. That's the Lady Emily, a close friend of Chentene's, a distant relative from the Sudaland border, I think. They spend a lot of time together."

"I bet they do." Maryan bit her lip. The sudden need to beat smug little Emily to a pulp filled her. She wanted to tell her to keep her claws away from

Chentene. Violent thoughts stayed with her until she reached the training ground.

"Well, my little Serenian storm-cloud, are you here to train, or to sulk?" Harlon stood grinning, with his jacket hooked on one shoulder, his cocked hip stretching the tight black fabric of his breeches.

"Train."

He threw a blade to her before moving to the centre of the practice ground. True to his word, the courtyard was empty. Only the sound of their clashing blades bounced back from the walls. Determined to punish somebody for her frustration, she attacked Harlon furiously

Instead of panicking under her onslaught, Harlon's grin widened. "Little pussycat is angry."

His teasing words infuriated her more. She stabbed clumsily, her blade whipped from her grasp and bounced across the paving stones. As the tip of Harlon's sword touched her throat, he danced close enough to peck her with a kiss.

"Weapon Master!" Patricia squealed.

"Moods and tantrums have no place in a duel. I thought you'd brought a doxie for me to play with, not a warrior."

Red-faced, Maryan collected her sword. Fredrick emerged from a far door. He shook back his curling hair and smiled at her from across the courtyard. She drank in his every contour before turning back to her tutor.

Harlon's brooding glare was riveted on the young blade-master. He shook himself, barely returning his attention to Maryan. She slapped his rump with the flat of her blade. "Moods and tantrums?"

“That man …”

“Fredrick?”

“Yes. Make sure you keep clear of him. He’s trouble, especially for women.”

“Might be difficult, we’ve met before.”

Fredrick sauntered across the training ground and posed with his hands on his hips. Unleashing a gleaming smile, he flicked his unruly fringe back from his face. “Hello, I heard you were here. I thought we might try to get some ‘training’ of our own sometime.”

“I think your tone is inappropriate,” Patricia said. “I suspect the Ambassador might have something to say.”

“These days, the Ambassador and I have an understanding.” Fredrick squared to Harlon. “Sometime soon old man, sometime soon.” He spun on his heel to march away.

“Why not now?” Harlon growled.

“We should use proper weapons.” Fredrick turned slowly, his grin still in place. He nodded at Harlon’s training blade. “Not toys.” He unsheathed a gleaming sword with ornate working on the hilt. “A gift from an admirer.”

Harlon stepped backwards to the low wall covered in swords. Without shifting his attention from his foe, he slipped a plain looking blade out of its scabbard. Fredrick sneered at the simple weapon.

“Rules?” Harlon said.

Fredrick lunged straight at Harlon’s chest. The weapon master slapped the thrust aside. His blade flashed, tearing a single line across Fredrick’s shirt-breast. Fredrick touched the blood-tinged edge of the fabric. "Farther than first blood, I think." His blade danced in a bewildering assault.

Despite the younger man's speed, the weapon master dominated. He fought with an intensity that frightened Maryan. Pressing Fredrick cruelly, Harlon unleashed an assault of deadly blows from every direction. Dropping any finesse, he went about his work like a woodsman clearing stubborn growth from amongst the trees.

The superb efficiency of the plain blade left Fredrick no opportunity to pose. The ornate sword flew from his hand. Obviously outmatched, he dropped to one knee, his arms raised.

With a push of his foot, Harlon rolled the youth onto his back and towered over him. "Stay clear of those I care for."

Keeping his head down like a whipped dog, Fredrick limped across the courtyard, vanishing through the door on the other side.

Face flushed in exaltation, Patricia gloated at the back of the vanishing youth. "For once, Weapon Master, I thoroughly approve of your behaviour."

Harlon retrieved his training blade and returned his attention to Maryan. "I've noticed you seem to skip when you advance. Perhaps acceptable behaviour in a daisy field, but it has no place in a battlefield. Try to move your feet in a glide."

Neck deep in the bath, Maryan lifted her hand, watching the water run down the length of her arm. It felt odd not steaming the grime from her skin, but apparently, Garalandian ladies didn't use steam rooms.

She had to meet Chentene to discuss the wedding, but thoughts of Fredrick tumbled around her head. Patricia's reaction baffled her. The older woman had muttered something about a girl, a veteran's daughter. Maryan smoothed soap across her body. The addition of a few scars had hardened Fredrick's looks. Confidence had replaced his hesitance. He'd certainly been over-confident in his challenge of Harlon.

A bell striking in the town shocked her. "Gorath!" She dried herself on the soft bath sheet before allowing a maid to help her to dress.

Holding her skirt so that she wouldn't trip, she hurried along the winding corridors making her way to the private dining chamber. A door opened slightly.

"Maryan," Fredrick hissed.

Stopping abruptly, she looked up and down the passageway. Nobody was around. Fredrick eagerly beckoned her to join him. Darkness draped the room visible over his shoulder. She moved closer. Blood started to pump in her ears. She wanted to feel his arms around her again, she wanted …

"There you are. I wondered if you'd forgotten me." Chentene's voice froze Maryan. He stood with his arms wide, waiting for her at the far end of the corridor.

Her head snapped around. The door closed without a sound. Could he see it? She ran her hand up the woodwork of the surround. "Such artistry." She tried to glide toward Chentene. His gaze absorbed her every movement and she wished her hips would swish her dress.

“You’re flushed.” Chentene touched her cheek, his expression that of a puppy seeking attention, uncertain if it’s due for a scolding.

“Just confused by all this …” she waved her hand.

“Becoming the most important woman in the realm?”

She glanced back to the closed door before linking his arm, allowing him to escort her to the private dining room.

Maryan felt helpless, trapped beneath Chentene’s relatives glaring down from the pictures. She allowed the servant to fill her plate before taking her cue from Chentene about when she should start to eat.

“You seem so glum?” Chentene said.

“Isolated. I’ve never been alone for such a long time before.”

“I’ve never been anything but.”

“Didn’t you go to school?”

“Good lord, no! A prince of the realm has private tutors. Just occasionally, we nobles would be shipped off to each other’s houses to allow us to mix. Really, just an excuse to get the girls introduced to the boys.”

Maryan felt her shoulders rise at the thought of a young Chentene playing with an already scheming, child-vixen, Lady Emily. She tried to smooth her features before looking up at him. When she did, he was staring past her shoulder, grinning like a cat in a dairy.

A squeal of delight pierced the sombre atmosphere of the ancient room as Stella burst upon her from behind.

Maryan leapt up from her chair to hug her friend, but found Stella’s swollen abdomen in the way.

“I know. Frightful isn’t it.” Stella pushed her already distended stomach prominently between them and lovingly caressed the bump. Justin hung back, allowing them their greeting. Stella clasped her husband’s hand bringing him into a shared embrace. “Son of Justin, we hope. Although from the kicks, I’d swear it’s a she in there.” Her husband wore a silly smile and nuzzled his face into Stella’s luxurious black hair.

“You’d like some food?” Chentene signalled for the servant. “Bring some cuts of meat for our guests,” he commanded. Then he threw back his head and laughed, gesturing with his knife. “This man’s house was one of the favourite ones to visit.” He openly appraised Stella. “So, this is the woman to tame you. It all bodes well.” Chentene raised his glass. “To barbarian brides.”

Maryan studied his guileless face. He didn’t have a clue how Mordacai held her captive. He looked so happy. She watched Stella’s swollen breasts wobble when she laughed and wondered how disappointed Chentene would be when he saw her poor figure. Unaware of her thoughts, he grinned across the table at her, his face alight with pleasure.

Stella gripped Maryan’s arm. “I’ll come to your rooms in the morning and you can tell me all of the court gossip.”

Chapter 11

It was mid-morning of the next day when Stella shattered the quiet of Maryan's cosy boudoir. "So tell me everything." She squirmed, trying to get comfortable in one of the overstuffed armchairs.

Maryan dropped into the chair facing her on the other side of the fireplace. The maids had stacked the large grate with logs, but Maryan refused to have them lit.

Patricia slid a tray of drinks onto the table. "I'll be in the next room. Speak up if you want anything, I can easily hear in there."

Maryan knew the meaning of her words and didn't dare do anything to cause Patricia to report to Mordacai. She waited until the thin assassin left the room.

"She's a sour one, isn't she? I'd get rid." Stella grinned wickedly. "So tell me, what's Chentene like between the sheets? He looks absolutely built for fun." She flicked her long black hair back over her shoulder.

Maryan shook her head. "We haven't …"

"Gorath! What are you thinking?" Stella slapped her palm against her forehead. "You wouldn't buy a horse without sitting on it. If he can't find his way around the passages of Manda Torre he doesn't stand much chance finding his way around yours, does he? I assume he knows what he's supposed to do."

"I think so." Maryan hesitated. "I suspect he's been quite close to some of the women in the court. There's one in particular worries me."

"You'll need to get those vixens cleared out." Stella barked a laugh. "Take control. I ejected a whole nest of rivals when I got here. Their damned families still keep sending doe-eyed doxies to visit."

Maryan glanced around before moving her fingers. Few knew the ancient secret of Serenian hand signals. Although no longer used in battle, Steppis had insisted they learned them. "I'm a prisoner. Help me," she signalled.

"Don't panic," Stella signed. She threw back her head and screamed loud enough to shatter crystal. "Friggit! The child's coming!" Another ear-piercing scream assaulted the room. When Patricia peered in from the next room, Stella pointed at her. "Fetch Justin," she shouted, panting frantically. "Go! You infernal twerp."

Patricia dithered for a moment, trying to decide what to do, but Stella's next agonised wail compelled her to go in search of Justin.

Stella smoothed her straight, black hair back into place. "He's down in the men's bath house. It'll take an age for her to find him." She allowed herself a triumphant smirk. "Now, what's happening?"

"Etelan drugged me so that she could ship me off to wed Chentene. The ambassador says he'll kill everybody I care about, you included, if I show anything but happiness." Maryan ran her hand back over her head, tugging at her plait. "Not just that, Fredrick's shown up. He still looks gorgeous."

"Let's get things in order here." Stella held her hands up. "You say we're all going to die and then start babbling about Fredrick?"

Maryan nodded.

"Fredrick's bad news. Really, stay away from him. When Justin found what he was really like, he dumped him like hot dragon shit."

"Justin *would* say that. Fredrick's different from them, not a courtier."

"He's dangerous and just as bad as Barag was."

"I think I love him."

"You're so stupid Maryan. If I could stand up, I'd slap you. You've fallen for the act."

Justin burst through the door. Almost naked, planes of muscle moved beneath his tanned skin. His powerful chest tapered down to the towel he clutched at his waist.

Stella signed, "We'll speak more." Smiling winsomely up at her husband, she played her fingers along the length of his forearm. "False alarm, darling." She dropped her gaze to admire the towel, "Did you run all the way like that?"

"Actually," His face crinkled. "I only just wrapped this around before I entered." He cradled her chin, obviously rapt in her beauty.

"It's caused quite a stir through the corridors," Patricia said emerging from behind him. She studied the two Serenians through narrowed eyes, but said nothing else.

Stella tugged Justin into a passionate kiss. "Now run along and play. We've got a wedding to plan." She took Patricia's hand. "I'm so sorry. I had such a panic. Please forgive me."

"I'm sure she will," Maryan said. "I didn't get a chance to introduce Patricia. She's not really a servant, but the Ambassador's sister." She emphasised the last words. "She's helping me to adjust to life in Manda Torre and prepare for the wedding."

"How wonderful!" Stella turned the full, glorious beam of her attention on Patricia, "We'll have to work together to get our girl here safely to the altar, won't we?"

"**It** has to be a traditional wedding dress," Helena said.

Maryan felt sorry for the woman. Fabled throughout the city as unflappable, the statuesque, royal dressmaker had been tugging on a fistful of her silver hair for most of the morning. Her usually alabaster skin had developed blotches at her throat. Cosseted in her rooms high in the palace, she had possibly thought herself immune to the tantrums of highborn femininity. The encounter with lowborn Serenians was obviously proving a trial.

"And what do I do with this?" Stella pushed her stomach at her. "I'm supposed to match and you're not getting this into a waist-pinching bodice."

"I'll be skinned alive …" The dressmaker grabbed a charcoal stick, sketching flowing lines down the page. "If we allow the robe to sweep down from just under the bust …"

"What bust?" Maryan rested her head onto the workbench and tumbled her hair over her face. "I've had enough, I'm beaten."

"You'll look wonderful, don't worry." Helena rubbed Maryan's back.

Stella added a couple of lines to the drawing. "This would work." She nudged it back for Helena's approval. The dressmaker added a thin shawl before holding it up for them.

"Okay, we're done here," Stella said.

After helping Stella down from the stool, they made their way out into the corridor where Maryan leant against the wall. "I'm going back to my room. Can you make my apologies to Chentene and Justin? Tell them you're working me too hard."

"A wedding needs to be organised."

"I really don't have a choice, do I?" Maryan shook her head.

"I think Mordacai has every angle covered. We couldn't change things even if I told Justin, which you've asked me not to do. Do you want me to come to your rooms and stay with you?"

"I just want some time alone. I'll see you in the morning." She felt let down by her friend. Stella seemed almost as hell-bent she would marry Chentene as Patricia did.

Time slowed to a snail's pace, but evening finally arrived. Maryan lingered in her suite until the others would be at dinner. The corridors were empty. Every footstep seemed to echo. Raised on tiptoe, she sneaked down the corridor leading to Chentene's rooms.

The door where Fredrick had signalled to her was half way along the darkened passage. She knew this was silly. What was the point? Nobody would be inside. Illuminated only by the moonlight etching criss-cross shadows across an old desk, the room appeared empty. She could make out the shape of two high-backed chairs. The room smelled of the musty books lining the dark walls. Poised in the gloom, she allowed the door to click shut.

"I hoped you'd come." Fredrick rose from the chair, a silhouette against the window.

A tingle ran through her and she was in his arms without a thought. His mouth covered hers. The passion of his embrace drowned all reason.

He lifted her, sweeping her back and forcing her onto the desk with her legs straddled wide around his hips. One hand gripped behind her head, holding her in a kiss, the other pressed against her breast before sliding along her body, moving lower, prying at the folds of her garments.

"Stop!" She jerked her head aside to break his kiss.

He kept his weight pressed against her, but lifted from the kiss to study her face. "Why? Why wait?"

"I'm to marry Chentene."

His hand kept searching, probing, touching. "He'd never know."

"I would."

"We could run away. I've collected a lot of money over the last few months. We could work as guards down in Baraland."

Shadowed in the gloom, she thought she could still see traces of the boy she'd loved. She sat up from the desk, holding him against her. Nestled into the muscle of his shoulder she listened to their twin hearts beating.

Finding her earlobe with his teeth, he raked his fingers across her back. The heat of his breath drew her farther into wild imaginings. She could feel the bulge of his erection against her, a forbidden and sensual pressure. Mere fabric was all that prevented him from entering her. He started to fumble at his waist to loosen his belt.

"No!" She shoved him back and stood up.

"I bet the others have poisoned you against me, haven't they?" He swept one hand back across his shaggy hair. "One damned mistake." His eyes flickered away from hers.

"Tell me about that one mistake."

He shrugged in the dark and sighed. "She led me on. I thought it was what she wanted." He gripped his hand into a fist. "You women get us so wound up and then won't …"

"Like now. I don't want you to go on, but with her you decided *your* needs were greater."

"You twist things. It's not like now. I'm here offering to sacrifice everything for you. Mordacai's been good to me, but I'd still turn my back on him for you. What will you give?"

"If I run, my friends will be executed."

"And? They're not important. We are."

"In battle, I'd give my life in an instant to save them. What's the difference?"

He stroked his fingers along the line of her breast. "When you're wed, we could still meet. Do you think Chentene will cease his trysts? He'll make a fool of you, probably already has."

"You need to go." She slapped his hand away.

"When you need me, remember, I'm waiting." He started for the door. She wanted to call him back, but knew she had nothing to offer him.

Walking the corridors without recollection, she stumbled into her rooms feeling as though she'd just killed something innocent. A choking sob exploded from her throat. Couldn't he understand? She had to dedicate herself to this life. It was time for a wedding, time for her to do her duty as a warrior of Serenia.

"Tell me, can we get a message to the others before the assassins seek them out?" Stella said. She was waiting hidden in Maryan's reception room, brooding in the shadows cast by the single candle.

Maryan shook her head. "I've told Fredrick to go. I can't believe I did it, but I think it's the only way." She dropped to her knees, curled at Stella's feet.

"It's not as if bedding down with Chentene is the most repugnant thought in world." Stella hugged Maryan against her taut belly. "Let's have a wedding and celebrate things properly."

Although the idea of marriage filled Maryan with dread, she could see the affection the court had for Chentene. It buzzed with excitement. Teams of workers toiled to bedeck the grand hall. Wagons full of provisions rolled into the castle from the outlying areas. Stella and Patricia joined forces, snarling their way through any obstacle the tradesmen created.

All Maryan had to do was turn up dressed in the creation the royal dressmaker was assembling in her workshop. As she made her way along an upper balcony to yet another fitting with Helena, she glanced down at the dais at the far end. If only it had been Fredrick … No, she had to push those thoughts aside.

In the dressmaker's chambers, Helena peeked out from behind the multi-layered dress. Escaped strands of hair hung across her face. "Strip off over there," she said around a mouthful of pins. She finished attaching a frill of lace to the hem and smoothed her hands across the front of her apron.

An attendant helped Maryan out of her gown, leaving her almost naked. She hugged her arms about herself, forever envious of the women of the court for their feminine curves.

"You should eat more," Helena said, reading her mind.

"Weight never goes where you want it to, does it?" Maryan twisted, pressing her hands on her hips, trying to imagine her figure with breasts.

A team of assistants helped to lower Helena's dress onto Maryan. The cut of the gown showed too much flesh and she started to tug the revealing neckline higher.

"Don't even think of touching or adjusting things." Helena slapped her hand away. "That is my job. Tomorrow, all will be perfect." She barked a short laugh and her blue eyes twinkled. "I'm sure that Chentene will enjoy unwrapping his wedding present."

"You should get a good night's sleep tonight, if you can." Helena took her arm to lead her to the door. "We'll be along in the morning for the final fitting."

The wedding morning rushed onto Maryan too quickly. Stella appeared at daybreak. Helena followed just behind, her small army taking over the large dining room in the apartments.

The ladies of the court bustled into the room. Dark haired Lady Natalie, easily as tall as Maryan, the additional height of her wig made her loom over everybody. She wore golden, earthy colours to match her complexion. Behind Natalie, came Sophie and Rachael. Plump sisters from lands a few leagues outside Manda Torre.

Each of these ladies had a suite of rooms allocated within the castle visitor apartments. Their existence in the court provoked numerous whispers amongst the servants. Whatever the reason for their presence, they were rapidly becoming close friends to Maryan.

"We prepare you for our Prince," Helena said.

"And we'll try to make the best of these primitive facilities." Stella winked at Patricia. "When she's married, can we get a steam room fitted?"

"Steam makes the skin go wrinkly." Patricia pursed her lips in disapproval as Stella guided Maryan into the large bathing chamber.

After dropping her nightclothes in the corner, Maryan lowered herself into the brimming pool. She watched Stella peel away her own garments and was shocked at the changes pregnancy had wrought on her friend's body.

Stella stroked her hand across her taut belly. "Don't laugh! You'll have one of these soon."

Maryan floated in the deep water of the bath allowing her friend to work soap into her hair. Unable to decide how she felt, her stomach tumbled. Out in the city, Fredrick would be moping. Somewhere high on the borders, Sami would think she'd been abandoned. What was love? Sworn to secrecy, only Stella knew her heart.

Moving in a dream, Maryan climbed out of the bath, then helped Stella up from the pool. Her throat wouldn't work. Tears ran. If she failed, all of them would die. She grasped Stella in a hug and forced herself to smile.

Stella summoned the servants and they faced each other as the maids ran drying sheets across their skin.

Stella's lip curled. "Trained to fight in any terrain, but we're not expected to know how to dry our crevices."

Wrapped in a thin dressing gown, Maryan opened the door. A wave of perfume mixed with the pungent odour of spirit hit her.

Lady Natalie posed with a comb that looked like a garden implement. "I've brought all of the essential things." She'd prepared what looked like a torture chair. Hovering beside it, the ladies Sophie and Rachael lurked wielding small vials of nail paint.

Once Maryan lay back with her arms and legs spread to allow them to paint her nails, Natalie started to work a wide-toothed comb through her hair. After her restless night, the rhythmic combing eased Maryan into a much-needed sleep. She shut her eyes, relishing the sensation, until a wicked bee-sting on her forehead almost threw her from the chair. "What did you do that for!" Maryan squealed rubbing her eyebrow with a finger.

"Don't be a baby." Tweezers ready, Natalie squinted to assess the next hair to pluck.

From then, Maryan remained wide-awake, watching every part of the preparations. Patricia's face creased into a superior smile when she succumbed to a little paint on her lips.

"The bride is ready," Natalie declared.

The ladies of the court departed to make their own preparations, leaving Maryan to Helena. The dressmaker supervised her team as they lowered the magnificent dress over Maryan's head.

"And finally." Patricia held out a set of manacles joined by a length of chain.

"I thought we agreed I didn't need to do this?" Maryan said, twitching her glare between Patricia and Stella.

"All Garalandian brides do this," Patricia said.

"Even I did," Stella added. "The breaking of the chains is the climax of the ceremony. Don't be a grump, it's so romantic."

The corridor to the great hall narrowed and closed around her. "I bet this is what it feels like when a warrior walks down the Tunnel of Heroes into the arena," Maryan said in a subdued tone.

"And later, in the bedroom, there should be as much screaming, but hopefully not as much blood." Stella squeezed Maryan's hand. As the closest thing to family, she'd present Maryan during the service.

The silence of the corridors emphasised the excited buzz within the great hall. The hubbub behind the door hushed and a wave of anticipation hit her. Maryan grasped Stella's hand in a fierce grip.

"Bring me a bride!" Chentene called from inside the hall.

Maryan's mouth went dry.

"Where is my woman!" he shouted.

Stella leant close. "What would they do if I slipped you a pair of blades? A virgin warrior in full battle fury, I bet he wouldn't do so much demanding then."

"Possibly our traditions would seem stupid to other people," Maryan whispered.

"I demand a virgin!" Chentene yelled.

"I don't know how I kept my face straight at that one. It's time. Let's put him out of his misery." Stella stepped in front of Maryan.

The ladies, Sophie and Rachel swung the huge doors open, gracing the throng with beaming smiles before beckoning Maryan to follow.

A sea of faces stared at her. Stella walked in front, her entire bearing haughty and challenging. Maryan followed, holding the golden chains binding her wrists out in front. The distance to the dais evaporated and too soon, Maryan found herself in front of Chentene, with her arms outstretched.

"Is this woman of noble birth and pure of body?" Chentene asked.

"She is perfection." Stella projected the words out across the hall. She pressed on Maryan's shoulder, forcing her to her knees. She then bent into a curtsey to arrange the chain across the chopping block. The scars of a thousand years marred its ancient surface.

A priestess of Deepala handed an axe to Chentene. He lifted it to his shoulder before severing the chains with a resounding thud. "I take her as mine."

Maryan lifted her gaze to Chentene taking his proffered hand and rising to her feet. Adoration filled his stare. A tingle ran from her chest to her groin, she yearned to be with him in every sense. As if responding to her unspoken desire, he embraced her.

Amidst the cheers, Maryan saw the exultant expressions on all present. They loved the Prince. Her heart pounded in the realisation that she did as well.

Although every urge in her body demanded taking Chentene to her bedchamber, they had to complete their ceremonial responsibilities. Chentene took her hand, leading her through to the rarely used state banqueting hall.

"Gorath," Maryan murmured when the doors opened. Brilliant hangings covered the drab walls, transforming the room into a riotous festival of colour. Tables created an aisle running the length of the room. Around the walls, liveried staff waited to serve.

Leading the party, Chentene guided Maryan, closely followed by Stella and Justin. Stiff backed and triumphant behind them, Mordacai and Patricia also took seats on the top table.

"You might as well eat something. This is going to be a long night," Chentene said.

"You promise?" Maryan replied, squeezing his hand.

"Sadly, not quite as we might hope." He pulled his face. "We've got to eat at least one hundred courses and greet every dignitary from every land who has travelled to the wedding."

"And then …"

"And then, we lead the dancing festivities."

"And then …"

"Then." Chentene blushed.

A braided major-domo escorted each table of guests to congratulate the couple. Maryan's face ached from smiling. Her hand throbbed from too many handshakes.

"Time to move on again," Chentene whispered. He took Maryan's hand to guide her through to the ballroom.

Thousands of candles burned in the chandeliers bathing the gilt-framed mirrors on the walls in warm light. A million crystals twinkled setting the room alive with glittering reflections.

"You have practised haven't you?" Maryan whispered.

"I'm sure I'll pick it up." Chentene laughed at her shocked expression. "I've been trained from birth for my wedding dance. I'm hardly likely to forget it now, am I?" His arm snaked around her waist to guide her into the centre of the room.

"Everybody's watching. I feel silly," Maryan said.

The orchestra in the gallery struck a stately melody and Chentene swept her into a whirling dance around the room. Blurred faces whipped by, the mirrors reflected the room away into infinity. Matching the rising tempo, their speed increased. He ended the dance with a flourish, before throwing his arms wide. "Let the dancing commence!" he shouted and the floor filled with swirling couples.

Chentene took Maryan up onto a double seat set high above the dance floor. The couples whirled past, a constant stream of silken dresses and crisp uniforms.

"I'm joining you." Stella waddled from the melee. "Justin, I just can't do it, not if you want your son born at home. One more turn of that dance floor and you'll be sending for the birthing nurse."

"I just …" Justin followed, but stood gazing out across the room, his foot tapping in time to the music.

"Couldn't you dance with one of your family?" Maryan said. She pointed to Lady Emily, who had taken a position not far from the royal party. "She's unescorted. Don't you know her?"

"Not that I recognise. Not one of the normal circle."

"I thought you and Chentene spent a lot of time together as children. She's one of his relatives."

"Not one of ours." Justin shook his head. "I'm sure I'd know her." His face brightened. "Now that one."

Heads turned to watch Natalie parade the length of the ballroom. "Hello cousin." She dropped into a deep curtsey. "Would you care for a turn on the floor?" Her purring tone, as well as her plunging neckline drew a blush to Justin's cheeks.

He cast an uncertain glance at Stella, waiting for her agreement before he took Natalie's hand.

"Come wife. We must do our duty," Chentene said, dragging Maryan out to dance.

The steps he guided her through appeared strangely archaic, with the men and women parading the length of the room in time to the music. Chentene led Maryan whilst the members of the court followed.

The music changed tempo many times until Chentene signalled to her that they could risk slipping away. The musicians played on and the guests continued to dance, unaware the couple had departed.

She could sense his tension as they walked through the corridors of Manda Torre. Staring down from the walls, the eyes of Chentene's ancestors followed them, apparently envious of what tonight would hold. Eventually they reached the Prince's chambers. He tilted his head to kiss her, plunging his hands into her hair.

After an age, he broke the kiss and opened the door. "Well goodnight then." he gestured down the corridor. "Your rooms are that way."

"I thought …"

“I told you that I wouldn’t touch you until you asked.” His face remained stoic. “Indeed, I insisted that you *demand* I do. So, until you make such a demand I suggest we sleep apart.”

She gripped behind his head and tugged his face close enough to bite his lip. “I think, I ask.”

“Do you demand?”

She pushed him inside the room, closing the door behind them.

“I demand.” she tugged at the wedding dress. It had taken four attendants to stitch her into it. Chagrined, she noticed Chentene was smiling like an idiot.

“Helena sent these with a diagram.” He flourished a pair of long dressmaking scissors, twirling them around his finger.

The image in front of her shifted. She saw Asti, blood spattered and furious standing over a whimpering Barag. Her veins filled with ice. This land had stripped beautiful Arlaine of life. It had robbed her of Sami and snatched her away from all that she knew. A pretty dress and a fairy tale wedding couldn’t erase that pain.

Chentene felt the mood change. The gleam faded from his eyes. He tried to embrace her, but she brushed his hands aside. “No Chentene, this is wrong. I shouldn’t be here.”

He gripped her biceps, driven by the madness of lust. “I could … I want to …” Maryan remained frozen to his need. Her demeanour drained his passion until he sagged away from her. “Go!” he spun on his heel, vanishing through the far door with a slam. Completely alone, she wound through the corridors, back to her suite.

Chapter 12

Harlon's blade cut so close to her face, Maryan could have kissed the steel. Cursing, she stumbled to recover. Even after months of training, he could still slip effortlessly through her defence.

"Hold," he said, keeping his guard in place until she lowered her blade.

"Look at the silly girls." He surveyed the training ground through his medallion. "Great idea though, wearing such a revealing training outfit. It thoroughly rewards the effort of accommodating them."

Maryan smoothed her short skirt. The saddle maker had made it from fine leather and had merely shrugged when she'd demanded he cut it off at thigh length.

A select set of the ladies of the court had started to join the sessions, with most of them copying her skirt. Equipped with ancient swords from the family armoury, the Ladies Sophie and Rachel worked hard, hewing enthusiastically at wooden blocks set in the ground. Their plump rears quivered beneath the straining leather and their chubby arms wobbled like Stump's fledgling wings attempting flight.

"I wonder which poor man they imagine they're hacking at?" Harlon said.

The thud of steel thumping deep into wood jerked their heads around in unison. Armed with a brace of heavy daggers, Lady Natalie studiously buried each one close to the centre of the target. Her hip-rolling walk to retrieve her knives drew an agonised sigh from Harlon. "Now that one, I need to give her extra attention."

“Stop lusting and get back to training.” Maryan slapped his arm, feeling the solid muscle of his bicep. Although he affected the air of a fop, his body betrayed his years as a warrior culminating in becoming the weapon master for the court.

She pushed him off balance and sprang into an attack, forcing him to dance away from her rapid sequence of forms. Her moment of glory ended when he slipped his blade through her guard to jab lightly on her breast.

“How do you do that?” She barely restrained from throwing her swords to the ground. That would be stupid. For one, the blades were beautifully balanced, an expensive gift from her bemused husband. Secondly, a tantrum would incur a repeat of Harlon’s patronising taunts regarding female temperament. She tugged at her plait in exasperation. “I’ve trained almost from birth, but I’ve never been able to keep both of these blades under control the way a warrior should.”

“Should? There is no should. In sword fighting, there’s only what is.” Harlon tilted to one side, his cocked hip stretching his breeches tight. “I’ve an idea that I know what your problem is.”

“Really, after the best tutors in Serenia couldn’t see anything wrong?”

“They weren’t watching the way I do.” Harlon curled the edge of his lip. “To be certain, I’d need to see you without your blouse on.” He raised his keyhole medallion. “Oh yes, without that, I’m sure I could spot the problem.”

“Rogue!” Maryan punched at his jaw, but he brushed the blow aside and flashed his infuriating smile.

“Okay, I’ll just have to try something else, come with me.” He crooked his finger, inviting her to follow him down the short flight of steps leading to his private rooms. “Leave the door open if you don’t trust yourself,” he shouted back from the doorway.

Needing a chaperone, she quickly tried to assess the suitability of the women training in the courtyard. Lady Emily was practicing with a bow. As one of the few who hadn’t succumbed to the fashion of wearing a short skirt, her long dress swished across the gravel of the pathways. Could she be trusted? Instead, Maryan raised her voice to call out across the courtyard. “Lady Natalie, would you come here please?”

After collecting her knives, the sumptuous woman made her way across the training ground.

“May I ask you to stand in this doorway to assure the ladies of the court nothing untoward occurs?”

“And if it does, should I tell?” The crack of a tight, white smile gleamed between her plump lips.

Harlon’s rooms stretched a good way beneath the wall, but Maryan remained in clear sight from the training ground steps. The collection of books lined up on a shelf surprised her. He’d hung a number of drawings around the room. She gasped. One of them was a pencil sketch of the painting showing Asti the Red and her mother. She squinted to study the detail. The artist had divided her mother’s face with feint lines and the curve of Asti’s hip remained formed from an arc of a circle.

"You've spotted my secret treasure then." Harlon leant over her shoulder to unhook the frame from the wall. "My brother, Oliver, drew it. He's an artist." Harlon traced along the line of Asti's body, his fingernail hovering a hairbreadth above the parchment. "To meet a woman like this ... that would be a dream."

"A dream!" Maryan snorted. "Gorath, it'd be a bad one for you. You know who these are?"

He shook his head. "He said they were the champions of Serenia, virgin warriors."

"The one on the left is my mother, Amara the Magnificent. The other is Asti the Red. She's not beautiful anymore. My mother took her face off in a fight."

Still cradling the frame, Harlon dropped onto a hard wooden chair. "Asti the Red," he murmured before narrowing his eyes. "Your mother's a virgin?"

"It's complicated." Maryan flushed. "Many virgin warriors birth a child." Desperate to change the subject, she asked, "Your brother drew this. Would he have done the inscriptions as well?"

"What inscriptions?"

"Along the bottom an inscription read, 'Strength through eternal love,' and across the top were runes that sometimes became words, 'Now you are queen, forgive me,' signed with an A."

"They shifted at night?"

"Yes."

"You're describing candle and moonlight writing, done using a magical form of ink. It's his most precious secret. Ask him what it means when he arrives in a few weeks. He's coming to paint you for the Prince." Harlon replaced the frame, straightening it with loving precision. "I need to get some things from the other room."

He returned from the storeroom carrying a sheet of leather and a selection of weapons. Using shears, he fashioned two leather triangles, joining them with strips to form a crude bra. "Put this on. If I can't see you naked, I need the next best thing. I have a suspicion about your muscles." Harlon winked and took the weapons out to the training ground.

After a moment's hesitation, Maryan slipped off her blouse. Lady Natalie made her way down the short stairway. "He's a gorgeous piece of meat isn't he? Few would have called for a chaperone if he'd asked them in here."

Maryan fitted the bra across her chest. It barely concealed her breasts.

"Deepala help me," Natalie muttered, helping her to adjust the single strap. "I hope that dressing in these doesn't catch on the way your skirt has. I'd need half a cowhide to cover myself adequately."

Although she'd trained naked in Serenia, Maryan feared she'd disappoint Chentene if she showed her body in public. Garalandians were so prudish in these matters. Bracing herself for the comments, she ran up the steps to where a small circle of spectators waited.

"Now, take your blades and attack me." Harlon grinned.

She swept forward, keeping both blades moving in synchronised forms. Harlon countered. She tried to spin her swords into an Amaran defence, but he blocked the move.

"Now try this in your right hand." Harlon threw her a longer, heavier sword. "It will feel slower, but use your left hand as a guard."

The sword felt awkward, but soon, a rhythm started to flow through her. The extra reach helped her to stay balanced. Harlon held up his hand up again.

"That's better, now I want to watch you work against the block. I'll stand behind."

Sweat started to run down her back. She glimpsed over her shoulder, conscious the crowd had grown from the few women of the court into more than twenty palace lackeys.

"Wait!" Harlon commanded. He swapped the heavy sword for a battle-axe. "Try this."

She turned the ancient weapon in her hands, half mace and half axe. Shaped like a lion's paw, steel claws hooked out from the end. Where the pads would be on a paw, there was a spike long enough to pierce a skull.

"Your back muscles aren't flowing correctly for a sword in your right hand, probably a muscle tear that didn't heal properly. You need a heavier weapon with less finesse."

Harlon took a guard position before gesturing for her to attack. The axe felt out of control, its weight twisting in her hand.

"Your delicate wrist needs a bit more work," Harlon said through gritted teeth. "Tame it. Make the brute your slave. See, you can catch a sword between the toe claws and parry with the haft. Use the Serenian blade as a guard and hold that beastie ready to attack."

She cocked the axe back, using the light blade in her left hand to weave a defence. Circling and feinting, she waited until she'd moved his weight onto his back foot. The devastating weight of the axe swept out, almost catching Harlon's calf muscle. He leapt, but found her sword tip pressed against his chest. The small crowd of onlookers cheered, the racket bounced around the training ground.

"Good girl!" Harlon brushed the blade aside with the back of his hand and swept her into a bear hug that threatened to crack her ribs.

"My Lady!" Patricia's disapproving glare made Maryan step back. "It's time we returned to your rooms. I think you should acquire a robe before walking through the palace."

That night Maryan ate with Chentene in the dining room attached to her chambers. "I understand you put on quite a display today," Chentene said from across the table.

"You disapprove?"

"Not at all, I'm only sorry I didn't get to see the outfit everybody is talking about." He shook his head at the thoughts. "Lady Natalie in that leather skirt is already causing quite enough of a stir through the guards. If she took to dressing as they describe, I'm not sure what would happen. I can only hope that you haven't started another fashion."

Uncertain of how to react, Maryan cut silently at the meat on her plate. Why had he immediately mentioned Natalie? There were rumours about him meeting secretly with women before their marriage. She wondered if she was naïve, thinking it had all stopped since their marriage. Despite her fears, she tried to push the thought aside. Natalie had become a close friend.

Pictures of cow-eyed women hung around them, smiling enigmatically out across the room. The news that Harlon's brother would add her to the gallery had been a shock. A mischievous thought struck her. "If you'd like to see the outfit, maybe I'll wear it for my portrait."

Chentene gestured with his knife at the paintings. "I think these poor ladies would faint from their frames at the thought."

Maryan fed a small piece of meat to Carl perched on her shoulder. He balanced using one paw gripped into her hair.

"You do know there are women walking around the town with stuffed rats on their shoulders, don't you?" Chentene popped a small tomato into his mouth and spoke around it. "Thankfully, they can't get their hands on a dragon pup." He glanced at Stump, curled in the corner of the room. The adolescent dragon silently regarded them. Grown larger than a hunting dog, his multi-faceted eyes twinkled in the candlelight. "My jacket!" Chentene shouted spotting a shred of cloth peeping from beneath the dragon. Stump had scrunched the golden threaded jacket beneath him.

"Tell him to get off it." Chentene leapt up from the table.

'Gold.' The single word rang.

"Do you know how much that cost?"

"Dragons like to sleep on gold." Maryan shrugged. "It's what they do, gather treasure to lie on. You shouldn't have left it out."

'Mine.'

"Not yours, mine." Chentene tugged at the sleeve protruding from under the dragon.

'Treasure!' Stump coughed a blaze of flame, driving Chentene away. Maryan ducked under the dragon's head, wrestling him off his hoard. Golden spoons and bowls clattered across the floor.

Chentene grabbed his jacket and held it up. The weight of the young dragon had creased the metal thread beyond recognition. "His, I suppose." He threw it back to Stump.

"He's going to get too big to live in the house soon," Maryan said.

"I'm having doors fitted to the end of the long gallery. Come here, I'll show you what I'm thinking of doing." Chentene guided her to the window. "See, if we knock out through the top floor there, he'll be able to get in and out."

He caressed her shoulder, the heat of his hand burned through the silk of her gown. She spun to face him allowing his weight to press her against the window frame. Each time they were close, her feelings grew. She wanted to wrap her arms around him and ask him to stay, but worried in case she panicked as she had on their wedding night. Watching his eyes in anticipation of their kiss, Maryan guided Chentene's face to hers. A sharp rap on the door jerked them apart.

"Come!" Chentene commanded without shifting his attention.

Damon, the guard commander entered. "I'm sorry to disturb your meal, but something is going on out in the villages and I didn't think it could wait." The broad-shouldered soldier glanced between the royal couple.

Chentene sighed slightly, but nodded. "Of course." He allowed his gaze to caress Maryan before gesturing for Damon to come further into the room.

The commander coughed. "A lion's come down into the farms. He's taking sheep and the villagers are trying to capture it. If we don't get out there, somebody is going to get hurt."

Quietly watching Chentene's reaction, Maryan's heart melted. As ruler, he shouldn't care about peasants. All of the tales of uncaring nobles were wrong. This man, her husband, was a good man who showed concern for the lowest of his people. His sad expression tugged at emotions she didn't understand.

"I'm going to ride out there tomorrow and take a few of the guards." Chentene turned his back on her to face the older guard. "Assemble a dozen men and we'll put an end to this."

"Can I come?" Maryan asked.

He spun with his hand already outstretched ready to object, but paused, recognising the determination in her face. "Is there anything I can refuse you? Be ready at dawn."

The grey sky, heavy with the threat of rain almost sent Maryan back to bed, but the promise of a gallop, tugged at her more. Although she'd ridden horses, she'd never imagined the pleasure of owning one. Her life had changed when Chentene had presented her with a white mare, Ruby.

She dragged on a robe and went through to her sitting room where servants had laid bowls of fruit and porridge. She glanced at the unlit fire grate knowing sometime soon she'd have to succumb to lighting it.

"Carved from ice, with blades of fire," she muttered to herself. Chentene had been true to his word, he'd left her alone, but she remembered his weight pressing her against the window frame last night. Her breathing quickened acknowledging her feelings. Maybe, she wouldn't need the fire, just yet.

Back in her bedchamber, Carl lay curled in his open cage, still sleeping after a night roaming the palace. *'You need some air,'* she thought at him.

The large rodent rolled over to display his ruined back legs. '*Too tired.*'

'We're going to the stable, come on, all that loose grain,' she crooned, before cupping her hands to lift him. 'Did you know that there are silly women around here who think you're not real? They're wearing model rats.'

Downstairs, a groom walked the mare out to hand the reins to Maryan. The courtyard where the mounted guards waited reeked of horses and liniment. Chentene appeared in the doorway wearing polished riding boots. The sight of him in his gleaming breastplate quickened her pulse, making her skin flush.

Although Chentene did a double take when he noticed the rat on her shoulder, he waved a greeting. "Good morning, my darling, let's hope for a good hunt." He swung into the saddle and spurred his mount to lead the guards out of the courtyard. Maryan nudged Ruby onto the end of the line.

The air felt damp, a sure sign of rain. Carl muttered dark thoughts, but she'd grown used to ignoring the animal's complaints. Bred for castle life he didn't trust having so much sky above him.

After a time trotting in single file, they reached a forest where the road curved off around the edge. She nudged Rosy into a canter to edge past the line of troopers and catch up to Chentene. "Why don't we ride through?"

"Witches and other things. The Forest of Dreams isn't a good place to be."

"The Forest of Dreams sounds delightful, why avoid dreams?" Maryan blushed remembering her recent nocturnal fantasies.

"Think of your worst nightmare, double it and then make it real. That's what's waiting inside there. I've known guards take a drunken bet to spend a night in the forest. Some never return, but those who do, come back changed by the experience, fearful of ever falling asleep again. No, we ride around."

The patrol followed the tree line along a well-trodden pathway. Memories of Kait slipped into her thoughts. She'd have been unable to resist such an encounter with magic. Maryan smiled, imagining her wild friend bewildering the staid old wizards of Idrahail. Carl became agitated and his claws caught her skin. She slipped her fingers into his fur to calm him.

'She wanted to open me up and poke around inside.'

'But she saved you.' Maryan soothed him back on her shoulder.

The party stopped in the centre of a village. Small alleyways led away from the main square. The tavern even had a second floor and a slate roof.

Chentene and Guard Commander Damon dismounted to face the village elder limping out to greet them. The old man started to lower himself to his knees, but Chentene immediately caught his elbow to haul him to his feet.

"Not like that, dear chap, not today." Chentene spun on his heel admiring the crude buildings around him. "A fine village square you are creating here. One day, Garalandia will be proud of this place. Now, tell me about this lion."

The elder tugged his rough jerkin straight. "There's a group of the young ones chasing him, my Lord."

"Your Highness," the guard commander corrected. "The Prince is addressed as Your Highness."

"Damon, there's nought amiss with any lords in Garalandia. I don't object to being addressed as one," Chentene said. "Let the man speak unfettered by fear of offence."

Maryan's pride blossomed. Chentene worked so hard at being a part of his people. She wondered why he tolerated the likes of Mordacai. The old man directed the patrol through the village to pick up a winding track across the fields.

They spurred their mounts into a trot. At the edge of the village, Chentene glanced across at her. "If we don't stop them somebody will get killed. They're talking of corralling it into a ravine and trying to kill it with spears."

"And the problem?" Maryan remembered her own people fighting a dragon in a similar way.

"These are farm boys, not warriors. They're ale-brave, all pumped up to impress their harvest sweethearts. They don't know one end of a spear from another. An injured son means the crops don't get collected. Uncollected crops would mean the family starves. We have to act."

Their path descended into a high-sided gash in the landscape. As they progressed, the rocky escarpments reduced the view they had of the grey sky. The clouds grew darker and Maryan felt the first damp pinprick touch her cheek. Within a heartbeat, curtains of rain raked the length of the valley, forcing them to cover their faces. She tugged her hood over her brow leaving Carl nestled deep behind her head. The trail brought them to a niche in the rock where excited shouts led them to the hunting party.

Chentene dismounted and made his way into the cut. Maryan followed. "You have him cornered," Chentene said to the backs of the youths.

"Aye, trapped by his danglies," shouted a rough looking lad keeping his attention riveted on the mouth of the canyon. Too late, he realised who stood so close. "Your Highness, no offense meant, but he's trapped like a rat." He dropped to his knee, keeping his head down.

Maryan ignored the mental snort from Carl, but the rat's next words chilled her. 'The lion's scared. He already has his first victim planned. It's strange, I can't see anything.'

"Chentene," she interrupted. "The lion's about to pounce. If you fear for their lives, call the villagers away immediately."

After studying his wife for a moment, Chentene barked. "Pull all of these youngsters back." He laid his hand on the lad's shoulder. "We're grateful you've cornered the beast, but this is for us to sort out."

"Your Highness, what do you suggest?" The guard commander looked to Chentene for his lead.

"I'm not sure." The Prince rubbed his chin. "We need to tempt the lion out to allow your men a clear shot." He squinted against the driving rain to survey the ravine." Could you work some archers up there?"

"Possibly …"

"May I suggest something," Maryan said. "I've got Carl chattering in my head about the lion feeling strange."

"I think civilians should leave this kind of matter to the guards," the commander snapped, not shifting from studying the rocky escarpment.

"Have any of your men hunted a full grown dragon?" Maryan hissed at the commander's back. His shoulders hunched and she calmed her voice before speaking again. "The poor beast is terrified. He's not to blame for what's happened. Just let me …" Before they could object, Maryan squirmed between the two men and plunged into the bushes across the mouth of the canyon.

"Maryan!" Chentene said.

She ignored him, turning her attention to Carl. *'I hope you're right about this,'* she thought, conscious that she hadn't been completely truthful about her experience hunting dragons.

'He's watching us, but not with his eyes. It's all dark and blurry,' Carl said. 'He's definitely aware that we're coming closer. Wait here.'

Carl scrambled across her neck and past her face. *'Why you think this open air thing is good for you …'*

The warm fur of his rump brushed her cheek before he tumbled onto the damp undergrowth. The rat vanished, his ruined back legs hardly slowing him at all.

After what felt like an age, Carl's voice reappeared inside her head. *'He can't see, that's the problem, you can come closer now.'*

Maryan dragged herself through the undergrowth. The cold, damp grass smeared the length of her riding cloak. She wrinkled her nose at the filth sticking to her clothes. *'I can't see you.'*

'Look up into the rocks above you.'

Pulling her hood back, she peered into the canyon, the rain spattered against her face. Movement closer than expected revealed a young lion ready to spring. Its teeth looked too large for comfort.

'You're safe enough. He likes the smell of you,' Carl said.

'I like the smell of roast lamb.'

The lion's muscles bunched beneath his sleek, tawny coat as he flowed sinuously from the rocks. His milky eyes stared blindly. Maryan's legs trembled when she forced them to take her weight.

'I'm letting him look through my eyes." Carl sat perched like an oddly shaped hat between the lion's ears, his head twitched from side to side. "He's not been able to see or hunt properly for a long time. The gnawing hunger is driving him crazy.'

Maryan ran her hand along the flank of the lion feeling his ribs through the fur. The lion cowered away. She could sense Carl chattering and if she concentrated, could see the cascade of images he kept projecting to the lion. She focused on breathing slowly, trying to stay calm as she made her way from the gorge. When Maryan reached the edge of the canyon, the anguish visible on Chentene's face shocked her.

"Maryan." He surveyed the full devastation of her mud-smeared clothing, shifting his attention between the beast at her side and her face.

"Now, move away slowly, so that we can finish him," Damon said.

Chentene shook his head. "I think I know the expression. That isn't the look of a hunter. My wife's found another pet."

Chapter 13

"**If** this starts another fashion, we're leaving the city. I'm not having women wandering around with dangerous animals at their heels." Chentene pulled his hands over his hair, tugging it tight. "What are we going to do with a lion?" He spun around seeking support from the small group.

"Cleaned up, I think the pair shall prove noble companions for you." A rare grin split Damon's face.

Smeared head to foot in mud, Maryan placed her hand on Chentene's arm. "I'm sure we can figure something out, but we need to get him some food. All of these animals and people are aggravating his hunger." The lion roared, shaking his head, she could feel tension quivering through his flank pressed against her leg.

"Commander, I think we're camping here tonight," Chentene said. "Request some provisions from the village."

Crude bivouacs quickly sprang up in the valley, filling the spaces between the bushes and the rocks. Guard Commander Damon set up a small encampment for the royal couple separated from the soldiers.

"You know that Damon really doesn't need to go to too much trouble. I'm happy to fit in with the troops," Maryan said.

"It's more for the troops comfort, than for yours." Chentene grinned. "They're a little worried about the mud-smeared enchantress who tames beasts." He nodded at the lion gnawing at a haunch of meat. "What are we going to do with him?"

“He can’t fend for himself and I’m not going to let him die of neglect.” She pressed herself against Chentene, nuzzling into his neck. “I won’t abandon him.”

“I suppose that’s what I expected. In the morning, I’m going to ride ahead to start preparing things.”

The nervousness of the lion dictated the slow pace of their journey to Manda Torre. Damon split the troop to the rear and front of the main party. Maryan sometimes rode, but often walked with the beast at her hip. That night, when they called a halt within hailing distance of the walls of Manda Torre, Chentene rode out to meet them.

“I’m not sure they thought I was serious about this.” Chentene scowled back at the city. “I’ve had to knock a few heads, but I think we’re ready for the cursed thing.”

Their short morning journey brought them to the gates. Maryan dismounted to stride beside the lion, allowing it to nudge against her. Word had run ahead like wildfire. The streets were empty, but the upper windows bulged with people desperate to see their wild Serenian Princess and her lion.

Chentene walked alongside, glowing with adoration. “You are something special. I doubt I’ll ever be able to thank Mordacai enough for bringing you to me.”

The mention of the Ambassador slightly dampened Maryan’s happiness, but she buried her feelings and tugged Chentene closer. “I really need to be with you,” she whispered.

The Prince waved up at a group of people hanging out of a window. A smug expression played around his lips. “I believe, my lady, I said you had to do more than ask. I said you needed to beg me.”

“I think it will be you begging me once we get to *our* chambers.” She squeezed Chentene’s hand digging her nails into his palm.

The lion at her hip roared and Carl’s words intruded. ‘Stop that. The tension is exciting him. Can we get him settled before you two start rumpling the nest?’

Without being absolute ruler, housing a young lion in a working castle might have proved difficult. Chentene had evicted the mapmakers from their ground floor rooms, commanding them to find other accommodation. He’d redirected workers from renovations onto erecting a corral to section off a small courtyard. Mac, as Maryan had decided to name the lion, took up residence with remarkable ease.

“Despite your protests, you’ve arranged things well.” Maryan snuggled close, draping Chentene’s arm around her.

“I just don’t think I should have something quite this wild roaming the city.” He raised her hand to his lips. “Speaking of wild animals …”

Hand in hand, Maryan and Chentene hurried through the corridors of the palace. An official opened his mouth to ask for an opinion on a document, but Chentene’s answering palm stifled the words on the man’s lips. The doors to the royal apartments flew open and suffered the indignity of being closed with a kick.

After a fierce kiss, Chentene led Maryan through to the bedchamber. He’d barely turned to face her when her full weight hit his chest, forcing him onto the bed. Straddling him, she ripped the decorative dagger from his belt and tapped her teeth with the point of the blade.

Eyes wide, Chentene reached out, but she caught his hands and pressed them down to his stomach. “Wait. I need to feel in control.” She curled against him, sucking his earlobe between her lips, nipping it. “Please,” she whispered. “I’m not sure of this and I don’t want things to go wrong.”

By tilting his head to the side, Chentene met her gaze. “I’d give you anything you ask. I only crave your happiness.”

“And I yours.” A growl escaped her and she sank her teeth into the crook of his neck before sitting upright above him. His attention flickered between her face and the dagger.

“I’ve never been held at knife point. You don’t plan on injuring me too much, do you?”

“I want to hear you scream.” The blade sliced through the threads holding his shirt fastenings.

Wriggling open-legged along the length of his body, the pressure of his erection unleashed a delicious craving deep within her. His hips lifted beneath her and she brandished the dagger. “I told you. I need to be in control.” Carefully avoiding the taut bulge, she cut his waistband. The material parted and released him.

She played the steel blade across his chest, running it through the fine hair toward his waist. The size of his member fascinated her. Although she’d often detected his arousal, this was the first time she’d ever seen it. The thought of it inside her made her tingle. It lifted like a beast rousing from slumber.

“Not a movement!” she hissed.

“I’m afraid, My Lady, there are certain movements a gentleman cannot control.”

He groaned, clutching the neckline of her dress as if to rip it from her. Maryan took his wrists and pressed them onto his chest. “Let me.” Stretching up, she peeled her mud-spattered clothes over her head. Doubt niggled. Would he be disappointed? There could be no more waiting. She dropped the robe to one side. The reward of his adoration quelled any fears. She cut the side bands of her undergarment and remained poised above him.

Naked and holding the dagger, she returned her husband’s admiring stare. “I’ve heard how Garalandian folk imagine Serenian women behave.” She drew the blade slowly down between her small breasts, allowing the delightful trace to arouse her nipples. “Why not close your eyes and picture what we might have done?”

“I’d rather …”

“Trust me. Lie back and close your eyes.”

“And miss this?”

“You’ll not miss a thing.” She leant forward. “Raise your arms, and try to stay still. Not a movement.”

Trailing the blade in a sensual circuit, she stroked his wonderful body. They were so different. His muscles were taut hawsers, like the ropes tethering a ship at dock. His skin was much darker than hers. His broad chest had a down of hair. Even as she teased his nipples erect, they remained tiny. She touched her own. Although her breasts were small, her nipples had swollen hard and felt connected to her groin by a throbbing line of excitement. Wondering if it could be the same for him, she returned her attention to his, the sigh he emitted suggested it might be. She lowered herself, allowing the pressure between her legs to answer the call she'd awakened.

Discarding the dagger, she raked her nails along his body. "I want this moment to last forever," she murmured, dipping to taste his skin, drinking his masculine odour. Pressing her face against his chest, she could hear his heart pounding. Or was it hers?

Madness of passion gripped her. Her crotch pressed against him. Slick moistness allowed her to savour the mounting excitement. Her hip thrusts became more urgent. Feeling the room start to spin, all foreplay stopped and instinct drove her.

He reached up, inviting her into a kiss, licking her neck and nipping her ear. She could feel his erection probing. His breath burned hot on her damp skin. He massaged as he guided her to where he touched the spot. All thought of holding back vanished. Every part of her focused on a single point. His shaft entered and she allowed herself to accept it. Pausing, with her gaze locked on his, she savoured their shared anticipation. Unable to restrain any longer she lowered her weight, forcing his length inside.

Powerless to hold his passion, Chentene's movement became frantic. He gripped her waist, pounding all thought away and drowning her in ecstasy. Nothing else existed, no future or past, just a rising, wonderful, wave of pleasure.

Back arched, Chentene locked, frozen in a spasm. Slick warmth filled her and joyful in the long-denied pleasure of closeness, she wept.

When he could move, Chentene brushed away her tear with the edge of his finger. “I’ve been selfish. In my haste, I took only for me. Forgive me.”

“No, I teased you too much, didn’t I?” An empty pit of disappointment filled her. The whole mechanics of lovemaking with a man seemed too confusing. The concern on his face warned that her next words mattered. Secrets Sami’s mother had shared so long ago surfaced. “I think, as a first course, you have tempted me to dine some more.” She kissed him, exploring with her tongue inside his mouth. Shifting to lie alongside him, her nails played through his hair, barely touching his scalp and trailing lightly down his neck and shoulders.

“I …” he started to speak.

“Shush.” She dug her fingers into his muscles, working down his back and flanks, moving her attention ever closer to his waist. Sliding her hand between them, she found him. Although he remained swollen, it had softened. Still slick, she cupped him and started to move slowly.

Curled in a chaos of bedclothes and knowing how much this mattered, Maryan held herself in a languorous state, restraining from demanding the satisfaction her body yearned for. Chentene accepted her urging, tangling her legs in his and mussing her hair. The kisses moved across her neck, shoulder and down between her breasts, washing away any lingering doubts of her femininity. She cradled his head. The tenderness she and Sami had shared in their lovemaking had been special and she wondered if she would ever feel complete again.

Urgency crept into his caress. "I must set aright my shortcomings." He caught her wrist to ease her onto her back. His shift trapped one of her arms beneath his body. The other, he pressed against the pillow.

Holding her defenceless, his free hand trailed slowly, drawing a fiery line of suspense. Shifting, he found her nipple and his tongue drew a circle of excitement around it.

Her anticipation rose. A deeper call growled somewhere. Wild intoxication pulsed through her. Memories of Sami churned. One instant, it was her blade-sister's luscious body pressed against her, the next, Chentene's solid torso. Closing her eyes, the confusion multiplied, whirling into a melee of every sensual delight.

Maryan found herself already lost in frantic arousal before he lifted himself across her and slid inside. The weight of his body pressed her into the bed. His face buried into the crock of her neck and his hips moved with a determined rhythm, drawing her into a fantasyland.

So much heavier than Sami, he controlled her. The power of his frame emphasised his dominance, revealing the delight of submission to love. Maryan opened to accept him more fully. He manoeuvred, twisting to kneel, whilst keeping the length of his shaft inside. His touch hit the exact spot. Feeling her frenzy rising and unable to stifle herself she groaned. A scream tore from her throat. A powerful spasm shook her. For an instant, her heart stopped and her body shuddered into blackness.

Wrapped in a delicious reluctance to move, Maryan lay with her head on Chentene's chest listening to the pounding. She allowed herself a smile. Sex could be as good with a man.

Chapter 14

"**I** think this is appropriate," Patricia said from the doorway of Maryan's bedchamber. With only her feet visible, the slender woman struggled to hold a crimson ball gown off the floor.

Daylight barely peeked through the drapes covering Maryan's window. She ran her arm across the mattress, but found the other half of the bed cold and empty. Chentene had visited her rooms for a farewell kiss that had led to other, more absorbing intimacy.

The dress meant that Oliver, Harlon's brother, had arrived. She buried her face into her pillow before twisting to brush damp tendrils of hair from her mouth. "If he's that good, surely he can simply imagine me wearing whatever he wants. Show him the dress and tell him I'll be along after training." She knew she sounded childish, but hated the thought of her frozen image staring across the dining room for the coming centuries.

Silently stubborn, Patricia held out the gown until Maryan kicked her covers aside. After wrapping a blanket around her shoulders, she crossed the room, threw back the drapes and pressed her forehead against the cold window. Her thoughts soared out beyond the wall of Manda Torre to where she imagined Chentene leading his troops to face the trouble on the borders.

"Thankfully, you two might now have a child. Mordacai isn't the most patient of men and he's been enquiring regarding the situation." Although Patricia always sounded friendly, as Mordacai's sister, she remained an assassin waiting for Maryan to slip.

"Why me? Why did you choose me?"

"Because your line have only produced girls for how many generations, ten, maybe more?" Patricia wrung her hands. "Mordacai needs a royal daughter to a match with his son. In a stroke our house will be in line to the throne."

"What do you get out of the arrangement?"

"It's how the system works. I'm expected to support our family."

Maryan glanced out of the window to where she could see traces of snow on the distant hills. Now winter was biting, she'd finally succumbed to allowing fires in her apartments. The water laid for her to wash felt warm, but the air in the room still nipped. Dropping in front of her mirror, she started to weave her hair. By ancient Serenian tradition, two braids symbolised love and devotion. She flushed, knowing she would never again wear a single plait, the style reserved for the elite virgin warriors of the Serenian legion.

After fixing her hair, she allowed Patricia to lace the monstrous gown into place. "Carl says 'rumpling the nest' is the only way to keep warm in these damp winters," she said with a pout.

"We're supposed to take advice from a rat, are we?"

"He's very intelligent and deserves his place in the painting." Maryan scooped Carl out of his cage and sat him on her shoulder.

"My Lady, you cannot be serious!" A nervous laugh escaped Patricia.

“Completely serious. From our canvas, we’ll stare defiantly at all those cow-eyed women on the opposite wall for years.” Before Patricia could say another word, Maryan left her rooms to head for the studio.

Despite her objections to dressing in fancy silks, the wide passageways of Manda Torre allowed Maryan to enjoy the fabric swishing against her skin. Over the last few months, she’d modified her servant’s walk into something more akin to the sway of the ladies of the court. Holding her back as rigid as possible, she made her way to the older part of the castle.

A visitor might imagine Manda Torre frozen in time, but she wondered what Chentene’s worthy ancestors would make of his innovations. Pausing, she studied the new aspects of long gallery, the latest victim of his modernisation. At one end, he’d ordered doors be fitted on the first floor. Although they could be closed, they usually hung open allowing Stump the luxury of flying straight from his new lair out across the city.

At unprecedented expense, he’d converted the other half of the gallery into an artist’s studio. Despite all protestations, he’d badgered the craftsmen into constructing a roof and wall assembled using squares of the purest glass. From the corridor window, she could see a figure already moving inside the room. She wondered what Oliver would be like. Harlon had described a pompous older brother. His words inspired the mischievous part of her.

Maryan crossed the courtyard, lifting her gown to keep it from trailing in the dirt. A glorious wash of natural light filled the new studio. Chentene's choice of pale oak gave the room a vibrant feel.

Facing the windows, Oliver sat at a wide table working on a pencil sketch. The smell of paint already tainted the air. An oddly shaped lute leant against one wall, beside it, a battered sword.

"You've been made comfortable?" She smiled tightly at the man's back. She wanted to dislike him, but also yearned to quiz him regarding her mother.

"How could I complain?" The artist waved to the huge expanse of glass panels.

"Some people can complain honey isn't sweet enough." Maryan remained non-committal. Having become unused to waiting for people to attend to her, she tapped her foot beneath the voluminous gown. He still refused to shift his attention.

Seeking a distraction, she crossed to examine an unstrung, man-high hunting bow on the floor behind the sword. Compared with the short Serenian bow, it was a monster. She lifted it carefully and despite using all of her weight, found she couldn't string it. Instead, she rolled it along her palms noting the signs of recent use.

"There!" He put down the pencil and stood up. "Apologies, My Lady, but sometimes, the line flowing from my head through to the paper cannot be broken." He illustrated by running his finger from his forehead along his arm, turning the gesture into a bow. Oliver was possibly a hand taller than Harlon. He wore his reddish blonde hair much longer than his brother did and tied it back with a simple band at the nape. His tanned skin emphasised blue eyes that absorbed her completely.

"Allow me." He lifted the bow from her hands. Pressing one end against his foot, he hooked the string into place. "It's a knack." He handed the weapon back to her.

"Gorath!" she hissed. The strength required to draw the bow was immense. She held it positioned to shoot, but could barely flex it.

"It'll take a stag off its feet at close range," Oliver chuckled. He reclaimed and unstrung the bow before stowing the weapon behind his sword. "Now, to the painting."

"How do we do this?"

He scrutinised her, his gaze passing up and down before settling on Carl. "I've heard about this fashion. Actually, I quite like it. Have you any other foibles?"

"How does a pet dragon sound?" she asked, disappointed by how well he'd accepted Carl. "Or my lion, Mac?"

"I suppose something as simple as a horse would be out of the question?"

"Yes, I have one of those as well." She laughed, recognising the charm he shared with his brother. "Can we work them in?"

"Come, introduce me to these animals." Oliver stroked his finger across Carl's fur. "Can I hold him?"

'He's a good man. Trust him,' Carl thought.

She lifted the rat from her shoulder onto Oliver's. Standing so close, she noticed that his clothes smelled of the outdoors, hinting at a wilder side than a court artist might usually possess.

Uncertain of Carl's balance, Oliver held his hand pressed against the rat as he followed her along the corridor leading to Stump's loft.

Even though a cold wind blew into the room through the new double doors, chemical odours from the inner workings of the dragon greeted them. Stump lay curled on his growing collection of golden treasures, now the size of a large horse, he kept his wings furled against his body.

"By Gorath, he's beautiful. Look at the colours," Oliver said.

'I like him. Does he have any gold?'

Oliver spun on his heel, checking for tricks. "Did you hear that? This is wonderful. I can see the image forming already." Tears of excitement ran down the artist's face. He practically danced in a circle. "A lion, you have a lion. This is going to be special."

Threading through the castle on the way to Mac's corral, they walked through the main dining room. Maryan gripped Oliver's forearm, jerking him to a stop beneath the dark portraits of Chentene's overbearing ancestors. "You won't make me look like those will you?"

"I promise. Your image will be *the* centrepiece of Manda Torre for a thousand years."

Trying to catch him off guard, her words came out in a tumble. "Why did you add the inscription in moon writing to the painting of my mother and her friend?"

"I don't know what you mean?" Oliver shook his head slowly.

"Harlon says it's your great secret." She waited to see if he flinched from her stare.

"Then Harlon should learn what the word secret means." His guileless blue eyes returned her gaze.

Maryan hurried along the corridor to the royal chambers. She fluffed out the front of her white blouse before opening the ancient double doors to Chentene's apartment.

Although he was obviously worn out, she ignored the stench of horses and flew into his arms, sealing his mouth with a kiss. When she finally allowed them both to breathe, she asked, "What's happening on the borders?"

"The farmers up close to Serenia are reporting trouble with goblins. There's something strange going on out there. Etelan needs to get her troops moving."

"They're trained. We get all kinds of odd things heading out of Garalandia into the mountain caves."

"But this is big. It's as if something is calling them to mass. If Etelan doesn't act she's going to be in trouble."

Maryan wouldn't lose any sleep over troubles falling upon Etelan. Chentene remained unaware of her kidnap and the plot by Mordacai to gain the throne for his family. He wouldn't listen if she told him. In Chentene's opinion, Mordacai could do no wrong.

"Will you need to go out again?" she asked.

"It's my duty. I have to lead my troops. That's how we do things in Garalandia."

"Then I'll come, I can help."

"And that's *not* how we do things in Garalandia."

The tension in his stance silently told her she couldn't win this argument. Instead, she hugged close to him. He reeked, but she didn't care. "I worry. This is the first time I've felt this way about a man and I don't want to risk losing you."

“I’ll be careful.” He unwound from her embrace. “I need a bath. Are you joining me?”

Maryan held her nose. “I’m not sharing your dirty water. You go ahead and get clean. I’ll help dry your beautiful body.”

He grabbed his feathered hat from the stand and bowed deeply.

“And if you leave that feather around, I might show you a trick Stella mentioned …”

The next day, Maryan headed for the studio. Discarded sheets of parchment surrounded Oliver. She dropped into a chair and picked one up. She found her face constructed from faint circles. The similarity to the draft in Harlon’s room struck her. “Did you spend long with my mother?”

He didn’t falter, but touched her chin, tilting her head to catch the sunlight. “Yes. Your queen paid me to create an image of your greatest heroes. They happened to be young, beautiful and charming. Would I rush it?”

“Charming? I never thought of them that way.”

“A child wouldn’t. Your mother’s a beautiful woman and her friend oozed sensuality.”

“Do I detect traces of infatuation?”

“An artist always falls for his subjects, even when they’re truly ugly.”

The start of an idea nagged. Identifying who had been the ‘A’ on the picture could unlock the mystery of her mother’s disappearance. She had to know if it was Asti, or Amara who had written on the portrait. “Did you teach one of them about moon writing?”

Oliver lifted his pencil, but kept his eyes on the page before him. “Why would I do that?”

"A good looking woman …"

"The greatest virgin warriors Serenia ever produced." His lip curled into a wry smile. "Artists might pursue unrequited love, but the idea of waiting for one of them to fall for my charms is too futile to contemplate." His attention returned to the page. "Now, there was a family down in Bara where the daughter of the house …"

Even though she'd wanted to hate him, his charm shone warmer than a summer day. When he spun a tale, the most mundane of words danced to his bidding.

"Each day her father would pay a guard to ensure nothing untoward happened. Maybe he knew her mind." He brushed the hair from her neck. The skin of his fingers was callused, as a warrior's might be. "One night, when I lay abed, she arrived at my room, dropped her cloak and presented herself naked before me. What could a man do?"

"And what did the man do?"

"I always stand for a lady."

She held her breath, uncertain how a lady of the court should react to such an awful play on words. A snort blew out into a laugh. "Oliver!"

"I tell you, I earned every penny her father paid for the portrait." He paused. "When you laugh, I can see your mother behind your eyes. You missed so much by never knowing her properly." His skin flushed red at some thought and he twisted to watch Carl snuffling along the skirting. "Should I make sure I drop bits of food for him?"

'Tell him I like cake.'

Oliver tipped his head. "I heard something!" He scurried over, scooped Carl up and stared into the rat's button eyes.

"I can feel something, like a tickle on my mind. I'm sure it's him." A wicked grin slipped into place. "Could you imagine the things a rat gets to see around a castle like this?" Oliver lowered the rat gently to the floor. "It's no wonder Harlon found himself trapped by the allure of the place."

Maryan bit her lower lip. His mention of her mother had triggered something. She guessed a memory had caused him to change the subject.

"Which of them might have begged Etelan's forgiveness?"

"That's an intrigue that escaped a lowly artist. I never met Etelan. It was the old queen who commissioned me."

"Why did you give the drawing to Harlon?"

"I don't need it. I carry every line here." He tapped his heart and picked up a scrap of paper. His charcoal swept across the page and within a few strokes, the recognisable form of Asti and her mother stared out. She felt certain that if she placed it beside Harlon's copy they would match exactly.

"Every picture?" She studied his features, serious in their returned stare.

"The important ones." He crossed the room, took up his lute and picked an intricate flurry of notes from the instrument. Setting his head back, he sang. His voice was rich, easily reaching up to high notes and sweeping down into bass. "The women of Bara are honest and true …"

"A tavern song from the famous artist?" Maryan teased when he finished.

"An artist must eat and a song is quicker than a painting to sell." He put the instrument aside. "I hear you wear quite scandalous clothes to train in."

"In Serenia we frequently train naked. I doubt Chentene would approve."

"You'd be surprised how often the husband pays to have his wife painted fully dressed only for the wife to demand I secretly do a second portrait of them wearing less."

"No!" Maryan remembered the brooding nude hanging over Stella's bed. "Why?"

"For a lover or maybe simply to shock. One time, the wife of a noble someway darkward of here …"

When Maryan left the studio, her face ached. Oliver's tales of misdeeds rivalled his brother's. She wondered how the painting would look with tears of laughter rolling down her face. She also recognised Oliver was a master at deflection who had evaded her questions far too easily.

Chapter 15

“**You’re** going to train in this weather?” Patricia scowled through the window as though her glare could intimidate even the cruel Garalandian climate.

“It’s rare for an enemy to attack when conditions favour the defenders.” Maryan continued to dress in her training clothes. She grabbed her weapon harness from the closet and made for the door. Only Patricia’s restraining cough caused her to grab a full-length cloak to drape around her shoulders.

The wind whistling around the castle provided an eerie counterpoint to the click of Patricia’s heels as she followed Maryan through the lower corridors. When they reached the heavy outer door leading to the training ground, Maryan had to use her entire weight to force it open against the buffeting wind.

Swept by the foul conditions, the training ground looked dismal. None of the companions had braved the elements. Maryan struggled to stop the door slamming into Patricia. She stumbled awkwardly as a powerful gust tugged it from her grip. An unexpected thump shocked her as an arrow pinned her cloak to the door.

“What?” Patricia’s open-mouthed stare snapped from the arrow, up to Maryan and back to the arrow. Maryan tore free, bundling the older woman to the ground as another thud hit the door.

Patricia started to raise her head above the small balustrade around them. “Keep under cover!” Maryan yelled, dragging her to safety.

Patricia's normally white complexion turned grey. She clutched at her throat muttering. "Help me, help me, we're being attacked."

"Will you shut up and help!" Maryan was shocked at the usually cool-headed woman's behaviour.

Ignoring Maryan, Patricia kept up her babbling chant. "Help me, help me."

Abandoning the woman to her ramblings, Maryan needed to work out how to escape. Sprinting for cover in Harlon's rooms would mean too long in the open. They had to get back inside, but there was no quick way to open the door. If she tried, the archer would have time to take aim. The wind whipped the tattered strip of her cloak against the woodwork. Whoever it was, must be good, or desperate, to attempt such a shot.

"Give me your cloak," Patricia demanded.

"What?"

"I'll use your cloak to cover us. You get the door open." She tugged the wrap from Maryan's shoulders and stood up with it held wide above her head.

Maryan used both hands to heave the door open. The force of the arrow hitting Patricia bounced her off the door. Even though the old woman screamed in agony, she held the cloak aloft to camouflage their exact whereabouts. Maryan yanked Patricia into the corridor and let the door slam behind them.

Once inside, Patricia collapsed into Maryan's arms. Her bony back was sticky with the blood oozing around the shaft of the arrow. Maryan lowered her to the ground, carefully placing her to prevent the arrow from doing more harm.

Clattering footsteps announced the approach of Ambassador Mordacai. He dropped to his knees, squinting as he made a cursory examination of his sister's wound. "She'll live. Get that arrow to me as soon as it's been removed." He stood up and squared his shoulders ready for battle. "Servants will come. Keep her warm."

Hissing an incantation, a shimmering light sheathed him completely. He threw his weight against the door and stepped outside, leaving Maryan alone cradling Patricia's limp body.

She wondered how he'd known of their plight, but spotted the glowing brooch clasped at Patricia's throat. The woman hadn't been panicking, she'd been crying out for help, too little help, too late. One thing was certain though. Without this aging assassin to watch her back, she'd have been dead.

Chentene stood in the reception room of Maryan's apartments. The moment he'd heard of the attack he'd come running to join her, even insisting on helping the servants move Patricia to the healing rooms. "Who would do such a thing?" he said.

Maryan had changed from her training clothes into a bulky red dressing gown. She faced him with her arms folded. "What about one of your ex-lovers?" She held him in her glare, challenging him to turn away.

"You mean?" He matched her fury without flinching.

"I mean Emily. She's practiced with a bow and I don't like the way she watches me."

"Emily is family."

"Everybody in this castle is family. A bunch of Friggit-cursed inbreds! It's odd that nobody other than you knows her. Send her away."

"No! And wait for it. I know what's coming next." He dropped into a falsetto whine. "If you love me …"

Maryan clenched her fist behind her back. If he imagined he could get away with talking like that. A knock on the apartment door interrupted the rising argument.

Mordacai wore a studded waistcoat of rich, black velvet. His white shirt billowed at his shoulders in extravagant ruffles. He kept his head high, constantly moving to survey the room. "My sister will return to your service within the next few days." He rolled the arrow across his palm. "This revealed certain facts."

"What facts?" Chentene asked.

"I can sense the thoughts of the bowman. It was professional and political."

"Go on." Chentene shifted to stand beside Maryan, wrapping his arm around her.

"He was scared. Somebody of great power drove him, even though the timing was wrong. If he'd been allowed to wait for better weather, you'd be dead."

"That settles it," Chentene said. "You're not to leave the castle."

Chentene tried to hold her, but Maryan squirmed free of his grip. "I'm not hiding away for the rest of my life. I'll be careful, but we're going to find out who did this."

Mordacai grimaced. "My Lady, the production of an heir …"

"Will occur." She turned to Chentene. "You have a border to sort out. Wouldn't I be safer with you?"

"You're safer with Mordacai to protect you."

A heady mix of exotic perfumes pervaded the dressing room of Natalie's suite. Although smaller than Maryan's, the apartments were sumptuous. Craftsmen had stained the wooden panelling to a pale shade of pink. Intricately drawn murals of grape-laden vines growing up the walls added to the frivolous feel of the room.

She had sufficient wardrobe space to clothe a nation. Cupboards bulged with robes, blouses and shoes. Arranged alongside, she had shelves full of wigs in various styles, even different colours to match mood or outfit.

"Why do you need to do this?" Natalie said. The tall, dark-haired woman wrapped Maryan in a hooded cloak, but held onto the edge of the fabric as if she might snatch it back.

"I'm supposed to wait around within the castle under Mordacai's watchful eye." Maryan sniffed as she tucked an errant blonde lock under the ostentatious mountain of hair Natalie had pinned onto her. "No, I need to go into town."

"Have you thought this through?" Natalie gripped her hand. "Somebody did try to kill you."

"And I've a good idea who." Maryan pulled away, using a mirror to inspect the dark makeup she'd covered herself with.

"Women don't do that sort of thing, not with arrows. We use poison."

"She might not have taken aim, but she plotted the attempt." Maryan held out her hands in appeal to Natalie. "Be honest. You know everybody, but do you know from what branch of which family tree Emily fell from?"

"No, but that means nothing. She might be the result of a love tryst. A parent's delight, kept secret, but adored nevertheless. It's the kind of thing that happens all the time. Don't you read any books? "

"Of course I do." Maryan shook her head. She'd seen the books circulating between the women of the court and couldn't understand why anybody wasted their time on them. "I read the tale of a great hero, Shirl the Smith. She journeyed far from Serenia to experience the horrors of the outside world."

"Oh! Just like you, our own Shirl." Natalie wrapped Maryan into a fierce embrace before dramatically touching her forehead with the back of her wrist. "Out here, facing the wild people brandishing wicked things like wigs, perfume and baths."

"We had baths!"

"Either too hot or too cold, by the sound of it." Natalie shook her shoulders. "If there's nothing I can do to persuade you not to be so foolish, I could come with you."

Maryan sighed and repeated the plan. "No, I'm here in your rooms to learn about makeup, embroidery and feminine stuff. I've left instructions that we mustn't be disturbed, so, you can't be seen." She gripped Natalie's hand. "It has to be today. It's market day. The town will be busy and nobody will notice another person wandering around."

Crestfallen, Natalie gave in. "I'll remain here and catch up on some more reading. Rachel has passed this latest book to me." An impish grin dimpled

Natalie's cheeks. "It has a wicked monk who gets up to all manner of things in a castle."

Although Maryan had suspected such a shop would exist, it took most of the day to track it down. Each query had sent her deeper into the winding passages of the outer keep. The tiny shop smelled of the countryside.

"My Lady, what help can I give?" The skeletally thin man behind the counter spread his wrinkled hands on the ancient, wooden surface.

"I'm looking for somebody who can make up a potion for me?"

"Potion?"

"A truth potion, that works."

"You've been listening to too many stories. There's no such thing."

"Oh yes there is." Maryan eased the hood back over her hairpiece before approaching the old man. "I have a friend who can mix them. I've been told you can contact the people of the wood."

"The people of the wood are a legend." The man's eyes flickered to the side before meeting hers. "Like truth potions. Is there anything *real* I can help you with?"

"You suggest your sister isn't real? There are too many tales about her to claim that."

His shoulders dropped and avoiding looking up, ran his hand across the worn counter. "One mistake, that's all she made. If she'd been high born, she'd be a wizard, respected by all, but we're lowly folk and so she's a witch."

"I mean no harm, but I need her help." Maryan nudged a gemstone across the counter. "I'm sure this would be of use to her."

On leaving the shop, Maryan tugged her hood over the ridiculous hairpiece before ducking beneath the lintel. The bustle of the low-town activity on market day had died away, leaving the streets deserted. The surly-faced locals paid too much attention to a lone woman wandering the alleyways.

She scurried along a grubby alleyway. Foul odours assaulted her senses. For the briefest moment, the air smelled of flowers. Perfume? She snapped around. A slender woman wrapped in a grey cloak vanished into a doorway. What would Emily be doing here?

Her back itched between her shoulder blades. Horrific images of an arrow crashing through her spine drove her on. She hurried to the next junction, checking the windows overhead. All of her attention jerked to every shadow, fearful of spotting the glint of steel betraying a concealed bowman and equally scared of not spotting it.

Should she take an unexpected route to remain safe from ambush? That might be what they planned. They could be tricking her into the maze of passages to come at her in a rush. She cursed herself for bringing only the smallest of daggers. The weight of the battle-axe or a good sword would have proved more reassuring, but would surely have attracted attention.

Every face in the crowd seemed filled with crazed intent. The alleys gave way to a single, wide boulevard winding up to the main entrance of the castle. She had no choice, but to follow it. Every instinct nagged her to run, but that would attract too much attention. By the time she reached the castle walls, sweat poured down her forehead.

Two guards moved to block her. "And you are?" The older one squinted into the gloom of her cowl.

Encountering trouble re-entering hadn't been part of her plan. Since she'd been in Garalandia, the castle doors had been open to most. She swept back her hood. "I'm Princess Maryan. Stand aside."

"And I'm Prince Chentene. Would you like a dance?" The older guard reached for her shoulder. His smile vanished when she batted his hand away. He straightened his back to match her height. "None of that, dearie. Nobody comes in without me knowing them. Not anymore."

"Quite right," Chentene said. He'd appeared behind the guard. Although the set of his shoulders betrayed his tension, he kept his voice cheerful. "Did you enjoy your trip to the hairdresser my dear?"

"It was enlightening." She brushed her hand across the hairpiece. "Do you like it?"

"I think we'll discuss my feelings in private."

Although he wore a smile, the tension showed in his silence. He linked her arm, more dragging than guiding her through the corridors of Manda Torre. They reached her apartments where he held the door open before following her into the reception room.

"What in the name of Thrippas do you think you are playing at?" Chentene shouted the moment the door closed.

"I can't just sit around waiting. Somebody tried to kill me. I need to do something."

"Mordacai can't keep you safe if you wander off like that."

"Mordacai …" The words stuck in her throat. She knew Chentene wouldn't hear a word against the man. Instead, she slipped close, wrapping her arms under his.

"Mummf," Chentene said and spat out strands of horsehair. "Where did you get this damnable thing?"

"It's one of Natalie's." Realising she needed to tell her friend she was back, she unwound herself from his embrace. "I have to return it to her."

"And scrub that awful makeup off as well."

"I thought we might do that together in that nice big bath of yours. I could stop by your room on the way back."

Chentene gripped her biceps. "Please Maryan, I'm worried about you. Just stay in the castle."

Regardless of what Chentene said, that woman had been prowling around and she needed to prove Emily had made the attempt on her life.

"**You** should do what Chentene asks," Natalie said.

"I'll think about it. I've got to go and smooth his feathers." She made to leave, but stopped. "I won't tell anybody, but is there a secret pathway from these guest wings to the royal apartments?"

"There might be." Natalie flushed red.

"Do you know the way?" Maryan tried to keep the simmering anger from her voice. She'd told herself a thousand times, whatever had happened before she'd arrived in Manda Torre wasn't her problem.

"There's a way through the unused rooms on the top floor." She led Maryan through to her bedchamber where she delved into a bedside drawer to produce a key. "They're usually locked, but if you go to the end of the corridor, there's a door to a tiny staircase. It comes out in the old servant quarters. At the end of the corridor, you'll find some stairs leading off in various directions. The very last one leads into the royal chambers."

Maryan held her attention on Natalie. She didn't want to ask, but the words refused to stay inside. "Why have you got a key?"

"They're not secret. They open the servant doors. Most courtiers have one."

She left Natalie's suite to make her way from the guest wing. The key clicked, opening the door with a slight creak. Lifting her hem, she ran up the stairs to where they joined a landing stretching in either direction. Along the dusty corridor, doors led to the abandoned servant rooms. Most of them were closed, but some hung open showing a glimmer of light from tiny windows set high under the eaves.

Behind her, she heard the scuffling of somebody else opening the door. Rarely used? Slipping inside a disused room, she pressed her face to the crack at the hinge.

A man appeared at the top of the stairs. He glanced around before stepping onto the landing. Hugging close to the wall, his head constantly swivelled in search of somebody. He was dressed in a guard's uniform. Moving with obvious stealth, he vanished from Maryan's restricted view.

She had no doubt he was following her. Trying to remain quiet, she removed her useless slippers, wishing for a pair of solid sandals. Her heart hammered inside her ears. She scanned the room, desperate to find anything she could use to defend herself. Struggling to control her breathing, she waited for movement. Almost silent footsteps creaked on the bare boards of the corridor. The door started to open.

Summoning every iota of strength, she drove her shoulder into the door, crushing him against the frame. She grabbed his wrist, fighting to twist the blade from his grip. A fist crunched into her jaw, snapping her head back. His knee hit her stomach, folding her double. A boot filled her vision. The power of his kick flung her against the wall.

Silhouetted in the doorway, her assailant paused before starting toward her. The dagger in his meaty fist flashed. His grim expression showed no mercy.

"Why?" Maryan yelled at him.

"You have to die. There can be no child."

Bracing herself to pounce, Maryan waited for him to come closer. He might top her in height, but she wasn't going to give up easily. A shadow moved behind him, Emily slipped over the crest of the top step.

"Come to check it's done correctly?" Maryan shouted.

The assassin turned in time to see Emily's bow snap into a firing position. The arrow hammered deep into the side of his chest. Staggering back, he slashed out wildly. Maryan kicked at his groin, but he managed to sink the dagger into her thigh. Undaunted, she caught his wrist and used all her weight to snap his elbow joint.

"Get away from her!" Emily shouted, keeping her bow pointed at him.

He lunged again. Another arrow hit his back throwing him off balance. Maryan wrestled him to the ground. They hit the floor with her weight on his back. Unleashing all of her anger, she pounded his face against the wooden boards until he ceased struggling.

"You go and get help," Emily said. She tugged the man's hands behind him, using his belt to lash them together.

"I can't walk far." Maryan pressed her palm on the stab wound in her leg trying to stop the blood pulsing between her fingers. "You need to go." Her head spun each time she moved.

Emily briefly hesitated before running back down the stairs.

Whilst Maryan waited, she hauled her dress up to see the injury. No matter how hard she pressed on the wound, blood kept oozing between her fingers. Her last thoughts were of Emily laughing at how stupid she'd been in trusting her to fetch help.

Opening her eyes and finding Mordacai's face a hand's breadth away from her nose stunned Maryan fully awake. "What?"

"Lie still. You've lost a lot of blood. This contraption of Galia's is rectifying that." He touched a brass contraption linked to a bottle strapped onto her arm. "Quite ingenious."

"What is this about? He said something about a child." Maryan winced at the throbbing pain in her thigh.

"I had a little time with the attacker before he died." Mordacai shook his head. "This is to do with Calamore and the old order."

"What do you mean?"

"The legends say he will return and as you know, I'd rather that didn't happen."

The door opened and Maryan saw Chentene talking to Emily before he came into the room. The small woman bowed a curt acknowledgment before backing away out of sight.

Chentene looked grey. "Is she alright?"

"She needs some rest, but nothing the castle healers can't take care of."

"What can we do to protect her?"

"Now I know the source of the problem, I can begin to take steps. Trust me. I can seal this place against the old order." Mordacai's attention shifted between the two of them. "With your permission I'd like to get started."

Accepting his dismissal from Chentene, Mordacai smoothed his beard, fixing his dark stare on Maryan. "I will protect you."

She fell back onto the pillow, watching Mordacai leave. Galia, the women's healer immediately appeared through the door. Her eagle eyes shone beneath a curling halo of wiry, fire-red hair. She wore a green dress that clung to her gaunt figure.

"I'll leave you to the mercies of Galia's care." Chentene lingered over his kiss before turning to face the healer. "Make sure our Princess is mended and try to get a little sense into that head of hers for me."

Galia hissed in defiance. "That would be man-sense or woman-sense, your highness?" Although phrased as a question her entire stance invited no answer.

Chentene's most charming smile lit up his face. "Why, Galia, just good old common sense will do nicely."

Chapter 16

"**Gorath's** toenail, Maryan, can't you control that dragon?" Rubbing the back of his neck, Chentene surveyed the debris of his coach. "He would have killed anybody inside."

Stump, now much larger than the biggest horse still claimed anything golden. He lived in the converted long gallery, overlooking the main courtyard of the inner keep. The driver had only left the state coach for a moment, but shards of gilt covered wood now lay around the courtyard.

Stump's neck craned out of the doors. *'Mine!'* His voice echoed inside every head in the courtyard.

"Not yours!" the braver ones shouted. Having adapted to the oddities of their ruler's foreign wife, they possibly assumed most people in Serenia kept at least one dragon.

Stump dropped onto the largest piece of debris, forcing Chentene to leap clear. *'Mine!'* He hauled the door of the coach up to his lair.

Attempting to defuse the frustration building inside her husband, Maryan hugged his waist. "It's part of his nature. He can't resist gold." She squeezed him. "You know what it feels like to not resist."

"It's just …" Chentene shook his head. "I can take the second coach. I've got to ride out, but I'll be back later." He eased himself away from her embrace. "That dragon of yours is starting to become a problem. Can't you set him free or something?"

"He is free. He simply chooses to stay with us."

Maryan went to the stables just as she had so many times before. For the last few days, she'd been making a show of how much grooming Ruby helped her take her attention off the attack. Today might prove interesting. It had to be today. Once Patricia returned from the healing rooms, the stick-thin assassin would crush any plot before it could start.

Even though many had claimed ignorance, she'd pressed the local herb-traders to discover a way to make contact with the people of the woods. One had finally helped her. Living in a cottage just inside the forest of dreams was the person she sought.

Savouring the rich equine odour, she drew her brush across Ruby's flank one last time before calling for the groom. "Saddle her. I'm going to walk her around the courtyard. Leave her by the trough whilst I finish up in here."

As soon as the groom left, Maryan ducked into the farthest stall to don her disguise. She settled a single Serenian sword into a hip scabbard and dropped the clawed battle-axe into a holster that sat high across her shoulders.

By choosing the red cloak of a court messenger, she virtually guaranteed escaping the castle unchallenged. Covering the weapons, she tugged the cloak's wide hood forward and strutted across the courtyard. Her every step imitated the arrogance she'd witnessed in the vaunted cadre of messengers. Hunkering down into the saddle, she charged Ruby out of the courtyard. If Chentene had known of her plan, he'd have locked her in the deepest dungeon and forbidden the guard from letting her out.

A shout ran ahead of them. "'ware messenger!" Ruby clattered along the high boulevard, plunging into the more confined streets of the lower keep. Her disguise served to clear a way through the crowds and soon she emerged from the town onto the single road leading away across the farmland.

Out in the open, she kept up the gallop expected of a messenger, but unable to match the demanding pace, Ruby started to falter. Maryan glanced back, checking that the undulating folds in the land concealed her from Manda Torre.

The moment she felt clear of the city, she reined Ruby to a standstill and eased the hood back to enjoy the touch of the autumnal sun on her skin. The air smelled sweet. A strong breeze chased clouds across the sky.

At the edge of the Forest of Dreams, she hesitated. The shopkeeper's instruction had been clear about where to leave the road. After following the treeline, she would encounter two old posts marking where a pathway led into the forest. She took a final glance in either direction before nudging Ruby beneath the leafy boughs.

All around her, gnarled trees intertwined with brambles to form a corridor. Barely a sound penetrated and the moist air smelled of damp earth. Ruby followed the meandering path, her hooves muffled by the carpet of leaves. The trail snaked over the hillocks that folded the ground. In these woods, an army could remain concealed a stride away.

She spotted her destination nestled beneath the spreading branches of an ancient tree. Dense foliage draped the cottage from roof to floor. Nothing of the original structure remained visible beneath its natural camouflage. The path terminated at a point where the thigh-thick vines divided either side of the door. Maryan tethered Ruby before making her way through the well-stocked herb garden to tap on the stout wooden entrance.

"Come."

Inside, green tinted light tumbled through the windows, barely illuminating the chaos within. The rafters hung with dried plants. Hangings and throws covered every surface. An old woman stood close to the far wall, her clothing, like the furniture, a riotous mixture of random cloth.

"It's not often we get a visit from the high born of Manda Torre," the old woman said. She slapped her palm to her cheek. "You're the foreigner they brought for our Prince!"

Maryan nodded.

"You shouldn't be here!" She rushed to the door to slap the bolt home. "They're watching for you. It's not safe."

"I took precautions. I wasn't followed."

"Stupid girl, they don't just watch with their eyes. The old order wants rid of you, wants it badly. Things in this wood will be waiting."

"Can you truly make the potion I wanted?"

"I have it, but we must hurry if we're to get you safely out of the forest."

Without waiting, she vanished into a store cupboard to retrieve a small bottle of purple oil. "Put one drop of this in his drink. He'll feel the urge to babble and spit out the truth. After a time, he'll doze, forgetting all about it."

The woman bustled to the door, edging it open to peek through the smallest of cracks.

"Remember, it makes a man tell the truth, not what you want to hear. Don't start complaining if he declares love for another." She checked the door again. "Now for both our sakes, don't come back, it's not safe, especially for you."

Maryan swung herself into Ruby's saddle, nudging the mare along the winding route back to the main road. The weather was turning nasty. Cold air nipped her face. The recently healed wound on her thigh ached and a warm bath beckoned.

A huge figure lumbered into sight, its massive arms sweeping the bushes aside. It had to be a troll. Although man-shaped, its eyes glowed red and its skin looked as rough as stone. Goblins tumbled through the damaged shrubs. The troll moved quickly, grabbing Ruby's bridle, preventing any chance of escape.

A voice hissed from the depths of the bushes. "Get down from the horse, or the troll will kill it."

Ruby shied, but the troll tugged on the reins, jerking her head down. The monster raised a balled fist the size of a blacksmith's hammer. Maryan knew Ruby would die if the blow fell.

"Stop! What do you want?" She slid to the ground.

"We want you, need you."

"I don't know who you are, but I'm not going anywhere without a fight." Maryan dropped her cloak and drew her weapons.

The hissing voice shifted. "Kill her," it commanded.

Wary of the vicious club, the band of goblins edged forward, circling just out of reach. The troll released his grip on Ruby to close on Maryan. He moved frighteningly quickly, blocking any chance of escape with his outstretched arms.

Constantly moving to keep her opponents in view, she remembered Asti's words. *'Speeches are for sagas. Concentrate and put your opponent down.'* Her Serenian blade separated a goblin from its head. The troll swung his massive fist. She ducked, allowing the blow to whistle past. The keen edge of her sword hit the troll's leg. The blade should have hamstrung the monster. It jarred her arm, failing to cut the skin.

She spun, killing another goblin. One landed on her back. She rolled into a somersault, crushing it under her full weight.

'Idiot child,' Asti's voice rang. *'Stay on your feet or die.'* A dozen tiny hands held her down. Sharp fingernails dug into her skin. She flailed the axe around her head, fighting to clamber upright.

The troll charged, but stumbled as a sleek shadow arrowed from the hedgerow hammering into its back. Mac raked the stone-hard flesh, barely harming the creature. The troll twisted, unable to reach the lion. Distracted by Mac's onslaught, he staggered, bringing his head within range of the fearsome axe. Driven with every fibre of Maryan's body, the single blow struck home. A satisfying crunch betrayed the brutal power. The single spike shattered the troll's skull, leaving the fallen giant twitching at her feet.

Screaming in battle-fury, she whirled to challenge the remaining goblins. Scrambling for cover, they vanished into the depths of the forest. A frustrated hiss faded away. Reckless in her a battle fury, she ploughed headlong into the bushes, but couldn't find any trace of the mysterious voice.

Back on the road, Mac stood guard, his head low, checking for interlopers. She sent out a probing thought. *'Carl, what are you doing out here?'*

'We often come out hunting. We didn't expect to see you. You're supposed to be in the castle.' Carl's thoughts whispered the accusation. The rat silently appeared at her feet, his button eyes staring up at her.

'How did you get here?'

'Through the tunnels that riddle the palace. Some just go between rooms, but others come out under the walls. People make such a fuss if they see Mac. We don't go through the town alone.'

'You shouldn't come out here at all. Chentene would go mad if he knew he had a lion roaming the countryside.' She sensed the mental sniff signifying Carl didn't care.

'We'll meet you back at the castle.'

Mac rumbled a snarl of disappointment before squatting for Carl to mount his head. His muscles rippled beneath the tawny fur as he powered into the night.

As she returned the battle-axe to the holster, she wondered what her tutors would have made of her fighting style. A fierce pride filled her. Few could claim to have downed a troll with a single blow.

Chapter 17

For the briefest moment, Maryan thought they'd acquired a statue of Chentene to grace the stable yard. Silently regarding her progress across the cobbles, the Prince gradually changed colour to an ominous shade of white.

The instant her feet hit the ground he plucked the messenger's cloak from her shoulders. "These are only worn by obedient servants to the crown."

"Servant?" She bristled, her voice rising.

His face reddened and taut hawsers of sinew bulged from his neck. "Obedient!" he bellowed. His gaze travelled the length of her body, taking in the devastation of her clothes before returning to her face. "I just want you safe."

"And I want to feel safe. But how can I, when I know someone is trying to kill me?"

"Mordacai can protect you inside the grounds." His embrace crushed the breath from her. "What do I have to do? I love you and I'm not going to risk losing you."

The pain in his voice tortured her. If not for the chance intervention of Carl and Mac, she might not have survived her little adventure. "I'm sorry," she mumbled, knowing her words weren't nearly enough to repair the hurt she'd inflicted.

"Then I think we should try to forget this upset, don't you?" He folded her into another fierce embrace.

"Well, I do need a bath."

It took almost no time to cross the courtyard and make their way through the palace. Giggling like children escaping lessons, they took the stairs two at a time. Maryan's shoulder hit the door to her rooms slamming it open. A lurking shadow moved. Her blade slashed the air as she dropped into a crouched defence.

"Where in the name of Friggit …" Patricia's features glowed white, but her anger mollified when she saw Chentene behind Maryan. "We didn't know where you'd got to."

"You are quite correct. My wife has been a rather naughty girl and I intend to punish her quite severely."

"If I may comment." Patricia nodded curtly. "That sounds about as likely as rumours regarding my impending elopement with Harlon." She dipped a short curtsey. "I shall leave you to your … punishment."

The bathing chamber Maryan had thought so peculiar when she'd first arrived had proved to be one of her favourite rooms in the castle. Although not as hot as the steam rooms of Serenia, the castle heating system warmed the water constantly ensuring that it always remained a delightful temperature.

With Chentene crowding so close, it made the dressing room feel small. He gripped either side of her head and forced her to look in the mirror. Twin braids hanging in disarray, smears of mud covering her skin, she looked more like a street urchin than a princess.

"What were you up to?" Chentene asked.

Her hand hovered protectively, trying to conceal the small bottle tucked inside her blouse. Chentene twisted it from her grasp. "What's this?"

"It's truth potion," she said. "I'm going to get the truth out of Oliver. He knows something about my mother. I know he taught one of them how to do moon writing."

Chentene waited, his eyes shaded beneath his brooding brow. "You risked your life for that?"

"I'm going to get the truth about that woman, Emily." When she confessed her aim aloud, it sounded petulant

He shook the bottle, studying the purple fluid inside. "What if it's poison? You could kill somebody?"

"I'm the target. It's me the old order is trying to murder." She pounded her chest with her fist. "My whole life feels as if somebody is always trying to rip happiness from me."

"Not me." Easing her head against his chest, he stroked her back, enfolding her in his arms.

Much of the burning passion had drifted from them, but Chentene slipped into the water to sit on a ledge beneath the surface. She lay back between his legs with the water lapping close to her neck. Once she'd unpicked her braids, he worked a lather of soap into the tangles, running his fingers through her hair, gently massaging her scalp.

"Why do you keep your hair in these braids? I'm used to women wearing wigs, or ringlets."

"It's a legion tradition. We replace the single plait of the virgin warrior with the twin plaits of a wife." She let her legs float and ran a soapy hand across her skin. "It means a lot to me. Where I'm from and who I am."

They went through to Maryan's bedchamber where she lay face down on the bed with her arms outstretched. Chentene dried her using a cloth, before starting to rub scented oil into her skin. His strong touch dug into her muscles, easing away any remaining kinks. He took his time over the massage. Kneeling alongside, he used his knuckles to knead along her spine. Using languid strokes, his hands worked across her buttocks onto her thighs.

With loving care, he bent her knee and held her foot against his face, caressing the length of her leg, rubbing between each toe. Maryan sighed at his touch. Each caress nudged her deeper into a blissful haze.

"Is this my punishment?" She rolled to look up at him. He towered over her. She touched him, but he caught her wrist, forcing it against the bed, wrestling her onto her back.

"You have been allowed entirely too much freedom. Maybe I should keep you chained here, awaiting the royal pleasure."

"Bound, and helpless like this?" Maryan spread her arms wide. She grabbed his neck, squeezing him against her. "If you wanted controllable, you shouldn't have sought a warrior." Using a handful of his hair, she tilted his face to her. The adoration she found lit a fire in her throat. It ran in a burning line through her chest to her groin. A mere hand's breadth apart, she shrugged. "Warriors surrender occasionally."

He shifted to pin her hands either side of her head, easing his hips between her legs. She could feel his length probe against her. Keeping their eyes locked, she lifted to accept him. “I’m your slave.”

“You’re my life.”

She tried to free her hands to rake his skin, but his weight held her trapped. Holding his gaze, she experimented. By rolling her hips, she drew him out, before opening around him and forcing him deep. Chentene closed his eyes. She watched him, so beautiful, yet so intense.

She wanted to dig her nails into his back. She wanted to wind her fingers into his hair and smother his face in kisses. She wanted to …

The exquisite torture of near helplessness heightened every sense. They weren’t two people. Every movement served a shared purpose. The only way she could show her desire was through her hips. Beneath him, she danced to an undulating tempo, grinding his length against her pleasure point. Each delicious withdrawal rang with sensual delight, each entry, called a throbbing awakening. This was more than lovemaking. This was creating something that would remain forever theirs.

A childhood memory bubbled into her thoughts. She was standing close to the forge watching the powerful hammer blows crash on the anvil. Each ringing impact exploded in a cascade of sparks. Constant, solid and irresistible, the pounding shaped the metal. Anvil or hammer? It ceased to matter. The white-hot shape of a sword seared her mind.

Existing in a kaleidoscope of delightful confusion, she was torn between holding herself on the edge of ecstasy, or plummeting into uncontrollable pleasure. Passion drew her on. Every muscle of her body surged. Nothing mattered. Somewhere, somebody screamed and the showering sparks of life splashed from the anvil.

They lay in a tangle of continuous caress, fingers tracing languidly over each other. Maryan nuzzled against Chentene's neck. "That felt different."

"Special?" Chentene said without opening his eyes.

"Very."

Wrapped in each other's warmth they dozed, entirely sated.

Naked, perched behind the head of a great dragon, Maryan flew at impossible speed. Delirious with joy, the beast between her legs unleashed a burst of flame. They plunged through the heat. The sky wheeled as the dragon banked in a spiral. She clung on by wrapping her thighs tight. The ridge of the dragon's spine ground against her crotch. The inner warmth of the beast spread from her groin up through her body. Her nipples tingled erect. Sinful delight beckoned. The slow pulse of the massive wings called her to bask in the growing pleasure. The dragon twisted, curling to allow its gem-filled gaze to sweep close to her face.

Maryan's eyes jerked open to find Chentene a hand span away.

"What?" she asked.

"You look so peaceful when you sleep." A smile wrinkled his features. "It's only when you wake up you become a real pain."

"Would you wish me different?"

"All I ask, the only change I crave, is that you let Mordacai keep you safe."

Unable to speak of her true feelings regarding the man who'd kidnapped her, she snuggled into the crook of Chentene's neck. "I'll try to behave."

"Good, because we're meeting him tonight to discuss what he can do."

The drabness of the small meeting room sucked most of the light from the ring of candles hanging overhead. Servants had laid out jugs of wine on the waist-high sideboard.

An angry knot tightened in Maryan's stomach at the sight of the dark, brooding shape of the Ambassador. Mordacai rose from his seat at the small table in the centre of the room. He wore a short jacket of rich black velvet with complex patterns traced in midnight-blue gemstones down the front. Being one of the tallest men at the court, the width of his padded shoulders emphasised his dominant stance.

He regarded her with eyes as dead as black marble. His sensual mouth pulled into a semblance of a smile. "Your Highnesses."

Patricia sat alongside him, dressed in a black buttoned-up dress. The slightest hint of warmth touched her face when she saw Chentene. She stood up and curtseyed.

"I'm glad you could both be present," Chentene said.

Just as Chentene spoke, Guard Commander Damon entered the room. "Sir, may we speak?" Obviously uneasy about the news he carried, his gaze switched rapidly between all of the people in the room.

Chentene gestured for Damon to follow him through to a small antechamber, leaving Maryan alone with her captors.

"So the table turns," Maryan said. "You, who stole me away from home, keeping me here under pain of death, now must protect me."

Patricia remained silent, but her lips drew into a thin line.

"We have never meant you harm," Mordacai said. "Your presence is an awkward requirement. If not for your family's trait of breeding girls, you would be of no consequence. You are a mere womb of convenience."

Maryan remained silent, calming her breathing until she could match his cold tones. "And now the ancient history of Garalandia itself appears bent on undoing your plans."

"The rule of Calamore was a dark time," Mordacai agreed. "The echoes still sound, but I think we have sufficient strength to ignore the rumbling."

A hiss escaped Patricia. "Brother, you are arrogant."

"Matters progress at a pace," Chentene said, heading across to the sideboard to fill a goblet with wine. "Etelan's in serious trouble. Her borders are leaking all manner of foul creature."

"We've offered aid, but she refuses." Mordacai shook his head.

"As my wife's homeland, but more as a weakness along our border, we should insist she does more. If Serenia is overrun it will be a knife forever pressed at our neck."

"I will deal with Etelan. I may still hold some influence, but our problem with Serenian stubbornness is much closer to home." Mordacai glared at Maryan. "I have wards on all of the gates. I have traps in the corridors. I can stop the old order, but only if you stay within safe boundaries." He held her in his stare. "You must agree to keep Patricia close. She is prepared with devices to raise a warning."

Touching the broach at her throat, Patricia nodded in agreement.

"But for how long will I be incarcerated?"

Mordacai stroked his beard in thought. "There is a focus of evil drawn to you. Once I've traced it, I will eradicate it. I can't say how long, but give me time."

Evil forming around her. His words echoed those of Kait so long ago.

"My wife will behave." Chentene exchanged glances with the Ambassador before turning to Maryan. "Won't she?"

Stella's white blouse undid at the front enabling her to feed her daughter. Balancing baby Gemma on her knee in the crock of one arm, she checked the buttons with her other hand. Her long black hair swept back from her forehead, framing her beautiful, dark-skinned face. She gazed contentedly at the bundle squirming on her knee, her movements bearing the casual grace of experience.

"Did you see the reaction from that prune-face, Patricia, when I said I fed her? Justin almost coughed up a dragon turd, but I said I'd stab any woman who tried to feed my baby." Stella rubbed her hand up and down the baby's back causing Gemma's tiny head to nod like a small, black-haired puppet.

"I can't get over seeing you being a mother like this." Maryan squatted alongside to lift Gemma's chubby chin. The baby's blue eyes focused, tugging at strings she didn't understand. Her hand strayed to her own abdomen.

"Don't get too close. She can't hold a sword yet, but she can hit you with vomit from an arm's length."

Taking the warning seriously and not wanting to ruin the red satin gown Helena, the dressmaker, had prepared. Maryan moved away. "Was giving birth as bad as they say?"

Stella grimaced. "I'd prefer Asti's flogging than going through it again. Tell me about this woman we're trying to trick."

"It's the whole reason for the gathering. I've asked the women of the castle to a party. They can make a fuss of little Gemma and I can slip truth potion into the wine of a certain Lady Emily."

"Why her?"

"She's … not right. Chentene says she's family, but nobody recalls which branch. I've discovered them in too many little head to head chats in odd places around the castle."

"She is the one who saved you though?"

Maryan rubbed her thigh through the satin of her gown. "I just want to know more."

By throwing the afternoon party, Maryan gave the cook a way to show off his skill. He'd excelled in forming sugar-coated pastries of every size. A table draped with white cloth suffered under the weight of custards, creams and jellied fruits. The master of the cellar had undertaken selecting wines suitable for the delicate palate of the ladies attending and provided a variety of chilled drinks.

As well as the women who now trained with Maryan, she'd invited many of the mothers, sisters and wives of the court. A meeting with the two wild Serenian women at the top of Garalandian aristocracy might have intimidated these minor nobles, but baby Gemma helped break the ice.

"Isn't she sweet, I can see Justin's nose."

"Does she sleep?"

"When will you have another?"

Gemma passed from hand to hand, entertaining the gathering by gurgling adorably.

"Emily wasn't it?" Maryan heard Stella open the approach. "Are you from darkward of Manda Torre?"

Before Emily had a chance to reply, Gemma lunged for the shoulder of her dress. "Oh, please, I'll try and get …" Juggling her wine goblet and her baby, Stella struggled to release Gemma's grip.

"Let me take those." Maryan stepped in to claim their goblets. She took them across the room, slipped the vial from her belt and dripped a measure into Emily's wine. After checking they'd managed to open Gemma's tiny fist, she returned with the drinks. "No harm done is there?"

"I'll just straighten up a little." Emily dipped a curtsey before heading into Maryan's bathroom.

"Good girl!" Stella kissed the top of Gemma's head. "This grabbing thing is driving Justin mad. Now what?"

"We wait and then ask her a couple of questions."

Anxious with anticipation, Maryan tried to remain close to Emily. Unfortunately, every women of the court suddenly proved eager to speak with their Princess. Overbearing mothers came trying to garner favour for their family and Maryan found herself separated from their quarry.

Across the room, Emily moved to talk to Sophie. The plump woman smiled, tipping her head in whispered conversation. As Maryan tried to manoeuvre closer, the two women laughed.

Like a galleon moving ponderously into battle, a determined looking woman, Commander Damon's mother, strode across the room. Maryan groaned, knowing she'd never shake off the infernal woman.

"I don't think we've been introduced." Stella darted to intercept, leaving Maryan free to stalk their prey. She made her way to join the small group where Emily stood with Sophie.

"What do you think of our training?" Maryan asked.

"Training?" Sophie bellowed. "I wouldn't show up if a gorgeous hunk of meat wasn't doing the tutoring." She graced the throng with a beaming smile.

A hush dropped across the room. Maryan choked slightly. Rachel's head spun so quickly, it looked in danger of snapping from her shoulders.

A grin spread across Sophie's face. "Oh come on. It's not just me who'd ride him like a wild horse." After draining her goblet, she slapped her buttock. "Giddy up and jump the fence." Pushing her knees wide, she stretched the fabric of her gown to breaking point. The thrusting movement of her round hips left little to the imagination.

"Excuse me, My Lady." Rachel squeezed in front of Maryan. "It seems that my sister might have taken a little too much wine."

"Nonsense. I was answering a simple question. Given half the chance I'd pin him to the ground, tear those tight breeches off his gorgeous butt and …"

"Sophie!" Rachel grabbed her sister's arm, dragging her from the room.

"What on earth happened to her?" Maryan muttered.

"As she said, I think she was merely telling the truth." Emily's tight smile showed white teeth peeping between her red lips. "My Lady." After dropping into an elegant curtsey, she deposited her goblet onto a table and glided from the room with an exaggerated hip-sway.

Maryan stood on the tallest tower in Garalandia gazing out in the direction Stella had departed several days earlier. Melancholia washed her into a mood as dark as the coming night. Chentene's arm snaked around her from behind, the warmth of his closeness spread down her back as he moulded against her.

"You haven't forgotten we're expected down in the hall." His breath warmed her neck.

"I wouldn't dream of missing Oliver's grand unveiling."

"Do you have to go through with the other thing?" Chentene shifted uneasily. "After all, poor Lady Sophie slept for a day after your first search for the truth."

"You knew?"

"I guessed."

"It'll be my last chance. After my painting's been unveiled, Oliver will be off to Bara for another commission."

In the grand dining room, her cloth-draped portrait loomed at the end of the table. This would be a private viewing, just Chentene, Oliver and herself, an ideal time, even if Chentene didn't approve.

Oliver stood beside the concealed canvas. He watched Chentene, waiting for the command to unveil. Although he usually oozed composure, Maryan could see his hands tremble when he reached out for the edge of the fabric.

Feigning gruff disapproval, Chentene grimaced. "Go on then, show me what I've spent my money on."

The cloth rippled to the floor, revealing his vibrant creation. The life-size heads of Ruby and Stump flanked a radiant Maryan. At her feet, Mac snarled, his open maw vivid and frightening. Carl squatted on her shoulder, his button eyes gleaming.

"Fabulous," Chentene murmured.

"Too beautiful," Maryan said.

The two men exchanged glances. "It is a perfect representation of my wife," Chentene said.

"I would not embellish or alter your beauty." Oliver frowned. "I paint what I see. You are the jewel of the land."

Studying the portrait, Maryan preened. The woman in the painting wore an expression of depth, but the twinkle in her eye hinted at the mischief hidden within. The crimson ball gown flared from her hips and nipped her waist tight. Instead of severe braids, Oliver had insisted on portraying her blonde hair hanging loose around her face. At her feet lay a shield emblazoned with the arms of Garalandia and in the foreground, her clawed battle-axe.

She laughed and went to the jugs arrayed on the sideboard. "I think you deserve some wine." She added a single drop of the potion to the artist's goblet before turning to face the men. "Please, drink, and let's eat."

Oliver, as usual, dominated the conversation with stories of his wandering. His words became more animated.

"Were you and your brother close?" Maryan tested his honesty. She knew that although Oliver always claimed they were, Harlon said not.

"The little rascal drove me mad," Oliver admitted. "He ruined my chances with the girls. He was a real terror, fighting everybody in the neighbourhood."

Maryan's heart pounded against her ribs when she asked her next question. "Who did you show the moon writing to?"

"Your mother." He shook his head slowly. Tears glistened on his cheeks. "I loved her and treasured every moment we spent together. I wanted her to run away with me." He spread his fingers on the table and narrowed his eyes. "Then she asked me for help. How could I refuse? I showed her how to mix the ink, how to conceal the words. It was the night after she'd wounded her friend. She insisted on moon and candlelight, claiming a need to atone for a secret before leaving." Oliver drained his goblet, refilled it and drained it again.

"Before leaving!" He barked an ironic laugh, his fingers plucked out the band holding his hair. "She tricked me. I awoke, hoping to beg her to join me only to find I'd slept for days. She'd drugged me and had already left for the games. I followed, but I was too late." His face glinted wet. "How could a woman drug a man like that?"

Maryan felt her cheeks burn.

"Never trust a woman," Chentene said, raising his goblet towards each of them.

"I got to Bara, but the games were over and she'd disappeared. I searched. Everybody did, but we didn't even find a hair." Oliver lowered his head to the table and started to snore.

His tale of heartache still tortured him. Guilt gnawed at Maryan for compelling him to relive his pain. She tangled her fingers into his golden-red hair, massaging gently to ease him further into forgetful sleep. Always the same story, her mother had vanished and nobody ever found a trace of her again.

"Does that help you?" Chentene's brow knitted, casting his expression into shadow. "Did it tell us anything?"

"Nothing worth that agony. I wonder what the secret was that she needed to be forgiven for?"

Chentene approached as if to kiss her, she closed her eyes, savouring his fragrance. Instead, he plucked the vial from her belt. "We won't need this again will we?"

"But …"

"No buts, you've done enough damage. It stops now."

Chapter 18

By the time summer finally warmed the stones of Manda Torre, Maryan's slim-fitting dresses had been stored, swapped for tent-like smocks to cover her swollen girth. After sitting for too long, she was now trying to ease her spine by flexing backwards with her hands pressed to her kidneys.

She jealously regarded the canvas hanging over the fireplace. Oliver's magnificent picture took pride of place in the main dining room of the castle. It had been the talk of the area for many months, but now served as a bitter reminder of how much change pregnancy had inflicted on her body.

Feeling her glare turn on him, Chentene raised his hands. His dark hair flopped either side of his face. "If I could take the pain, I would." He slipped behind to press against her and she leant back allowing him to reach his hands around her swollen stomach. "Another night of kicking?"

"I think he wants to come to war with you." She spun, forcing their baby between them.

"Or she," he said, stroking his hands across her taut bulge. "Remember our child has a warrior mother. Boy or girl, they will be a handful."

"You're not going to spend all of the campaign leading from the front." She cupped his chin, forcing him to meet her stare. "Are you?"

His eyes flickered away. "It's the king's role. Those idiots down in Sudaland keep encroaching onto our land. They're not bright enough to cultivate their own. Our people have worked for generations to make that farmland viable."

Bathed in the dying embers of the sunset, they left the central keep and climbed a turret to admire the surrounding landscape. Chentene had assembled the full army. Around the walls of Manda Torre, another town made of tents filled the fertile bowl.

"I doubt they'll have much fight in them once Stump flies a few passes. I think they'll retreat," Chentene said.

Turning to face into the central keep, their heads touched as they watched Stump stretch his long neck clear of the tower he clung to.

'There will be gold!' The dragon's head swayed, bringing his glittering, multi-faceted eyes to bear on them. His hungry thoughts rang inside their minds.

Every servant in the courtyard stopped at the words. "Yours!" The cry went up from the town.

'Mine!' The roof tiles rattled with his bugle call. He unfurled his wings and peeled away from the tower. The drop powered him into a silent glide. A single beat took him in a swooping circuit of the city walls. '*Mine!'* His skin changed hue from green to purple as he banked high, allowing Maryan to admire the magnificent beast he'd become.

With all her heart, she wanted to beg Chentene into leaving the fighting to others, but she knew that would be selfish. If he did, and things went badly, he would resent her forever. "Galia says I have two months before our child is born. Try to return before then."

He squeezed her hand. "No riding out into the forest. Mordacai has encircled the castle to defend you, but he can't do more. Stay within the walls and you'll be safe. I worry as much as you do."

Maryan crumpled Chentene's letter into a ball. The army had been so outstanding they had crushed the Sudaland rabble and pushed the invasion back to the border. Part of the surrender agreement had been to support an incursion against Bara to reclaim lands once rightfully theirs. The terms of the treaty were magnificent. He had no choice but to remain in Sudaland.

Poor Chentene, so determined to be home, but also painfully dedicated to his role as king. She paused before smoothing the page on the table. Her confinement would end within a few days. Carl shuffled along the back of the winged chair, landing on her shoulder. *'Stump says Chentene is devastated. He weeps when nobody else is present.'*

Although the telepathy from the dragon couldn't reach Maryan, Stump could still communicate with the castle rat. 'Tell him that I love him. His child will be waiting and he will get the opportunity to attend the births of our several children.'

'It is done.' Carl sat back on his ruined rear legs, his whiskers twitching. 'I think that you should call your nest mates. Your whelping is close.'

Without doubting the wisdom of her tiny friend, she rang the bell that summoned Patricia's nervous face around the door. "Is it time?"

Maryan nodded. Her tongue had stuck to the roof of her mouth leaving her unable to speak,

The thin woman's hands flew to her cheeks. "I'll fetch Galia." She made to leave, but a noisy bustle of chattering women swept her back into the room. "Ladies please!" Patricia shouted, trying to push through.

Tears pricked Maryan at the sight of her comrades from the training ground. The hours of practice had forged a close-knit friendship, but dreading rejection, she'd been afraid to ask them to be with her. Her emotions tumbled uncontrollably. Dark haired Natalie, the sisters, Rachel and Sophie, round limbed, but staunch friends, and behind them, hovered the mysterious Emily.

The palace female healer, Galia, a striking woman with long, strong hands and a hatchet nose forced a passage through the circle of women. Her stare as calm as a lion fixed on its prey, she lifted her mass of fire-red curls and drove the women back with a glance. Galia nodded once to Carl before turning her piercing stare on Maryan, "Could I persuade you to loan the animal to me when this is over? He describes your progress with remarkable clarity."

"I think I've started my contractions." A twinge nipped. "That wasn't too bad," Maryan said.

Pity touched Galia's smile as she shook her head. "Tell me that when you nurse a child." She fixed her attention on the ladies in the room. "We shall have tea and wait, but when I command it, you will leave. Are we agreed?"

Galia's pale-eyed stare stifled the chatter. Two attendants followed her carrying a table covered with equipment. They silently prepared Maryan's bedchamber, finishing by hanging a large water skin by the bed.

Time passed, Maryan's waters broke and the agony of mounting contractions wracked her. The women each took their turn to hold her hand. Galia bustled efficiently around the bed, occasionally wiping the sweat from Maryan's face. "Still too easy?"

Maryan took a drink before slumping back into the nest of pillows. She shook her head slowly, not wanting to waste the brief respite in chatter.

"How many children have you promised Chentene?" Natalie winced as she massaged her crushed fingers straight with her other hand.

"It's time for you all to leave." Galia shooed the women toward the door. "When you next see your friend she will be a mother."

Baby Leon arrived in the early hours of the morning. The ladies of the court napped outside, but their heads came up as soon as Galia opened the door to the bedchamber. "You may return."

The babe lay upon Maryan. Although exhausted, she couldn't keep the grin from her face. "He looks like Chentene, he's beautiful," she said.

"A boy?" Patricia squirmed through the ladies of the court. "You idiot. We need a girl!" She grabbed the healer's elbow, "Are you sure? You must be wrong!"

"I think I know a boy when I help one into the world."

"We must get rid of him." Patricia's twitching became wild. She gnawed on her knuckle. "Quickly, before Mordacai hears. We can find a baby girl in the town. Bring her here. It will be fine." She tried to snatch Leon. "Give him to me, I'll do it."

Natalie slapped Patricia's hands away. "You're mad, get out!" She caught the woman's wrists to hold her back.

Patricia squirmed free, making another dive for Leon.

"Rachael, grab her other arm, so we can get her out of here!" "Sophie hauled on Patricia's shoulders and dragged the struggling woman to the door.

Patricia shouted back over her shoulder. "Listen to me! You're all in danger, Mordacai won't accept this."

Carl's voice whispered. 'Chentene is pleased. He's dancing in front of the soldiers. Stump is puzzled and thinks the Prince is trying to fly.'

A tired smile slipped across Maryan's face at the idea of her husband's crazy joy. She wondered what the troops would make of their normally reserved ruler's actions.

Dull autumnal light had already edged into the room when a touch jerked Maryan from a deep sleep. Surprised to see Lady Emily at the bedside, she instantly checked the crib. The woman put her hand out to restrain Maryan. "He is unharmed, but we have a problem."

A rustle near her feet indicated that Carl was clambering onto the bed, his ruined legs slowing him down. Emily gathered the rat, struggling to hold him, but Carl squirmed frantically to free himself.

'Chentene is dead!' Carl's voice wailed. 'He's dead, killed in his sleep. Stump is berserk, he's raging and torching the countryside, things are crazy.'

Maryan threw back the covers to ease her legs out of the bed, wincing with every movement. *'Can Stump speak to Mordacai?'* She turned to Emily. "Can Mordacai …"

"Apparently, he's vanished." Emily interrupted. "Don't strain the capabilities of the rat and dragon. They do well, but they don't understand human politics. I do."

"Why are you involved?" Maryan shook her head. It felt stuffed with sheep's wool.

"It's my job. You imagine Chentene didn't know things were happening behind the scenes?" Emily went to the door to peep out. "Sadly, he didn't expect such a direct approach, but he did think an attempt on the child likely." The slim woman coolly regarded the royal crib, "We need to move you, but we have some time. Even flogging horses to death, Mordacai can't get here in less than ten days. By then, you and Leon must be gone."

"But he's the Prince. He needs to replace his father." Maryan clutched Leon fiercely against her. Shocked awake, the new Prince screwed his face up into a mewling cry, ramming his tiny fists into his cheeks.

"We're not going to argue." Emily's expression hardened. "You must do as I say." She unfolded a letter and held it out. The curling script was undoubtedly Chentene's.

Dearest Maryan,

If ever you read these words, I fear the worst has occurred. The person bearing this, Lady Emily, is a professional, especially recruited to keep you safe. Do as she bids and remember our love forever.

Chentene.

Emily slipped the letter back inside her skirt. "Chentene made your safety my priority. I want to talk to Patricia before she gets wind of what's happened. Send for her."

Struggling, Maryan pulled a gown around her shoulders and rang for a servant. The moment the girl put her head through the door Maryan screamed at her. "We need more heat in here. I need a fire. Fetch Patricia, this is unacceptable."

Even in winter, Maryan always complained when they stoked the fires too high. The confused servant ducked a short curtsy before backing out of the room.

Disturbed from his sleep, Mac prowled from side to side, before settling with his head resting on the bed. Unable to clear her thoughts, Maryan ran her fingers across his fur as she rocked Leon. The aging assassin arrived. Her attention hovered on the baby, but she smoothed her features into a worried grimace. "I have tried to be your friend, but you don't know what he's capable of." She locked her fingers together in front of her slim-fitting black dress.

"What is he capable of?" Emily asked, stepping out of the adjoining room.

Patricia didn't flinch at the sudden appearance. "Anything."

"Chentene's dead and Mordacai has vanished. How do you read that?"

"Help us all. That can only mean one thing." Strength drained from the older woman. She staggered back, reaching out to find a chair to support her weight. "We have to get away as quickly as we can. He has men gathered at his estate. Not enough to fight a pitched battle, but enough to attack without the army here." Patricia spared them a single pitying glance. "Fly you fools, flee. I don't want to know where you've gone to." She spun on her heel almost running for the door.

Emily tugged thoughtfully at a tendril of hair at her temple. "I'm going to gather our friends. We need to plan how we're going to handle this." She strode from the room leaving Maryan alone in her thoughts.

Baby Leon wasn't going to settle. Maryan tugged at the laces on the front of her gown and held him to her chest, brushing her fingers lightly through the child's blonde hair. He searched blindly before finding her nipple. Chentene dead? Grief tore a sob from the depths of her soul. Tears rolled down her face. She didn't know what to do. Go back to Serenia, or seek asylum in a foreign land.

She knew nothing of foreign lands, or of caring for a child. She carefully placed Leon onto the bed to change the diaper wrapping his tiny body. Although she'd practiced on a rag doll, the doll hadn't writhed amidst rumpled bedding. She struggled with the complex folds, stabbing the back of her hand with the ridiculous pin.

Already aware of the tragedy, her friends filtered quietly into the room. Maryan felt naked, with her nightgown unlaced and her hair unbound.

"Let me do that." Sophie took the diaper from Maryan. She folded it into a neat triangle, before expertly tucking the cloth around Leon. "Eldest girl in the family gets to do these things."

"We need to secure the keep, but we also need to make sure this wing is guarded." Emily was counting off the things they had to do on her fingers.

A nightgown felt inappropriate, Maryan had to be able to move freely. She ducked into her dressing room to find clothes. Regarding the leather skirt, she ran her hand across her stomach. It would be weeks before she could think of fitting into that. Instead, she chose thick woollen trousers to go with a baggy outdoor top.

Just as Maryan re-joined her friends, a thunderclap shook the room. Rachel squealed. “What was that?” She ran across to peek out of the window. “Oh save us, it’s Mordacai, look.”

In the courtyard, the ruined gates to the outer keep hung torn from their hinges. Mordacai strode towards the stairway leading up to Maryan’s rooms. Behind him, a squad of crimson-clad soldiers efficiently secured the area.

“He can’t …” Maryan said.

“He has. We’ve run out of time.” Emily cut her off.

“We’re not going to meet him in my bed chamber.” Maryan led the women out into the corridor and waited.

The door at the far end crashed back and Mordacai strode through. He looked old and haggard. His normally sleek black hair hung loose, shot through with grey streaks. His eyes were bloodshot and his face purple with burst blood vessels.

“That’s close enough,” Emily shouted. She trained a short riding bow on him.

He stopped, curled his hands onto his hips and laughed. Two crimson-clad guards crowded behind him. His laughter ceased abruptly and he reached out, rippling his fingers before folding them into a fist. “I’ve travelled the paths of the demons to get here.

You don't think a rag-tag of doxies will stop me, do you?"

The arrow flew true, but stopped arm's length from his chest. He flicked his hand negligently sending it speeding back along the corridor to skewer Emily through her throat. She crumpled to the floor, her gaze meeting Maryan's before fading into a dead stare.

Mordacai had so easily brushed Chentene's last defence aside. "It's time for a change." He started to walk toward them, the two flanking guards grinned insolently.

A third soldier dressed in the crimson of Mordacai's private army burst from the stairway. "Let me through. My Lord, stop! It's a trap."

The two other guards stepped back allowing the newcomer to dodge between them. Mordacai held his hand out to the women, commanding them to wait for the interruption to pass.

The running soldier landed a punch carrying the full weight of his momentum. Mordacai spun, his face smashed into the wall. Harlon slid to a stop in front of the women.

"Get the Prince out of here." His face lit up with his most wicked grin as he gave Maryan's arm a shove. "I'll try to hold them."

The two soldiers rushed forward. Harlon's blade slashed across the throat of the first before slipping into the eye of the second. Powered by every muscle in Harlon's body, his sword carved a glittering arc for Mordacai's neck. A blinding flash filled the passage. The sword shattered into a thousand pieces. Harlon catapulted back, landing awkwardly.

Footsteps clattered up the stone staircase. Harlon struggled to reclaim a sword from one of the dead soldiers whilst shouting over his shoulder. "Get moving, I can't hold them for long."

"I'll guard you." Natalie notched an arrow into the bow retrieved from the fallen Emily. She drew a bead on the staircase, waiting to pick off the first soldier to emerge.

Rachel pushed ineffectually against Maryan. "Go, we're all in danger whilst you stay."

Mordacai raised his hand. Magic swirled into a fireball, pulsing with evil.

"Get down!" Maryan dived back into her bedroom. Her final glimpse of the carnage outside the door was Sophie gripping the handle and slamming it shut. An explosion shook the plaster from the walls. She could hear Harlon shouting, buying her time, possibly at a terrible cost. Mac paced, raking the wooden panels. She tugged in vain, but the door was jammed.

'Over this way,' Carl's urgent words squealed in her thoughts. Moving as quickly as her aching limbs could, she rummaged for travelling gear, bundling a mishmash of clothes into a canvas bag. Then, she grabbed cloth to swaddle Leon and a handful of lengths to use as diapers.

What else? Her mind reeled. What else? Food! She gathered the meagre bowl of fruit from the sideboard. Galia's water skin still hung by the bed. She swung it off the hook and laid it across the top of her clothes.

The noise outside the room grew. A thunderclap shook the castle walls and the clamour of battle fell into silence.

'Quickly,' the rat urged.

After casting a single last glance at the room where she had known happiness. *'How do we get out?'* she thought.

'The tunnels! We go through the wonderful tunnels.' Carl sat with his ruined stumps behind Mac's head, his forepaws locked into the fur above the lion's brows. Mac's sightless, milky orbs swept across her and a deep growl escaped. *'Follow us!'* Mac threw all of his weight into a lunge at a panel by the soil closet. The wooden section snapped free to reveal a service tunnel and Mac's tawny rump vanished through.

Maryan lowered her head to peep into the gloom. *'How dark is it?'*

'Mac doesn't have a problem.'

'Mac's blind.' Maryan edged herself through the opening. A clever mechanism held the hatchway down. Once her weight moved off it, the panel snapped shut, plunging the tunnel into blackness.

Chapter 19

The wonderful tunnels turned out to be service hatches for the latrines. Maryan crawled slowly, in near-perfect darkness, her only assistance, the occasional touch of Mac's tail. Tortured by the height of the ceiling, she followed in an awkward stoop.
'How do we find our way?'

'Use your nose,' Carl said.

'I really don't want to,' she said, trying to breathe through her mouth.

The meandering passage continued downward until she judged they'd descended below ground level, possibly even beneath the castle cellars. Their path vanished through a brick-lined tunnel in the stonework, emerging in the drainage system running beneath the wide boulevard leading through the city.

Metal grids allowed the water from the streets to wash the debris of life towards the sea. Shafts of light speared through grates above them, bouncing off the swiftly flowing water of the narrow canal. The twinkling reflections on the stained brickwork showed how high the water sometimes reached. Swollen by rainfall, the oily brown surface flowed in a greasy torrent, heavy with the stench of human waste. Maryan tugged a cloth across Leon's face, praying the fumes wouldn't harm him.

Mac prowled ahead with casual grace. She could sense the constant stream of chatter Carl fed to the lion to guide him. Leon stirred, she lifted him to her and realised that some of the offensive smell originated from him. Nuzzling against her woollen shirt, his mewling whimper grew more frantic. *'I'll have to stop. How much longer are we going to be in here?'*

'Not long, we go through a narrow passage and then follow the tunnel out onto the fields.'

They emerged in a small thicket a distance from the walls. Maryan approached the edge of the bushes to peer toward Manda Torre. The dark gate remained closed, but she imagined pursuit bursting forth at any moment. Even though instinct told her to get away as quickly as possible, they had to wait for dusk. Any attempt to make her way across the fields in daylight would be suicide. She settled in the shelter of the stone entrance to feed Leon.

Maryan tugged her cloak around her shoulders before setting off across the fields. Her limbs ached, emphasising how unfit she'd become. Imitating the hobbling walk of an aging farmworker came naturally. Not daring more than a glance over her shoulder, step by painful step, Maryan progressed across the fields.

Finally, after an age of slow progress, the Forest of Dreams loomed ahead. Although it offered her only hope of concealment, her every instinct screamed not to venture beneath the dripping boughs.

Settling Leon, she paused to shrug her baggage into place before stepping off the road. A delicious, rich smell of fern, nuts and mushrooms washed the remaining odours of the sewer from her nose. Determined not to go too far into the woodland, she remained barely hidden by the trees. As full darkness descended, she had to go deeper into the woods to find cover for the night. In a small dip, she formed a crude shelter by hanging her spare cloak across a pair of saplings struggling to grow in the shade of a larger tree.

Cold, but at least sheltered, she tugged her hood down and opened her tunic to press Leon against her. Mac settled close, adding his warmth, Carl wriggled just below Leon. Memories of the day gnawed at her. She wanted to keep moving, but knew she had to rest. Her eyes flickered shut.

"Thank Gorath, I've finally found you."

A golden figure in a burnished breastplate appeared on the edge of the hollow. Easily as tall as Maryan, she wore her blonde hair scraped back into the plait of a virgin warrior, the Serenian stood with her hands on her tiny waist.

Maryan's dry mouth almost prevented her from speaking. Finally, she managed to croak, "Mother?"

The crooked smile she remembered lit up the warrior's face. "I've struggled for an eternity to find you." Amara raised her arms, inviting a hug.

Maryan wrapped Leon to protect him before clambering to her feet. Carl grumbled at being tumbled from his sleep. In comparison to Maryan's grubbiness, her mother gleamed with vibrant health. The Ultimate Warrior had arrived.

"Where have you been? The whole world's been looking for you," Maryan said.

"Never mind that." Amara stepped into the dip. The instant their fingers met, Maryan screamed. Her mother's face changed, her radiant beauty dripped like wax down a candle. Their hands merged. Maryan felt her own life force torn away. Through the raging agony, her mother's voice still crooned. "I love you. Let me hold you."

Wracked with pain, Maryan started to weaken. The ground hit her knees. Red filled her vision. The melted caricature of her mother screamed. It fell to the ground clutching at the gushing stump of its arm, leaving Maryan holding a severed hand.

Spinning and dipping, a red-cloaked figure shoved Maryan aside. A blade flashed, hacking the creature to the ground. It held its leg, unable to rise, but still crooned with Amara's voice. "I'm here for you. Help me."

A burning need for revenge gripped Maryan. Her hand snapped over her shoulder, her axe already swinging to destroy the cringing parody of her mother.

"Stop! Idiot child."

Frozen by the words, she halted her strike a mere hair's breadth from the monster's skull. Was she back at school? What kind of crazy nightmare had she fallen into?

"Asti?"

A scowl contorted the woman's ruined face. "We need to move. Don't kill her. They double up when you kill them. You can, however, carve them so they can't move very quickly." She nodded to a crowd of wounded imitations of her mother stumbling through the trees towards them. "I think we'll be safe if we get to the road." The shambling forms lurched ever closer. She crouched, helping Maryan gather her things. "Move! I'll bring these."

Leon's cry pierced the brooding silence. Mac rumbled, baring his teeth at the oncoming crowd of six, no, seven, if she counted the one that had attacked her.

"Why did it take you so long to realise they doubled," Maryan said.

"They just kept coming out of the dark. I didn't know what was happening until I'd cut them down."

Hampered by Leon, Maryan craned around, trying to keep the pursuers in sight. "We're not going to make it to the road. We're going to have to fight."

"I've been at this all night. You can't fight them, they're magical."

'Take cover!' Carl drove Mac crashing into the bushes. The lion whipped around, snarling at the pursuing figures.

"Get down!" Maryan relayed to Asti.

"What?" Asti gaped around in confusion.

Maryan bundled her to the ground, barely avoiding the flames roaring from overhead. Leather wings rippled as Stump wheeled in the sky. He returned, skimming the treetops, heading directly at the figures. Screams rang out before dragon-fire silenced them. The edges of the scorched woodland smouldered. Smoke blew across the bushes.

'They dare to attack? They attack you, my mother, they shall die, all die.' Stump's voice roared, arrogant and deep. He circled once more before dropping onto the road bordering the forest.

Rushing at him, Maryan flung her arms around the dragon's neck. "Stump, I'm so glad to see you."

'I have claimed my dragon name, Tamas, son of Tamaar. I am now one of the great dragons, ready to take my place in the heritage of Shudalandia.' He brought his head lower than hers. His jewelled eyes pleaded. 'Mother who has raised me … may I fly to the breeding grounds?'

This question obviously meant a lot to Stump, Tamas, she corrected herself, pausing before speaking. "I need help. Can you watch the road to prevent Mordacai from following?"

A blaze of flame flashed in the dull morning light. 'That evil creeping worm, it shall be my pleasure to roast him alive.'

She leaned her head against Stump. "He has strong magic. Don't fight him, but keep Carl informed of any troops you spot. Once we reach the borders, then I, the mother who raised you, insist you fly to the breeding grounds." She dropped her voice to a whisper. "You do know where they are?"

Tamas sprang into the air, his scales changing hue. 'Of course. When we become adult, all dragons possess all dragon knowledge. Isn't it the same for humans?'

"No, it's not the same for us." Maryan shared a careful smile with Asti as they watched the dragon fly into the distance.

Because Leon needed feeding, they made a small camp just off the road. Asti started a fire using a smouldering branch. It felt odd to see her old teacher, her hair shaved in a high arc over her ears and the cruel scar contorting her once beautiful features. She wore an eye patch, but Maryan remembered the awful image of the uncovered socket. Holding Leon to her breast, Maryan spoke without looking up, "Why are you here?"

"I'm heading for Serenia. There's trouble brewing and they need warriors."

"It's the death penalty for you if you try to return. Etelan told me as much."

"It's the death penalty for all I hold dear if I don't. I can deal with her." Her lips curled into a sour grimace. "I'll be contrite. Play on her vanity. Let's be honest, there's plenty of that to go at." She rummaged in her pack. "I came to Manda Torre to give you this."

A small, gold-embossed book dropped at Maryan's side. Without reaching out, she studied the elaborate cover.

"It's your mother's diary."

"You found something! Why you, when nobody else could?"

"The others didn't think to twist Orlon's arm for him."

Orlon was the magician who helped the people of Bara to organise the games. None knew his history, but Maryan vaguely remembered a thin man with a straggling beard.

"How can you pressure a wizard?"

"The same as anybody else. If you catch them off guard they're as vulnerable as we are." Asti hesitated. "I went to Idrahail, the home of the wizards, but he rarely returns to there. He guards his solitude by wandering where he's least expected."

"Did you see Kait in Idrahail," Maryan said, her mind still darting.

"She didn't arrive. I asked, but they didn't know why she hadn't taken her place amongst them."

The idea that Kait hadn't gone to Idrahail puzzled Maryan. She thought about the night Kait had left and her hesitance to leave.

Asti carried on. "I tracked Orlon to rooms in Bara. He had taken charge of your mother's belongings. I searched them myself. I knew Amara's mind and how she hid things, feint within feint, within feint, the same as fighting her." Asti stroked where the scar cut a ragged fold in her almost black skin. She nodded at the book in Maryan's hand. "A diary, hidden inside a book, inside a box, inside another book, all inside a locked box."

"Does it tell us anything?"

"No, but it says how much she'll miss seeing her daughter grow up. As though she knew she wouldn't return from the games."

"She didn't even come to see me before she left. There was a lot of fuss and preparation. It all happened so suddenly."

Asti coughed a cold laugh. "She wasn't going. Until she did this, I was supposed to go." She lifted the eye patch and rubbed the flat of her palm against the raw socket. "I've no idea how she beat me. One moment I'm on the offensive, the next, I'm in the Infirmary without a face. That didn't rate more than the slightest mention. 'Today, I stopped Asti from competing.' Was all she wrote."

'People are approaching,' Carl warned. Maryan reached for her axe. Asti regarded her quizzically.

"He's our guard." She nodded to Carl. "I can hear his thoughts and he says someone's coming."

Carl rocked back on his haunches, almost bowing to Asti.

"Your source, sir rat?" Asti returned a short nod.

'My ears warn me. Why doesn't she try using hers?'

"He says he has better hearing than we do."

A small patrol of soldiers appeared. The crimson uniforms looked rumpled as if they'd searched all night. "She's here!" They came forward at a run.

Asti scowled. "You hold the baby. There are only six of them." Her twin blades whipped into a defensive blur.

"Who's that?" one of the guards shouted. "You! Woman, who are you?"

Asti continued to stalk slowly forward. Maryan knew her tutor wouldn't speak during a battle, but she could. "The woman you face defeated your champion, Barag. She ground him to humiliation in the arena. I would introduce you, but I don't think you'll live long enough to make the effort worthwhile." As an afterthought, she added, "Asti, leave one alive, we need to speak to him."

Swords ablaze in the dull morning light, Asti sprang amongst them like a fox amongst chickens. The men tried to encircle her, but for Asti, it proved a training exercise. Her whirling blades locked and struck. Each time they did, a man fell screaming to the floor.

Only two remained standing. "Which do you prefer?" Asti shouted. Distracted, one of the men glanced at Maryan. A whirling blade flashed. He grasped his neck, suddenly desperate to stop the gush of blood pumping from his throat.

A wrist flick whipped away the final assailant's sword. In a single fluid motion, the twin blades crossed beneath his chin stretching his head rigidly high.

Maryan balanced Leon on her hip as she approached the soldier. Mac prowled at her thigh, his snarl rumbling almost beneath hearing.

"How did you get past the dragon?"

Beads of sweat pricked the man's forehead. His eyes rolled, trying to meet Asti's grim stare whilst also watching Maryan. "The Lord Mordacai gathered us into small bands and made us march into these things, gateways, he called them. They shimmered. All around, fell creatures tried to paw at us. He said that if he could endure it for hours, then we could manage a few minutes. We dropped out on this road, I guess the others are scattered all around."

"Your instructions?" Asti said, lifting the razor edges of her swords.

"I'm not telling you, unless you promise to let me go."

"You can't bargain, but I'm not a mindless killer, serve well and you will be rewarded."

"Lord Mordacai said to bring back the head of the baby. Do what we liked with the woman, but leave her dead."

Maryan clutched Leon. How could anybody issue such orders? She shrugged. What else did she expect? "Let him go."

Relief flooded the man's face. Asti released the pressure on his neck. He spun, but the ebony-skinned warrior moved like a snake, reaching from behind and whipping her sword across his throat. She held him for a moment before letting him drop.

"Do you think he'd have said no when they lined up to abuse you? We couldn't let him give away our position."

Even knowing Asti to be correct, bile rose in Maryan's throat. She watched the blood pool around the dead soldier. Without the uniform, he would be a simple working man, a farm labourer.

"Where are you heading?" Asti said.

Where would she go? If she stayed in Garalandia, it would only be a matter of time before they found her. She didn't have a home anymore. "I haven't a clue."

Veiled in a misty drizzle, they walked along the lane. Moisture dripped off the rim of Maryan's hood. After a time, Asti said, "I think you should come home with me."

Maryan wondered if anywhere would ever feel like home again. In one day, she had gone from being a princess in a castle to barely owning the clothes on her back. All her worldly riches were in the pouch tucked in her bag. She knew nothing of life.

The day wore on and Asti repelled a second attack, then a third. They debated cutting directly across the fields rather than following the road, but decided against it. Instead, they trudged the gloomy pathway until the descent of night forced them to seek a place to rest.

The bushes crashed apart and a circle of guards quickly surrounded them.

Asti glanced at Mac, "Is he any use in this?"

'She's not very bright is she? It's only his eyes that don't work,' Carl said.

"Carl says the lion will assist you."

Mac leapt into the fight, Carl urged the beast forward before rolling clear.

Asti dipped and flowed through the soldiers, her blades unleashing death in every direction. A trooper still concealed in the bushes hit her with a crossbow bolt. She spun, blood exploding from her arm. He bent to reload the weapon, but Mac powered into the undergrowth, tearing at his throat.

Flailing her claw axe, Maryan struggled to hold off the three men closing on her. With a baby slung across her chest, she couldn't get her blade into the fight. Mac swept away her adversaries in a single leap, giving her time to lower Leon to the ground. He cried out on the wet grass, but she could finally act.

Mac tore at one of the soldiers, but two of them scrambled free and came at her. She caught the blade of the first between the toes of the claw, turning it away. Her sword pierced his eye, deep enough to kill, but not far enough to wedge. She spun, using the full momentum of her body, the central spike crashed into the second soldier's temple. The power of the blow kept moving, tearing away the front of his face, cascading blood and brains across the road.

Asti lay sprawled between two dead soldiers. Maryan tugged her off the road and propped her up against the bank. "We can't go on like this. We need a plan to get us away." She examined Asti's torn muscle. "This needs treating."

No matter how much Asti declared herself fit, her rambling protests became more incoherent with every stride. The crude field dressing failed to staunch the bleeding. Anxious to keep moving, Maryan hauled the woman's good arm over her shoulder.

Limping on, they reached a trail leading off into the fields. A silent farmhouse stood in darkness on the far hill, but there was a barn much closer. Assessing their plight, Maryan surveyed the road and the track. They desperately needed a safe place to tend Asti's wounds.

The interior of the barn was well organised. The smell of animals and stored grain scented the air. Maryan debated asking at the farm for help, but knew that would put the family at risk. Besides, not a single light shone from the house and she didn't want to travel all that way only to find the place deserted.

The last leg of their journey had drained Maryan's strength. Asti slipped from her grip, smashing her head on the floor. Blood oozed around the makeshift bandage. Her ex-tutor would die if her injury wasn't cleaned and wrapped the correctly.

After settling the older woman in a bed of straw, Maryan rummaged through Asti's pack. She found rations, a small cooking set and a roll of field dressings. She scraped out a shallow pit on the far side of the barn and set water to boil on a small fire. To salve her conscience, she left a small gemstone as payment for the chicken she killed. Uncertain of how to cook it, she tore the carcass into strips, laying them on stones close to the fire.

The water boiled, allowing her to tend Asti's arm. The raw flesh oozed at her touch. Asti groaned, her head lolling. It took an age, but finally the wound looked clean enough to bind with a dressing.

Using the remaining water, she bathed Leon's tiny body, carefully cleaning soil and grime from the folds in his skin. She fed him, crooning nonsense melodies to ease him back to sleep. Once he settled, she scrubbed his clothes and set them to dry.

A creak betrayed the door of the barn opening. Standing in the doorway, dressed in the ambassador's crimson livery, a broad-shouldered man with a shock of dark hair craned his neck. "Maryan?"

After studying him for a moment, Fredrick's boyish features emerged from the rough demeanour. "Here," Maryan said.

Chapter 20

The last year had given Fredrick solid muscles, bulking him even wider than she remembered him. Numerous scars now added ruggedness to his once boyish face. He swept her into a crushing embrace. "Thrippas be blessed, I've found you."

His mouth sealed across hers. One hand gripped her neck holding her in the kiss, his other explored, searching between the folds of her blouse.

"Fredrick!" Maryan pushed him away. "I'm in mortal danger. I've just had a baby and you want to, want to …" she waved her hand, twisting away.

He caught her shoulder, spinning her to face him. "I'm about to risk my damned life for you." He glanced at Asti, unconscious on her bed of straw, before his eyes crept across to Leon. "Mordacai said bring him the baby's head and do what I will with the woman." He gripped her shoulders. "My will is to keep you for my own."

"But the price is Leon's life?"

Fredrick couldn't meet her stare, but nodded.

"The Ambassador said to leave me dead. I know his instructions."

Fredrick grinned at Asti. "We strip her and burn the barn. One charred corpse is the same as another. I'll be the one to find the body. Nobody will know."

"I'll be safe?" Maryan whispered, moving a step nearer.

"Safe." Fredrick opened his arms, drawing her into his broad chest.

Her knee jerked for his groin, but blade-master reactions saved him. After deflecting most of the power, his foot swept away her legs and his full weight crushed her into the ground.

Startled by the sudden ruckus, Mac roared. The lion stalked closer. Fredrick pressed a knife close to her eye. "Tell it to stay away, or you're dead."

She glanced at Carl. Mac rumbled ominously, but held his approach.

Shifting the dagger to her throat, Fredrick's free hand tugged at her clothing. "Bitch, I'm going to screw the princess and take my reward from Mordacai." He pushed the blade against her jugular. She couldn't fight him.

"Please Fredrick, no. I've just had a baby. There's no love in this." Everything whirled. He seemed to grow more hands. His leg pushed between hers, forcing them apart.

"Love?" He tore her blouse, squeezing her breast as though he was wringing out a dishcloth.

The shadows behind him shifted. An ebony fist closed on the wrist of his dagger hand. Asti fell on them sinking her white teeth into his ear. Her long black legs wrapped around his body as she rolled her weight back, inexorably tugging him off Maryan.

Helpless, he thrashed his elbows to either side, thumping into her protective breastplate. His head jerked back into her face, but growling like an animal, she held on. Mac pounced, his teeth finding Fredrick's throat.

A torrent of blood washed across Asti, but she clung on, making sure Mac could finish his dreadful execution. After a gruesome eternity, she released her grasp. Protective of his prize, Mac painted a bloody smear as he tugged Fredrick across the barn.

Maryan helped the warrior to her feet. Her skin and breastplate glistened with blood. Spotting a water trough, she tumbled into it. The surface boiled as she scrubbed herself clean. "Metal and leather, is far more practical than fabric." She laughed like a maniac.

"I'll sort myself out a little less drastically," Maryan said. The pan of water was still warm and she used her tattered blouse to scrub away the stench of Fredrick.

The smoky taste of the charred chicken possibly wasn't the worst thing Maryan had tasted, but it came close. Asti took a bite and grimaced. "It's pretty obvious you didn't have to cook for this man of yours."

A creak warned them as another crimson clad figure slipped into the barn. Asti flew at the interloper, her one good arm whipping her sword into a blur. The soldier easily disarmed her, but she leapt at him, teeth bared, her fingers curled to claw at his face. He dropped his shoulder into her stomach, catapulting her over his back. Spinning, he tugged a medallion from his shirt. "Thrippas, is that truly Asti the Red?" He peered through the keyhole as she struggled to her feet.

"Harlon!" Maryan sprang at him, wrapping her arms around his neck. "How did you find us?"

He gestured down his body to emphasise the uniform and ran his hand across his shaved head. "I became one of the guards. They're mercenaries and don't know each other. We have to get a move on. Mordacai has worked out your direction." He pointed at the remains of Fredrick. "Using magic, he tracks those he sends out and knows when they die. There's a large force of mercenaries coming up this road behind me. We have to go in another direction. Come on, we've a carriage."

"We?" Maryan's voice rose.

"The Lady Sophie." Avoiding her gaze, he headed for the door. "She was the only one to escape."

Outside, the moon threw a silver sheen across the wet meadows. Harlon ran down the track to bring the coach up from the road. The coachmen of Manda Torre would have wept for their sumptuous touring coach. The axles creaked ominously as he struggled to work it close to the barn. Mud and worse smeared the lacquered black panels.

"Civilisation is coming to an end." Sophie said, as she opened the narrow door. She waited for a moment before lowering herself. "Travel without staff is the worst."

Maryan swamped her in a tearful hug. "Oh Sophie, I'm so sorry. You shouldn't ..."

"Stop." Sophie held up a hand. "Those animals will not get away with this. Now, where's Leon? Are you caring for him?" She bustled past Maryan, in search of the young Prince.

Harlon checked the team of horses before helping Maryan to lift Asti into the carriage.

"I can ride on top and help," the injured warrior grumbled as they forced her through the narrow doorway.

"Let's hold you as a surprise for any we encounter," Harlon said.

Sophie sniffed. "Anybody opening the royal coach to find this travelling circus would die of fright."

The coach lurched drunkenly off the farmland onto the main road where Harlon nudged the horses into a fast trot. Sophie kept a careful eye on Asti, apparently trusting a lion more than she did the wild warrior of legend.

At the first stop, Maryan passed Leon into Sophie's care and joined Harlon on the driving seat. It had passed midday, but the cold air forced her to draw her hood tight. "How long before they catch us?"

"Not long. I was prepared to set off the moment I knew the direction. It takes time to despatch a troop, but some of them are bound to ride ahead."

"If we evade the soldiers following us, can we make it to the Serenian border?"

"I think so. The mercenaries are refusing to use Mordacai's demon-filled tunnels. The monsters ate a full squad in full view of the men waiting. They'd have lynched him if he hadn't wielded a fireball.

"Then let's stop them. Pull over here."

She'd chosen a narrow ravine breaking a craggy escarpment in the landscape, looming not much wider than the coach itself, the walls climbed steeply on either side.

"I hope this will work," Harlon said. "You're putting an awful lot of faith into that dragon. Last time I saw him, he was dropping on anything that glittered."

"He's grown. This is how they used him when he fought with Chentene, trust me."

After blocking the narrow gulley with the carriage, the four of them waited for the soldiers to arrive. The squad galloped into the narrow chasm, reining their mounts in as the leader called a halt by raising his arm.

Asti strode to the front. She stood with her hip cocked, a sword in her left hand, her injured arm hooked casually on her belt.

"That woman is too damned arrogant," Harlon muttered to Maryan.

"Arrogant doesn't even start to describe her," Maryan said.

"She behaves as if she's the only one here who can use a sword. I do have a little skill," he took up guard alongside Asti.

Maryan and Sophie flanked the other two. In the distance behind the troop, the shape of a bird approached low across the fields. Growing from a starling, to an eagle and finally, a full size dragon, Stump swept towards them. The heat of the flames forced Maryan to cover her face. The dragon swooped through the raging blaze and landed between the carnage and the carriage. In an instant, the troop vanished, filling the air with the smell of roasting flesh.

Stump approached awkwardly along the narrow gulley. He lowered his head allowing Maryan to hug him. She held on, allowing his inner warmth to run through her body. Finally, she said, "Thank you. You may go in search of the breeding grounds."

'You aren't yet safely to the border.'

"I have these friends with me. It's not safe for you in Serenia. They kill dragons."

Tamas snorted in disgust, smoke curling from his nostrils. *'I don't fear them.'*

“If you possess all dragon knowledge, then you realise it is a dangerous place,” Maryan chided. Flames still licked the gruesome pyre at the far end of the gulley. The dragon’s multi-faceted eyes twinkled and his colour-shifting skin rippled from green to purple. She clung to him until Harlon had drawn the carriage out of the narrow valley.

“It is time for you to leave,” she said, turning to catch up with the coach. The dragon followed her, his scales rasping against the rocky walls.

At the mouth of the canyon, they stood in awkward silence. Maryan rubbed her hand on the dragon’s eye-ridge. A rush of love filled her. “Go, find a wife.”

The dragon’s voice rang loud inside her head. ‘I will return, mother who raised me. I will bring you my bride. Dragons don’t know about family, but I believe they should learn.’ He leapt into the air, the downdraught almost pounding Maryan to her knees. She straightened to watch him soar across the fields.

The fastest route to Serenia ran ahead, but Harlon steered the team onto a track. “If we’re lucky, Mordacai will chase up the highway and lose our trail. Our escape lies in stealth not arms.”

Night had started to furl over them as the carriage rolled into the market town. It was the kind of place that had made Chentene proud of his rule. A large monument to Jarr, the god of farmers, stood in the centre. An ancient wooden tavern faced a newly built hardware store to create the start of a town square. Garalandia had prospered under Chentene and she couldn’t hold back her fierce pride.

“Stop here,” Maryan said.

The instant Harlon pulled the reins Asti's head appeared out of the window. "What are you playing at, you moronic man?"

Maryan dropped from the seat. With her hands on her hips, she faced up to her ex-tutor from the hard-packed dirt road. "We need supplies, a decent sleep and some medical help to fix your arm. We stop here." She matched Asti's stare. "Harlon, check the tavern for rooms and ask what the nearest thing is to a healer in these parts."

Harlon emerged with a sly grin creasing his handsome features. "See that balcony?" He pointed to a wooden structure hanging from the gable end of the building. "The loft runs the length of the place. It's the only room the inn-keeper can let us have." He used his medallion to observe Asti's rump lowering from the coach. "We have to share."

"Share?" Asti spluttered. She glared at Harlon, who continued to peer maddeningly at her.

"And you think that I'd choose it? My dear, I'm quite mortified."

The entire space was a single dormitory styled to house drovers bringing flocks to market. It was clean, but the furniture had seen better days. The atmosphere crackled with tension. Determined to show that Harlon didn't exist, Asti stripped naked to wash using a cloth and a bowl of water. Although now healed, her back was horribly scarred by the flogging. A thousand other battle scars criss-crossed her limbs. Small, dark nipples surmounted her firm breasts. Her perfectly proportioned body appeared assembled of long bone and muscle. With dancer's grace, she raised her leg to scrub the water across her skin. Whether intended or not, glistening in the candlelight, the act of cleansing became a ballet of seduction worthy of any handmaiden.

Harlon feigned disdain, but continually peeped across. Maryan smirked as she fed Leon, recalling the tender way he'd held the drawing in his room.

Sophie rigged a curtain across the corner so that she could attend to herself in private. She emerged, immediately lifting Leon from Maryan's arms. Maryan started to object, but saw her friend's yearning. The round-limbed woman nuzzled her face against Leon's tiny scalp. "They smell wonderful … once they're washed. I'll do it." She closed her eyes. "It helps me forget the horrors."

Maryan wrapped herself in a cloak before going to sit on the small balcony. She slipped out her mother's diary, angling it to catch the candlelight spilling from behind her. The writing blurred, forcing her to rub her eyes. What she had read earlier rippled.

Asti, forgive me. I didn't mean you harm. Orlon told me that whoever went to the contest would not return. He claimed Serenia would fall without you as queen. Challenge Etelan and stop the madness. She cannot be queen. It must be you. Remember, whatever happens, my love for you is unwavering. If there is a way back, I shall find it.

When we fought, I didn't mean to strike such a devastating blow. I curse the wizard for interfering. He claims somebody else tried to kill you with my sword, that he did his best to turn my blade. Please watch over my daughter. Tell her I will be proud of whatever she becomes.

"Asti! Come and look at this." Maryan called out.

Wrapped in a blanket, the dark skinned warrior slipped onto the balcony and took the diary. Her face creased as she read it.

"Moon writing," Maryan explained. "Oliver, the artist who painted your portrait taught it to her."

"All of these years. All of the agony." Asti stumbled back into the room, dropping heavily on the end of her bed. Her shoulders shook with the grief. "That damned wizard must know more. I'm going to wring it from his hide."

Maryan settled beside her, wrapping her arm around the sobbing warrior. "You are meant to be queen. You have to usurp Etelan and how are we going to do that since you're not supposed to set foot in Serenia under pain of death?"

"Usurp Etelan!" Asti's head snapped around, her single eye bulging from its socket.

"Think about it," Maryan said quietly.

"I don't need to think about it. I'll be happy if they let me return. I don't want to be queen."

"But the diary says you have to be. My mother, your blade-sister, gave up her life so that you would be."

Asti waved her hand across the room. "And we invade with this ragtag?"

"Well, let's just get safely across the border."

In the morning, the local animal doctor properly dressed Asti's arm. The small man craned his neck to meet Asti's stone-like gaze. "Try not to use this for a few days," he said. "If the muscle doesn't knit it won't ever work again."

Asti grunted, but remained silent until he'd packed his bags and left. "You must go on. Each day here is another day that Mordacai can find us. You're in danger, I'm not."

"We'll move into the forest. We can wait there until you're ready to go on," Maryan said.

Sophie gave a small cough to draw their attention. "You can't take a baby into the woods for too long. It simply can't be done." Her stare switched between each of them. "Let's be honest, I don't contribute anything to a battle, but I can stay in a small room and care for Prince Leon. I'm sure I can find a wet nurse to help out with the feeding."

Maryan hugged Leon's frail, warm body. It felt wrong to leave him, but logic said they had no choice. She delved into her small pouch of gemstones. "Will we be able to change this for money?" She held out a large ring.

Harlon rolled it in his fingers. "I'll see what I can do. In the meantime, get ready to move out."

Chapter 21

*'**They're** at it again.'* Carl's words jolted Maryan awake.

Clashing swords rang close by. *'They're training. It'll be fine.'* She hauled the blankets higher, determined to relish the last moments before facing the sharp chill waiting for her. Forced awake, she rolled onto her back, trying to ignore the pressure of her bladder.

Green-tinged sunlight shone through the canvas. Keeping her blanket wrapped around her shoulders, she unpegged the entrance, despite the shield of ferns, the bright light of a crisp, blue sky made her squint.

The woodland was part of the ancient forest stretching from the edge of Garalandia across the Serenian border. All around their campsite, tall pine trees arrowed for the sky. Harlon had concealed their tents amongst richly scented, shoulder-high undergrowth in a niche beneath a rocky outcrop.

A river bounced down from the mountains. Maryan took a bundle of warm clothes down to the water's edge. Reluctantly surrendering her blanket, she gasped as she waded into the water to a point where it swirled around her knees. Squatting, every blonde hair on her body stood erect until washed flat by a handful of icy water.

The snow-covered peaks loomed close. According to the maps, The Academy pressed against the other side of them. Legend claimed a cave system wound through their heart. In the tales, Shirl had passed through them with the aid of an imprisoned sprite to light the way. Legend also said that if a dark evil ever crept into Serenia, this is where it would lurk.

After dressing, she followed the ringing sound of battle. Remaining concealed by the undergrowth, she paused to watch her companions spar.

"Come on old woman. You need to put more into your attack than that." Harlon forced Asti's blade aside and dropped, trying to sweep her legs away with a scything kick.

Asti still couldn't use her right arm and laboured to modify her swirling, dipping style. She sprang level with his shoulder, her foot hammering into his temple, battering him to the ground.

He propped himself up on both elbows. "Better." He grinned.

Her foot lashed at his jaw, but he caught her ankle and powered it into the air, crashing her down beside him.

Maryan winced at the landing and waited for the explosion. Instead, laughter bubbled from her old tutor's throat. Feeling like an intruder, she slipped back to the camp to build up the fire ready to prepare some gruel.

The bushes crashed apart and Asti stalked to the edge of the outcrop. Fists curled on her hips, she scowled at the rugged cliffs blocking their path. "I don't see why we have to go this way?"

Harlon emerged from the undergrowth a few steps behind her. "We could march straight to the border, couldn't we? The guards might not notice a scar-faced warrior famously exiled from Serenia under a penalty of death."

“Or a man who thinks he’s a weapons master trying to enter a land where men are forbidden to carry swords,” Asti snapped back.

‘They’ll be rumpling the nest if we leave them alone,’ Carl’s thoughts chuckled inside Maryan’s head.

Harlon squatted to help himself to a bowl of gruel. “After we’ve eaten, we’ll make the torches.” Juggling his bowl, he held his hands apart. “We need to find enough branches, about this long. Maryan, can you gather the spare sheets to tear into strips?”

Maryan went into each tent. Hers resembled a battle zone, with bedding and clothes tangled in a bundle. In comparison, Asti’s tent appeared empty, her pack positioned for a pillow, she had a single sheet folded square at the foot of her blanket. Although Harlon’s was almost as tidy, she smiled to herself when she spotted her mother and Asti staring out of the picture frame on top of his pack.

They laboured all day, twisting the strips of fabric into tight cords to bind oil-soaked cloth to the end of the branches. When they entered the caves, they each needed to carry a bundle of ten torches.

“It’s your turn to cook.” Harlon nodded toward Asti.

She’d been to the river to wash and had returned with a high arch shaved above her ears. Her arm muscles danced as she worked behind her head weaving a tight plait. “We still have cold rabbit. That’ll do.” Picking up her greaves, she produced a polishing cloth from her pack.

“We might not get a hot meal again. Woman, fetch something cooked.” Harlon’s insolent grin filled his face. Asti's shoulders rose, in preparation for the storm about to break.

Unable to face another bickering argument, Maryan slipped away beneath the trees. A short distance from the camp was a small clearing where she studied the mountains fading into the evening sky. Easing herself down onto a log, thoughts of her life washed through her mind.

"Worried?"

The unexpected weight of Asti's hand clamped on her shoulder. The scent of metal polish and leather awoke a memory of her mother from the depths. "I never knew how close you were to Mum. You even smell the same." Maryan rubbed her cheek against the warrior's hand.

"In another land, we'd have raised you as our daughter. Instead, a Serenian warrior hands their child to the care of an academy so that we can return to protecting the realm. It's ingrained into us."

"Yet tomorrow, we try to sneak back, maybe to overthrow the queen. Is that protecting the realm?"

"Not my idea. All I want is to get back to our homeland."

"The wizard obviously convinced my mother. She gave up everything she held dear."

"It was never easy to convince Amara of anything. I just wish she'd left a note to say how I was supposed to do it."

In the morning, they abandoned their camping gear to head for the tiny cavern at the start of 'Shirl's Path'. The entrance was well known. Even though it lay on Garalandian soil, many Serenians used it as a starting point if they went out into the world. Before a traveller left, they would scratch their names onto the rocks close to the narrow opening. A small shrine had stood here for centuries, but now lay smashed. The tokens it had contained were scattered in the dirt.

Harlon dropped to one knee to check the ground. A thousand small footprints rippled the surface. "Goblins."

After taking a final breath of fresh air and a last look at the mountain scenery, they lit a torch and stepped inside.

Encased within a tiny bubble of light, the darkness arched over them. At each junction, Harlon used a small pick to chip a mark. The cave system dripped with water seeping through the rocks. They stopped to eat, but didn't sit down. Torch smoke tainted the stagnant air with the fragrance of burning oil.

"Thirty torches and that's the first one finished," Harlon said, lighting the next one from the guttering flame.

"Stating the obvious," Asti sneered.

"Stating that we need to think about it. Once we've used fifteen torches, do we come back out, or do we press on, hoping to find our way through?"

"We'll decide in another fourteen, shall we?" Asti snapped.

After four torches, Harlon allowed the light to die. They ate in the dark. The impenetrable gloom wrapped them, filling every corner of Maryan's senses. She thought she could see flashes of light, but knew it was her eyes fooling her.

'This is an odd place,' Carl's thoughts floated into hers.

She ran a hand across Mac's head until she found Carl. Her fingers played, taking comfort from the feel of his soft fur. *'Why do you say odd?'*

'I can hear you, but there isn't anything else. It's as if the weight of the mountain is crushing the ability to speak with our minds.'

The oppressive sensation of somebody watching them nagged at Maryan, she strained all of her senses to search the opaque night around them. Detecting her unease, Mac rumbled.

'We shall guard you. If anything seeks to pass, they will need to cross our fangs,' Carl's, voice sounded muted in Maryan's thoughts.

"They make a good companion," Asti said. "Your injured pets bonded by their limitations, silent and trustworthy." Concealed in the dark, the warrior's armour grated on the rock as she shifted to settle herself. "Amara once kept a pet cat hidden. The tutors never discovered it."

"Will you tell me of her?"

"Your mother?"

Maryan heard the catch of bitter emotion locked away for too many years. She imagined the older woman turning away. Instead, Asti chuckled.

"There was one occasion when we had to go out to support the border guards. Your mother always wore that polished breastplate …"

Asti filled the inky night with tales. Maryan spread her thick blanket on the cold stone and smoothed her cloak over her tired limbs. Resting her head on older woman's thigh, Asti's fingers played through her hair. For a short time, she became a child listening to bedtime stories. She imagined the scent of Leon's scalp and the feel of his soft, dependent body. Cradled in the moment, sleep took her.

"We need to press on," Harlon's voice jerked Maryan awake. The rasp of flint on striker preceded a blue flame wrapping greasily around the oil-soaked torch. It grew in brilliance, lifting the darkness a short distance from them.

Somewhere, water bounced over stones. Sensed, rather than heard, a rumbling torrent thrummed in the caves. Maryan pressed her hand against the rock face and could feel the power vibrating. As they moved through the caves, Harlon checked the ground for signs. Each time he found something, he swept the torch in a wide arc to explain what he deduced.

"It's a chaos of tiny footprints. They're all heading in this direction and none flow back. Either it's the way out, or an army of goblins is waiting ahead."

After another four torches, they rested. Harlon's rolling timbre filled the darkness with tales of Oliver and himself as children. He talked of his own emotions, envy, jealousy and then finally, pride in his brother's skill with a brush.

"I've seen your blade-work," Asti said. "It is artistry far more useful to have at my side."

Harlon coughed a deprecating laugh.

A rustle of fabric said Asti had reached out to touch him. Maryan held her breath. If Asti knew of this man's age-old yearning for her, combined with his reputation, she might be more reserved. For all of her knowledge, the old warrior appeared oddly naive in the ways of the world.

At one point in the next leg, they encountered a crystal panel filled with light filtering down from the surface. Easily the width of Maryan's thigh, it slashed from the ceiling to the floor, creating a magnificent display in the jewelled-filled rock, like a frozen lightning strike. Maryan sighed. Even though the air remained fetid, she imagined a summer breeze brushing her cheeks.

"Cover your eyes," Asti said in a parade ground snarl. "Think of your night vision. It will take hours to recover."

The fourth torch of the day flickered into life from the guttering death of the third. Harlon tapped the small pick to mark the junction. The sharp report of steel against stone echoed into the thick black around them. A shuffle in the gloom replied.

They turned to each other. Asti slipped a single sword from her shoulder and Harlon lowered the torch, allowing his body to steal the feeble light. In almost complete darkness, they continued until they reached the next junction.

Harlon raised the torch, but the light barely reached the ceiling high above. The tunnel widened into a domed chamber. The cavern floor was smooth and clear of dust. The mouths of four tunnels waited on the far side, each exit arched higher than Maryan could reach. The torchlight failed to penetrate the waiting gloom. She started to cross, but Harlon stopped her with a touch on her arm.

"Before we step out, we should mark this passage," he whispered. "It's easy to get turned around at a junction like this." He waited for his companions' approval before tapping the potentially life-saving scar. The echo of the tap bounced ominously away. “Which one shall we try?” Harlon said, stepping into the wide space.

Maryan checked the left hand tunnel. The air felt warm, she brushed a tendril of lose hair that tickled her cheek. A breeze? The draft became a blast, an awful grating noise squealed through the caverns. She spun in time to see a huge shape slither across the entrance plunging her into darkness.

“Carl, Asti, Harlon!” She ran to the exit, hitting a putrid blockage of slime. She could see nothing, hear nothing and sense nothing. Trembling in the inky silence, she wrenched her pack from her shoulder to find her flint and tinder. Her hands shook. Unable find either, she lectured herself to stay calm, working methodically through the contents, feeling each item before putting it to one side. Finally, she discovered them. Plucking a torch from the straps on her pack, she struck the flint. A flame oozed around the cloth.

A wall of grey, mucus-covered flesh blocked the exit. She touched it with the flame. It hissed, but remained in place, sealed smoothly around the opening. Maryan screamed inside her head trying to reach Carl, but nothing came back. She slipped her claw shaped battle-axe out, tapped the rock and listened. All she could hear was her own pounding heartbeat.

The beast had blocked the entire tunnel. She’d not heard any screams, but either her friends were dead, or they’d sought refuge in one of the other tunnels. She was on her own. Her pack contained food and five torches. Insufficient to get to the entrance, even assuming she could return to their original path.

Brandishing the torch high, she made her way up the incline. At the first junction, she used the battle-axe to chip a small mark onto the rock. Her instructors would have winced at using a weapon this way, but if the others managed to follow her path, they'd see the mark.

Although desperate to sleep when the next torch died, fears of creatures lurking in the dark troubled her. She squeezed into a niche to hide, but immediately regretted it. Her thoughts filled with terror of the monster moving, sliding down the passage, leaving her trapped in the tiny space. She gave up trying to rest in favour of keeping moving.

At one place, the rock face became smooth. Hopes leapt when the shadows resolved into a huge warrior. It turned out to be a statue positioned to guard the exit. The doorway led onto a narrow platform facing a wide chasm. A delicate archway spanned the gap. It was a suicide bridge, so called, because a single warrior could collapse it by pulling the central stone from the arch.

Maryan edged along the rise to where the keystone, no wider than her hand, supported the entire structure. She raised the torch, willing the feeble light to illuminate as far as possible. On the opposite ledge, a path emerged from a tunnel. It wound up a spiral staircase to a platform at the other end of the bridge. Somebody had spent a lot of time carving these paths.

The next room stank of rotting meat. A corpse with its entrails spilled, hung limply from a spike. With its face destroyed and skull scooped empty, she was unable to work out if the body was male or female. The far doorway led back into rough tunnels.

A tendril of hair stroked her neck. She licked her palm and held it up, trying to figure out the direction of the draught. A slithering noise accompanied the mounting air pressure. She spun frantically, desperate to avoid any monster that lurked down here. The breeze dropped and the sound vanished.

She reached for her final torch, debating whether to light it, or try to make progress in the dark. Memory of the chasm spanned by the suicide bridge convinced her she didn't stand a chance without it. She tapped a mark onto the junction and lit the torch.

Chapter 22

Her final torch flickered into an oily, blue death, submerging Maryan into total darkness. She sent out searching thoughts to Carl, but nothing came back. Settling against the rocks, she slid to the ground, hoping the others strode through the tunnels close behind. After filling her lungs to bellow, the memory of the corpse in the torture chamber stifled the scream. Her breath slowly escaped. Who or what could treat another creature with such cruelty?

Crouched in the dark, she ate the last crumbs scraped from the bottom of her pack. Her water bottle barely splashed when she tipped it to soothe her dry throat. The maddening sounds of a torrent thundered, close, but unreachable. Somewhere above, students walked along corridors. Another four girls would be in her old dormitory. Possibly, they mused over the initials carved in the woodwork, trying to guess who'd been there before.

Her head drooped as she tumbled into a confusion of dreams. She was fighting Fleur with a sword too heavy to wield. All around, her friends pointed, their faces slowly peeling from their skulls. The nightmare bark of Asti's voice snapped her awake and the vivid sunlight-filled arena became unfathomable black.

"Thank goodness you've come back," Kait said.

Fingers touched beneath Maryan's chin, tilting her face up. Maryan grabbed the hand. "I didn't want to go away, Etelan made me." A halo flared behind Kait, jerking Maryan fully awake. The light around her friend blinded her.

Kait squeezed Maryan's hand before dragging her up into a crushing embrace. "It's so wonderful to have found you. I've searched so hard."

"I'm safe," Maryan said, clasping Kait in a tight hug. Her friend's perfume made her conscious of her own body stench. She backed away. "I've been in these caverns for so long I must smell like an ox."

"Friends don't worry about things like that."

"There's something evil in these tunnels. We have to get away to safety."

"Surely, you're imagining. Hunger can do that."

"No, I didn't imagine it. I've seen a massive grey creature, a giant worm or snake."

"That old thing!" Kait's laugh echoed incongruously in the gloom. "It rumbles around the caves, but it's not evil, just blind and stupid. Rather like the ruling council of Serenia."

"But that's not all. Somebody has tortured a poor soul back there."

"Follow me. You're upset, let's get you to safety." Kait led the way by keeping the ball of light hanging an arm's length ahead. It swung easily, swooping as it followed the twists in the tunnel, throwing bewildering shadows across the floor.

"Where did you go to instead of Idrahail?" Maryan asked.

When Kait twisted to look back at Maryan, darkness draped her face. "I found better teachers. Wait until you've rested, I'll explain more. We're here."

The floating globe of light whipped through a doorway into a wide room, coming to rest close to the low ceiling. The bright light from a dozen other globes forced Maryan to shield her eyes. A myriad of archways suggested a maze of tunnels. “Gorath, Kait, what is this place?” she said in a hushed voice.

“I am helping to shape Serenia.” Kait allowed a secretive smile to play around her lips. “The old order needed to be shaken, but Etelan knew we couldn’t take them on directly.” She gestured idly around the cavernous space. “I’m creating a paradise just below the surface. Just think, no more shivering in the snow.”

Kait guided Maryan into another room, where even more arches led away to other spaces. A sturdy table with four high-backed chairs made of light-coloured wood stood in the centre. Through one arch a neatly made bed was visible and through another, a kitchen.

“This is all too confusing.” Maryan rubbed her temples. “We have to go back into the tunnel.” She almost started to tell Kait about Asti, but the tutor was returning under pain of death and Kait spoke in friendly terms of Etelan. “Others are trapped. We have to find them.” She tugged the strap to tighten her pack.

“You should rest before we try to search.” Kait pressed Maryan’s shoulders, guiding her onto a sofa, kneeling to lift Maryan’s legs. “We’ll talk later.” Squatted by her side, she caressed Maryan’s face. “Sleep.”

The smell of cooking enticed Maryan back from a dreamless sleep. She stretched, immediately turning her thoughts to her comrades. Hoping for a reply, she projected a silent call to Carl. Nothing did.

"You're awake." Kait appeared from beneath the arch leading to the kitchen. "Now, it's time to bathe. I have a steam room just through here." She guided Maryan to the far end of the room where an archway led to a bathroom antechamber. There was a vertical cold-plunge, with a stepladder. A low dresser covered with multi-coloured bottles stood on one side. Close to the door, there was a rack of neatly folded bathing sheets.

Maryan peeled off her rancid clothes and stepped into the steam room. A subdued orb lit the white-tiled room. The heat of the gloriously damp air immediately soothed her aches. She leant back against the tiles and let the sweat run down her skin. When the heat became unbearable, she used a rough flannel to scrub the grime from her body.

In the antechamber, the ice-cold plunge crushed Maryan's breath from her lungs. She climbed out of the pool and rubbed herself vigorously with a bathing sheet.

Somewhere in the caverns, Kait sang a wistful melody. She appeared at the entrance carrying a large, steaming mug. "You might prefer wine, but this will do you more good."

Painfully aware that her abdomen still resembled a rumpled bed quilt, Maryan lifted the bath sheet to hide the soft flesh.

"Of course, you had a baby!"

"I've been loved by a wonderful man, but it's over."

"Now, you're lost." Kait's green eyes opened wide, "Many will think him the true ruler of Garalandia. Get dressed. I've cooked up a real treat for you." Kait swept away, ducking gracefully beneath the low arches.

Maryan gathered the rags she'd been wearing. The stench of her discarded blouse almost choked her. She rummaged through her pack to find her least-soiled clothes.

The exotic aroma of Kait's of cooking guided Maryan through the lounge into a large kitchen. Herbs and dried flowers hung around the walls. A pan bubbled lazily on the iron stove. Kait greeted her with a radiant smile. She wore a plain white gown with long sleeves, her red hair hung straight down her back. "Please sit. I'll bring you some stew." She filled two bowls and followed Maryan back to the table.

The fragrant steam made Maryan think of her friends in the labyrinth. Her spoon fell back to the table. "I can't eat. I've been selfish. We have to seek the others." She started to rise.

Kait shook her head. "A short rest and then we'll go … hunting. Please, taste your food. I've made something special for you. Tell me of your son."

"No, tell me about you. Where have you been?"

"When I left, I travelled towards Idrahail, but I always planned to escape. Some of us are born to delve into things others find distasteful. At my first chance, I headed out to the woodland witches in Sudaland. They have a different view of right and wrong." She peeled back thc sleeves of her gown, proudly displaying her tattoos. Not a finger's width of Kait's pale skin remained visible amongst the hypnotic patterns.

"Kait! Why would you do such a thing?"

"I found our moral code too rigid. I needed to lose my inhibitions to find myself."

She filled the oddly shaped goblets on the table with red wine. One slid silently across the table. Maryan picked it up by the golden stem to examine what she had taken to be marble. The wide rim felt awkward. The contents smelled too strong. She spun it, puzzled by the uneven shape. "Is this bone?"

"Stop changing the subject!" Kait rapped the table. "Tell me about your son. Where is he?"

"I'm not going to tell anybody where he is, friend or foe. The best kept secret is the one nobody shares." Maryan pushed away from the table. "I'm not hungry. I need to help my friends."

"Friends? You talk of friends, yet I ask a civil question and you snap at me!" Kait breathed deeply, controlling her voice. "You're sick from your ordeal and I forgive you."

Maryan tried to stand, but her legs trembled, threatening to fold. Kait slipped from her seat. A warm embrace of air wrapped around Maryan, lifting her weight off the floor.

"You are too weak to venture out. I'll take you to rest."

"No, we must …"

"You must rest. Leave the search to me."

The spinning room drove all argument from Maryan. She relaxed in the floating sensation. Her head settled onto the pillow and everything swirled into a mist.

Firm hands, ran across her body, luring her to wakefulness. "Darling, I'm back. Why did you run away?"

His face in shadow, Chentene's dark hair stole the light above her. His full lips hovered close, promising a kiss. She went to put her arms around him, but found them bound to the bedframe above her head. She tried move, only to find her legs also tethered. "What, why?"

"You were raving, screaming that you had to leave. I had no choice. You're not well and it's my job to protect you."

"Chentene, I'm alright. Release me."

"But surely, we could take advantage of this situation." He nuzzled her neck, his breath warm on her skin. His hand ran the length of her body, gliding over the thin fabric between them.

Maryan tried to squirm away from his touch. "No, I don't like this. Stop."

"You don't like it?" He pulled aside the single sheet covering her. A salacious hunger flashed across him before he nuzzled into her neck. He caressed her breast and ran his tongue the length of her body. His chin felt smooth as it slipped across her thigh.

"Please," she muttered.

He ceased, but scowled. "Since we spawned a child, you reject me. Where is the little monkey anyway?"

"Chentene stop. This isn't you. I'm not telling anybody where he is."

The vision of Chentene melted away. His features rotated into a different shape, the looming width of his shoulders evaporated exposing the reality beneath. It was Kait holding her breast. Her naked body entirely covered with a swirling riot of tattoos.

"Why?" Maryan sobbed. She felt sick at the cruelty. "Why would you do such a terrible thing?"

"I need your son and I hoped you might tell the father."

"And the rest, the kisses, the caresses, why would you torture me like that?"

"Torture? Once you lose every inhibition, pleasure can be taken in many ways." Shaking her head, Kait stepped away from the bed. "Do you remember how I used to predict evil was close?" She waited until Maryan nodded. "I was so serious, so sure of myself, so convinced it would be Fleur or Etelan. How could I know?" She touched a thin finger between her breasts. "It was me. I am the witch. I serve the Dark Lord." Her slender hand snapped into a fist. "I need you and your spawn finished!"

"What have I done?"

"Nothing yet, but your line could prevent the rebirth of Calamore."

"Is this what happened to my mother?"

"I don't know. Calamore has many servants working to clear the path for his return." Kait's head twitched as if she listened to somebody talking. "Gorath! Preparing an invasion of goblins … you wouldn't believe how stupid they are. When I come back, you will tell me where your brat is."

"Never."

Kait waved her hand at the wall. The grey plaster shimmered before it winked out of existence. The stench of excrement and decaying flesh washed out of the concealed part of the room. Bound to iron rings set into the rock of the mountain hung a warrior with her arms outstretched. A noose hauled her head high, keeping her standing on tiptoes. Sami's dark eyes peeped over a tear-soaked gag.

"Our friend has been listening to me play with you." Her forehead wrinkled. Immediately, Sami squirmed with pain. "She's getting a little boring, somewhat drained." On the floor, a half-filled demijohn was attached to Sami's throat by a thin tube. The surface rippled as blood trickled from Sami.

Kait stood with her hands on her hips. "When I return, we'll see just how much being a blade-sister means to you." The eye-wrenching swirls of the tattoos on her body emphasised her arrogant strut as she ducked beneath the arch.

Maryan strained to pull free, but she'd been expertly tied. The bed, made of solid wooden spars didn't even creak with the pressure.

'Mistress?'

Her heart leapt. *'Carl?'*

'She felt strange. We hid until she left. She's changed.'

'She's changed," Maryan sent. "Can you free me?'

A snuffling accompanied the tug on the sheets as Carl emerged over the edge of the bed. His tiny claws pricking her skin, he dragged himself up her arm to nibble the bindings. Mac prowled from side to side, filling the small space with the scent and sound of an angry lion.

Time passed. Whenever Sami's head slumped, the cruel noose snapped her awake, forcing her to refocus on her balance.

'Hurry up, Carl.'

'It's awful tasting leather.'

The binding gave. She struggled to reach the other hand, but couldn't. *"Carl, you've got to do it."* The rat scurried across her body. Swinging all her strength against the bindings, she kept her hearing focused, waiting for Kait's return. Finally, the bands snapped, tumbling Carl onto the bed. With her hands free, she shuffled down to unhook the loops holding her feet.

She needed to stop the blood draining from Sami. Battling her aching joints, she hobbled across, tucked her nails under the gag and eased it over Sami's chin. "How can I get you out of this?"

"You can't, if you unhook the drain I'll bleed to death. I watched her kill Violet this way. Go, run, before she returns."

"I'm not leaving you here." Maryan quickly dressed herself in the clothes discarded around the bed. Finding her weapon harness strewn carelessly to one side, she shrugged it across her shoulders.

The single blade made short work of freeing Sami. Maryan caught her as she slumped, lowering her weight down the wall. She held the tube, inspecting where it ran into her friend's neck. A brass fitting tapered to a hair-thin needle pressed through the skin. A cord tied the contraption to support the weight and prevent it from tearing free.

"The hole's tiny. Give me your finger, I'm going to pull this out and you have to block it." She understood the fear filling Sami's face. "I've seen a similar device used by Galia in the treatment rooms in Manda Torre. It will just come out. I know what I'm doing."

She slipped the needle from Sami's neck and guided her friend's finger to the puncture. "Keep the pressure on it. I'll get something we can fix over the wound." Trembling, her skin a ghastly shade of grey, Sami sat on the floor, unable to move.

As Maryan ducked under the arch to the kitchen, the sight of Kait stepping through the entrance froze her mid-stride.

"You don't have to die, I can save you," Kait said. Her voice became a crooning song. "All I need is the location of your son. Is that too much to ask?" She glided across the room with sinuous grace.

"Step away." Maryan bit her lip, using the pain to block the fog billowing into her mind. She pointed her sword directly at Kait's breast.

Without warning, Kait staggered, her nails tore at the white skin of her temples. She screamed and jerked erect. From beneath the curtain of hair, two snakes emerged. They lifted above her scalp, tongues flickering to taste the air. Two pairs of red, hate-filled eyes fixed on Maryan.

"Gorath, Kait, what are these things?"

Kait's imperious glare vanished, replaced by fear. "Maryan, help me, they hold me, torture me, twist my words and thoughts. Don't let them find your son." She dropped to her knees screaming. "No. Please stop, I can't make her." She twitched her neck to impossible angles, craning, trying to see the snakes writhing behind her.

Maryan drew back her sword, "I can take their heads off. Will it kill you?"

"You mustn't. No. The pain is terrible, I never wanted to hurt those people, believe me."

Unable to control the anger seething inside, Maryan's blade whipped the head from one snake, sending it spinning across the floor. Kait screamed. Another half dozen snakes burst from beneath her once beautiful hair. Before Maryan had chance to attack again, the snakes disappeared as quickly as they had appeared.

"That's enough of that." Kait smoothed her features. She raised herself carefully to her full height and flicked her hand. An unseen force slammed Maryan across the room. Kait flourished the two goblets from the table. "Violet and a friend of hers, Sami will contribute a third. With you, I'll have a complete set!" Raising one to arm's length she poured the wine into her mouth. It ran across her chin soaking into her simple white dress, making it cling to her slender body. She vanished and the goblets clattered to the floor.

Maryan spun bewildered. Catching movement above, she ducked away out of reach. Kait hung from the ceiling like a fly, her hair dangling, her expression leering. Once again, the snakes emerged from behind Kait's head, hissed and then disappeared. Like an acrobat, she let her hands fall, dropping in a somersault to land on her feet.

"I've learned so much since we last met."

A growl rumbled as Mac stalked into sight. His head remained low as he shifted his weight.

"A cat! You brought a cat into my caves." Kait hurled a fireball, but the lion sprang to one side and landed ready to creep forward again. Kait's glare whipped between Maryan and Mac. "A cat!" she wailed. Her hair exploded into a writhing nest of snakes hissing angrily at Maryan.

Kait's own personality forced to the surface. "Forgive me. Please end this. Please!"

The Lion's paw battle-axe answered her prayer. The central spike of the cruel weapon crushed Kait's skull, pounding her to the floor. A knot of snakes rolled out. Maryan stomped on them. One wriggled free, but Mac pounced, whipping it from side to side. Carl joined the battle, his sharp rodent fangs making light work of the creatures.

The glowing orbs flashed before winking out of existence, plunging the room into a full black night.

'Carl, can you see anything? We have to find the kitchen.'

'Follow me,' Mac's weight nudged against her. She sank her hand into the lion's mane for guidance. Moving slowly through the darkness, she tried not to imagine snakes slithering around her ankles.

Beneath the kitchen archway, the iron stove glowed in the dark. She swung open the oven door gaining sufficient light for her put together a torch. The first one flared and burnt too quickly, but she managed to use it to make another one. Soaked in oil and bound tightly, the way Harlon had taught her, it burned slower, giving her the chance to search the Kait's lair.

The light from the erratic flame painted lurid designs across the white walls. She found a slab-like altar with four temple candles positioned at each corner. She lit one and hauled the others into the dining room. After lighting another, she dragged one through to Sami.

Silently sobbing, Sami remained curled on the floor. Maryan massaged her hands up the length of

Sami's legs, trying to force life back into them. Despite the groans of pain, she dug her fists into her friend's thighs to knead the knotted muscles.

She felt Sami's hand on her shoulder. "Leave me here. I'll try to follow once I get moving." In the shadow-filled candlelight, they studied each other's faces.

"There are too many awful things down here. You're coming, or I stay."

'Stop wasting time.' Carl swayed, perched upon Mac's head, rocking like a sea captain on the prow of his ship searching for land. 'Come on, I can find my way easily. If we hurry, there will be delicious things waiting for us in the bins. We're almost home.'

'Have you sensed the others?'

'We lost you all. It's been very difficult. There are goblins in these caves.'

Maryan used the cord that had held the drain in Sami's throat to fix a wad of cloth against the wound. She silently promised Kait she would return to attend to her remains, but for now, she had to worry about her own survival.

With a grunt, she hauled Sami to her feet. Ducking to one knee, she caught her friend's weight across her shoulders. Wincing with the effort, she forced her legs straight. For all her diminutive size, Sami weighed almost more than Maryan could bear. Pressed against Mac, she started the awkward ascent to the exit of the labyrinth.

Chapter 23

The Labyrinth exit opened into a courtyard garden. Viewed in the dim light before dawn, ominous shadows filled the wide space between Maryan and The Academy. Although a sturdy iron gate sealed the entrance, it always remained unlocked to offer a final refuge in case of attack from the sea.

She peered through the bars, intimidated by the imposing outline of her old home. Would Etelan immediately send her back into Mordacai's clutches? There was no choice. The struggle up from Kait's lair had rendered Sami almost unconscious. Whatever the personal cost, they needed to reach somebody who could save her.

The latch moved silently, freeing the gate to swing inwards. With a final glance back at Sami, Maryan stepped into the courtyard. At her hip, Mac lowered his head into a prowl with Carl leant forward, fixed amongst the lion's mane.

"The witch, the witch has come to claim us! To arms!" Other voices took up the cry. A distant bowstring sang as lights flared in the windows.

"Hold your fire!" Maryan shouted, "The witch is dead!"

A bulky woman carrying the largest meat cleaver Maryan had ever seen lumbered towards her. Maryan knew her as one of the under-cooks. Her name had always raised a smile, Minnie. "Minnie, it's me, Maryan."

The huge cook ran the next few steps and crushed Maryan in her fleshy arms. "Poor child. What's happened?" Brandishing the cleaver, she shifted her attention to the circling lion. "Get behind me whilst I sort this out."

Maryan hooked a restraining hand on the cook's forearm. "They're friends, don't worry about them. Sami's injured. Please get help."

Unwilling to shift her gaze from the lion, Minnie backed into the tunnel. She dropped to one knee and pressed her hand against Sami's forehead.

"She's in a bad way." Minnie handed the cleaver to Maryan and forced her arms under Sami's near-lifeless limbs. She heaved herself upright, cradling Sami as if she weighed no more than a baby did. "Let's get her to the warmth," Minnie whispered.

The huge cook made her way back across the courtyard, nudging the door open with her elbow. The lower kitchen serviced the staff and students of The Academy. During the day, the activity would be frantic, but draped in shadow, the tranquil space felt spiritual. The high ceiling echoed their shuffled movements. The only light came from a fire burning in a monstrous grate. The warmth made Maryan's skin tingle and the smell of cooked meat aroused a gnawing hunger. Minnie lowered Sami onto a table.

Unable to shift her attention from Sami, Maryan heard Minnie stomp off along a darkened passage barking commands to rouse others from slumber. "Fetch the healers. We've got a sick girl in here." The sound of running feet clattered.

The smells revived memories of days when The Academy kitchen had been the source of all comfort. They'd filled the corridors with wholesome odours to welcome them from their training, provided good food, meals with friends and hot water to bathe aches away. Grateful for the homeliness of the kitchen, Maryan dropped into a chair and laid her hand across the top of Sami's head.

Four healers rushed in, two with a stretcher between them. The same old man who had treated Maryan so long ago pushed her aside to press his ear against Sami's chest. He examined the wounds piercing Sami's flesh before scowling. "This girl's been tortured. She's almost drained of blood." He snapped his fingers to direct the others. "Get her to the Infirmary." They slid Sami onto a stretcher and carried her away.

"How did this happen?" The tall healer cast an accusing glare at Maryan.

"The witch," Maryan said, touching her throat. "She had a drain." Tears welled up that she couldn't hold back.

"Stuff and nonsense. Blubbering won't protect you. We don't have a witch who tortures warriors. What happened?"

Barely restraining her anger, Maryan stood up and smoothed her features into haughtiness that matched the healer's arrogance. "We need to understand each other. I am the rightful princess of Garalandia, whereas you have never been more than an inadequate sawbones. I'll speak to one person. Bring Steppis." She reached for the hilt of her sword. "Now go!"

The man held his ground until the sword rasped from its scabbard. His pale skin blanched and he ran for the passage.

Minnie scattered a handful of grain for Carl and sniffed at a leg of meat before throwing it to Mac.

"Damned thing will be going to waste tomorrow anyway." She vanished into a storeroom, returning with a plate of cold ham, cheese and pickles for Maryan.

Although Maryan wasn't sure whom she could trust, she hoped her old tutor would be amongst those she could. Perched on the edge of her seat, she chewed and waited.

Steppis eventually appeared out of the gloomy corridor. She wore a breastplate moulded to contain her formidable chest. The greaves strapped onto her thick legs were polished to a gleam. The hilts of the twin blades swept high above either side of her head emphasising the steel grey of her close-cropped hair.

"What's happening? We have enough trouble with the goblins in the forest without you stirring things up underground."

"We need to send a search party into the caves. Ast …" Maryan stopped herself, before slowly choosing her words. "A group of friends might still be alive down there."

"Asti the Red is in jail." Steppis pursed her lips before speaking again. "The man is in the Infirmary." She glanced out of the window where pale sunlight had started to creep into the courtyard. "They'll both be executed by the end of today."

"What? No, this is wrong." Maryan leapt to her feet.

"Her life is forfeit for re-entering Serenia. She knew the law."

"But the man, Harlon, he saved me. He's a loyal friend."

"He can't be allowed to live. She surrendered immediately, but he wounded half of those trying to take her. I've never seen a blade wielded so." Steppis shook her head. "Archers had to bring him down. He still breathes, but the executioner will soon rectify that."

"He is a good man. If he fought, he had a reason to do so." Maryan thumped the battle-axe onto the table. Gore from Kait's skull still clung between the claws. "I am going to free them. Are you with me, or against me?"

Steppis stared unfocused toward the fireplace where the lion gnawed at the carcass on the stone floor. "Etelan is the third queen I have followed. None of them perfect, but they are the chosen leader of our nation. She has said they are to die."

"Our system stinks." Minnie crashed her cleaver deep into the ancient kitchen table beside the axe. She pointed at her larder. "If something is rotting in there, I get rid of it. We all know Etelan is going too far."

Maryan hefted the axe again, slapping the back of the paw into her palm. "You once told me of your failed efforts to find my mother. Now put the same effort into fighting for the one she believed would be queen."

"Girl." Steppis rose from her chair. "If you threaten me with that thing again, I'll ram it somewhere painful." Her twin blades swept into a perfect Amaran defence. "Who do you think taught your mother how to hold a blade, how to wield anger like a weapon?"

"Surely, you can see that executing Asti for returning is wrong." Maryan cocked her axe against her shoulder. “She came to help her nation. At least let’s put a stop to the execution.”

“If I agree, how are we going to do that?” Steppis snapped into a high guard.

“We need to get to the jail without too much noise.”

‘Then use the tunnels,’ Carl said from where he lay curled in the grate of the fire.

‘Could you lead us to the jail?’ Maryan asked. Steppis and Minnie both followed her gaze to the grate.

Carl scurried across the floor to nuzzle at the storeroom door. *‘Here, there is one, here.’*

“There’s a passage in there.” Maryan grinned at the two women.

“My larder?” Minnie coughed, “I swear there’s no passage in my larder.”

Maryan found the latch hidden behind the bracket supporting a shelf. As the wall swung back, cold air swept her face sending a chill down her spine. Mac’s sinuous body prowled into the passageway.

Slipping her sword from its scabbard, Maryan returned the battle-axe to the leather harness. Easily keeping pace with Mac, she felt at home in the ancient servant passages. Carl balanced between the lion’s ears twitching from side to side as he made decisions about the cross paths.

Minnie had to twist sideways to manoeuvre her bulk along the passageway. Masked in the shadow of the cook, Steppis moved silently. They came to a wall where a hole vanished downward with only brickwork handholds to clamber down. Mac backed away, snarling.

‘He can’t work out what I’m showing him.’

“I’ll lead.” Maryan stepped onto the first brick.

“No, let me.” Minnie tugged her back. “If you fall on me, I’ll grunt, but if I fall on you, we’ll both die.”

When Maryan followed, she stopped to let Mac sniff her. His warm breath smelled of meat. “Come on boy, follow me.”

After an eternity of descending the handholds into the dark, her feet touched the floor. She turned to survey the arched tunnel. Light filtered through grates running along the centre of the ceiling. They were under the passage leading to the jail.

A wild scurrying tumbled down the chimney. Maryan leapt clear just in time to avoid Mac crashing onto the floor.

Carl sat panting by Maryan’s ankle. His thoughts spluttered indignantly. ‘Stupid cat wouldn’t come down backwards. He thinks he’s a rat and tried to come down head first.’

‘Of course he thinks he’s a rat, that’s all he sees.’ She nuzzled against Mac’s fur to calm him. When they restarted, Steppis took the lead, guiding the party along the gloomy passage.

They followed in single file until the old warrior stopped. “You follow my commands and don’t kill anybody.” Keeping her face grim, she waited for their nodded agreement.

Rusting metal rings protruded from the ancient brickwork leading up to the iron grating. Steppis climbed the ladder before taking a deep breath. “We need to seal these,” she bellowed as she heaved her bulk against the grate. It clattered across the stone floor above. Grunting with the effort, she hauled herself into the guard chamber above.

"What's going on?" somebody challenged Steppis.

"Stand down. We're checking these damned passages."

Squinting up through the grating, Maryan watched Steppis square herself to the guard. "Etelan's right. She knew these tunnels led to the jail. I didn't believe her." She peered down and winked at Maryan, "Come on up."

Had Steppis given in too easily, tricking her into walking quietly to the prison? Her hands shook as she gripped the loops to climb up to the jail. At the top, she kept her face in shadow for as long as possible.

"Maryan?"

Rose reached for her sword, but Steppis moved faster. "Easy! I don't want to kill a fellow warrior." She pressed her sword deep into the folds of Rose's many chins. "But in your case, I'll make an exception."

Torches lit the guardroom. Fleur's old sidekick had bloated from an ugly child into a hideous woman. Her bulk strained the seams of her leather uniform and her complexion still flared with angry red blemishes. A ring of keys hung on Rose's belt. Maryan nodded to them. "The key to Asti's cell?"

"The key?" A slow grin creased Rose's face. As she glanced at a locked door, her hand hovered over the bunch on her hip. "Yes, it's here somewhere."

"Open it then."

Moving slowly, despite the sword pressed to her neck. Rose searched the keys, studying each one.

Maryan snatched the ring from Rose's grasp. "I'll do it myself."

Finally, the door swung back. A blanket lay rumpled on the single bed. Minnie burst between Maryan and Steppis to land a vicious blow on Rose's face. "Where is she, you miserable dung heap?"

Rose crashed against the wall with blood pouring from her nose. "You bitch. I'll kill you for that!" she said, but cowered when Minnie cocked her fist to oblige her with a second punch. "She's already been taken to be executed. You won't get there. She'll be dead by now."

The time for stealth had ended. Unwilling to give up and not caring about the noise, Maryan burst from the jail. Rushing across The Academy precinct, she fired a breathless thought at the rat. '*Carl, where's Tamas?*'

'He flies with all speed from the breeding grounds. His mate is with him. They come, but have a long way to travel.'

Knowing the execution would be at the arena, she hurried around The Academy. Steppis's heavy tread pounded behind her.

A guard emerged as they ran headlong towards the Tunnel of Heroes. Mac loped ahead, his velvet paws crushing her to the ground before she could even draw a weapon. Maryan finished the job, knocking her senseless with a single punch.

At the end of the tunnel, Maryan paused to prepare herself, her sword in her left hand, the battle-axe in her right. Concealed within the shadows, she surveyed the scene. Spectators packed the seats to capacity. In the centre of the arena stood the ominous platform used for punishment. Four soldiers held Asti and Harlon facing the Queen. Behind them waited a block and a headsman's axe.

Maryan lowered her head and sprinted across the killing floor. A mutter ran through the crowd as they spotted her.

"Stop her!" Etelan screamed.

The planks of the wooden staircase bounced as Maryan hit the step. She skidded to a halt and squatted, holding her weight balanced and ready to spring. "Move away from the Queen," she said to the guards holding Asti.

The battle-hardened troops sneered. The last time they'd seen Maryan she'd been a raw trainee. Nodding to her companion, one released Asti and drew her swords. "The Queen sits where she should be. Now run away before you get a spanking." The twin blades spun in lazy circles.

"Stand away or die," Maryan warned, still poised in a crouch.

The guard danced forward, her swords shredding the air. Instead of meeting the attack, Maryan rolled, sacrificing any chance of recovery. The spike of her axe buried deep into the woman's calf, tearing away a length of muscle. Still rolling, she hamstrung her foe's other leg, dropping her screaming in a deluge of blood.

Maryan sprang to her feet. One guard still held Asti and two held Harlon. Mac prowled from side to side behind her. At each roar, the guards faltered.

Blowing hard, Steppis strode onto the platform and stepped over the warrior writhing on the floor. "Terrible technique," she muttered before lifting her head to speak to the crowd. "There'll not be an execution here today. Go home."

"Traitors!" Etelan shrieked. "Any who stand against me, stand against the law. Kill them all!"

Harlon screamed. His eyes rolled back into his head and he slumped between the women holding him. As his weight dragged them down, Asti sprang from the floor, her heels smashing into the chins of his captors. Miraculously cured, Harlon surged from the ground, powering the top of his head into the remaining guard's stomach.

Steppis rolled the fallen guards off the platform before cutting the bindings holding the prisoners. Harlon grabbed the headman's axe, as Asti retrieved a sword.

"Etelan, your reign is over, give up now!" Maryan shouted.

"These are my people, loyal and true." The Queen gripped the rail on the front of the box. "Stay by the block, we'll be using it in a moment." Soldiers poured out of the tunnel, heading for the platform.

Nothing betrays the approach of a hawk to the mouse and silent as an owl in the night, two mighty dragons burst over the rim of the arena. Searing flame swept the killing floor. Warriors on the edge of the intense heat screamed. Those caught in the blast vanished, burnt to a charred smear.

The dragons wheeled around the platform, flaming any movement. '*Tamas, son of Tamaar is here for vengeance!*'

'Vestra, his mate joins Tamas. Fear us dragon-slayers. Know our fury.'

Such was the arousal of the dragons, the twin voices rang inside the heads of all for miles around.

"Just like your mother," Asti said. Her smile made gruesome by the puckered eye socket. Her words lacked the venom of her previous slurs. "Make an entrance and then wait for your friends to sort out the mess."

"Blasted Serenians. These damned wounds are going to drain me," Harlon muttered. He tried to straighten the dressing around his thigh, but tumbled to the ground. Asti immediately dropped to her knees to help him.

Frozen in the moment, Maryan stared at her old nemesis. Asti had proclaimed herself a wife by replacing the single braid of the virgin warrior with twin plaits. The gentle way she tended Harlon's injuries betrayed the object of her love.

'Mother?' Stump's head loomed over the edge of the platform. Maryan rushed to hug him, rubbing fiercely above his eye ridge. *'Mother, stop it. I have somebody for you to meet.'*

The second dragon nudged beside Stump. Vestra had a predatory gleam in her multi-faceted eyes. *'We can pillage the city?'* she asked, barely a question. *'Your son needs a worthy treasure.'*

"I think that would be unwise. You took these people by surprise, but remember how they hunt dragons." Maryan regarded Vestra. "You're carrying an egg?"

'Your son has convinced me to attempt this strange idea of a family and must support us.' The dragon's eyelid blinked slowly. Smoke seeped from her nostril as Vestra allowed a sigh to escape.

'Tamas, we should fly, it's too cold here.' A powerful beat of her wings lifted her out of the arena. 'Tamas.' The single word hung in the air.

If a dragon could shrug, Maryan swore that Stump did. *'You'll like her when you get to know her.'* He sprang into the air to follow his mate.

"We need to chase Etelan before she regroups," Steppis said.

Asti frowned at Harlon as he struggled to take his weight on his good leg. "You're going to slow us down."

He reversed the headsman's axe to lean his weight against it. "I'll keep up with you, old woman." He crouched to retrieve a sword dropped by a guard.

They fell into a protective formation. Swords drawn, Steppis and Maryan took the flanks. Ever vigilant, Mac and Carl took point, the rat swaying on his haunches, riding the flowing motion of the lion's gait. In the centre, Asti and Harlon remained close to each other. Minnie walked behind, brandishing her cleaver.

Filthy as barbarian raiders from a minstrel's story, they approached the most prestigious confines of the palace. The ornaments along the pristine corridors rattled with their heavy tread. Impassive gods watched from the ceiling murals. Finally, they entered the wide corridor leading to the throne room. At the door, two ceremonial guards drew their weapons ready to challenge the small invasion party.

"Don't be stupid," Steppis said. "If either of you think you can stand against us, you deserve to die."

Maryan added, "It's good that you're loyal to the crown, but if you don't step aside, we will kill you."

The guards silently held their ground. Sorrow filled Maryan's heart when she looked at each of them. "You don't need to die, please run."

A squad of warriors rushed into sight, their heavy sandals clattering as they burst from a side corridor. Asti and Harlon brushed Maryan aside, driving their swords into the throats of the frightened guards. They flung open the double doors open and crashed into the throne room.

Although the chamber wasn't big, the design made it feel like a temple. Tall columns swept high, tapering up to trick the mind into believing they shot to an even greater height. Above, a crystal dome filled the room with peaceful light. Around them, murals showed queens of Serenia beset by unimaginable odds. Bruised and bloody, they stoically fought the oncoming hordes.

A circular dais of five steps led up to the throne. Shrouded with a silken cloth, the chair itself remained hidden. Standing almost at the top, Etelan glared down upon them.

Minnie slammed the large double doors closed. An ornate door handle snapped polished brass rods into the top and bottom of the doorframe. She leant back against them with her arms folded to guard the entrance.

Etelan singled out Maryan. "You are a very wilful daughter. I might regret taking you into my family."

"I don't recall asking to be a part of your family. I'll happily offer to leave it."

"And you don't exist." Pure venom oozed from Etelan when she pointed at Asti. She ran up the final steps to the throne before facing them again. "This is my realm, I rule here."

Etelan yanked away the silken cover, revealing the throne in its glorious beauty. Ancient carving layered with gold and inlaid with gemstones. Upon the seat lay the golden crown of Serenia. Lifting it over her head, she stood in front of the throne. Her hair stirred into a halo of snakes. "Ours!" the sibilant voices hissed.

A thunderclap of disaster heralded a cascade of crystal. Tamas dropped through the ruined dome. *'Mine!'* The throne, the crown, the snakes and Etelan all vanished under the weight of the young dragon.

Chapter 24

Dust swirled amongst the crystal storm of the ancient roof settling like snow on Tamas's colour-shifting scales. He curled around the wreckage in a covetous embrace. Thin wisps of smoke escaped his nostrils.

'Gold!' His dramatic arrival had extinguished all of the torches, draping the room into sepulchral gloom.

Minnie's excess bulk wobbled in time with the pounding on the double doors. "They'll be through any second!" she shouted.

"You must surrender to me." Steppis turned her sword upon Maryan and the others. "It's your only chance."

Harlon growled, but Asti laid her hand on his arm. "You'll take this ox for treatment in the Infirmary?"

The aging warrior agreed with a curt nod.

Maryan exchanged glances with Asti. Harlon's awful pallor indicated he wouldn't last much longer. The muffled sound of the guards gathering outside confirmed they would all die if they tried to resist.

"We yield to you," Maryan said, "in faith of our good treatment."

Steppis stomped to the door. "Stand aside Min," she said before raising her voice into a parade ground yell. "Move back from the door. I'm going to open it and nobody will do anything stupid!" The pounding stopped and she signalled for Minnie to unlock the doors.

The guards burst through the huge double doors, moving boldly until Stump's head lifted to regard them. Their arrogant progress faltered beneath his multi-faceted gaze.

"We are all friends." Steppis held a hand out in either direction. "And we're all going to behave as such." Her grim stare searched the guards before turning to Stump. "How are *you* going to get out of here?"

'A dragon may rest where he chooses,' Stump's voice echoed in all of their minds. *'I think I shall remain here a time.'* He replaced his head upon his forepaw.

"You'll behave yourself this instant," Maryan said. Her finger lashed up, pointing at the gaping roof. "Get back to Vestra. We'll talk about this again."

Jerking his head erect, he sprang like an arrow upward. A tight flick of his wings lifted him through the roof, shaking the remaining crystal shards onto the ruined body of Etelan.

"Minnie, will you escort this man to the Infirmary?" Asti asked. "Make sure they lock the door. Warn them not to let him charm them. Gag him if you have to."

"But …" Harlon said.

Minnie's broad hand sealed his mouth. She touched her lips and drew her finger across her throat hinting what would happen if he spoke again.

Steppis coughed. "We'll house you in the visitor chambers. If they serve foreign dignitaries, they should suffice."

The rooms Steppis assigned to them approached the opulence of Manda Torre. Maryan had her own suite. A fire warmed the reception room and wooden shutters covered the windows. The small pictures peppering the gaps between the rich wall hangings screamed an unsubtle message to any visiting noble. All of them showed women in battle against huge odds. With grim faces, their swords dealt death to their foes.

In the large bedchamber, Maryan stripped away her clothes before tumbling between the clean sheets. She felt awkward in the softness of the bed. How long had it been since she'd enjoyed a comfortable mattress?

Filled with the urge to hold Leon, her last link to Chentene, sleep took a long time to come. When it did, it was full of dreams. In one, she crept into the room where Sophie nursed Leon, but when the woman glanced up, her head exploded into a halo of snakes. In another, Kait was packing her belongings into a crate. She seemed unconcerned her skull was torn open and blood ran down her white dress. She simply kept babbling about the magical secrets she'd be learning.

When Maryan awoke, her bedding was rumpled and her hair stuck out in tangled knots. She forced herself to wash and straighten her hair, plaiting it into twin braids. She was sitting on the edge of the bed sorting through her pack when Steppis arrived clutching an armful of clothing.

"I collected some things for you. I thought you might like to get out of those rags," said her old tutor.

Maryan selected a simple tunic from the bundle Steppis had brought. Out of habit, she donned her weapons harness.

The old warrior sniffed. “Clumsy thing that. You need to get back to the blades. Never forget that you’re from a solid line of heroes.”

“I’m not a Serenian warrior. I’m …” she hesitated. “Simply, Maryan, a citizen, I hope.”

“That shall be decided. We’re meeting in the dining hall. A full enclave has been called to decide the fate of Asti and that man.”

“He’s a good friend. I’m not going to allow harm to come to him.”

“If you’re a citizen, you’ll do as commanded.”

They collected Asti from her suite. Two whip-like braids hung either side of her nape. She’d polished her breastplate to a mirror shine. Her proud stride exuded the same dignity it always had. Any who saw them walk through The Academy watched in awe. The moment they passed, a hushed chatter of speculation exploded behind them.

The benches in the refectory had been pushed back, leaving a single table facing out into the room. Fleur sat alongside the heads of caste. Her brow furrowed when she saw Maryan.

“What place has she here?” Maryan whispered to Steppis.

“She’s done good service up on the borders. The warriors deem her tough, but fair. She’s become Opella’s trusted right hand.”

Opella, head of warriors, sat at the end of the table, a black cloak draped around her shoulders. Round-faced Bethan, the head of healing sat at the other end of the table. She was a gifted magician and the only healer Kait had admired. Her button eyes studied them carefully. Wearing a robe shot with shimmering gold thread, Sheelan, the head of handmaidens, dominated the centre of the table. Small bells hanging from her ears tinkled each time her head moved. Her wide brown eyes gave nothing away.

Maryan shook herself. The use of this room filled with memories was a ploy to make her feel like an unruly child facing discipline. She imagined her simple tunic to be a regal gown. Adopting a haughty demeanour, she swivelled her glare along the table. They couldn't bully the Princess of Garalandia. "Is this how we've come to greet visiting royalty?"

Bethan spread her stubby hands on the table. "When said royalty destroy the throne room and kill the Queen. I think this is adequate."

"Why have you returned?" Sheelan asked, focusing her attention on Maryan.

"I have no home. My life and that of my son is forfeit. Where else could I hope for safety?"

Fleur shifted, as if to speak, but Opella silenced her with a firm hand on her arm.

Sheelan continued, "We are told you plotted to have your husband killed. That this man, Harlon, whom you protect so passionately, is the father of the child."

"Told by Mordacai, I assume. His envoy of lies must have ridden hard to get here. I've done nothing wrong."

Sheelan nodded, switching her attention to Asti. "Why have you returned?"

"You need help. The forces of darkness are massing. I came to help."

"The great Asti the Red." Fleur's lip twisted into a sneer. "One woman will turn the tide, will she? You've no idea what we've faced in your absence."

"And you've no idea what is coming at you," Asti replied, matching Fleur's tone. "Not just goblins, the call has gone out to the wild folk. Witches and trolls have joined them. You need all the help you can get."

"My mother negotiated peace with the witch in the labyrinth. The freak controls the dark creatures." Fleur turned to the others on the table for support. "I get reports from Violet. Things in the cave system are in hand."

"Violet's dead," Maryan said, trying to keep her voice low. "The treaty with the witch was a sham. There was no control." She knew Etelan had been either a co-conspirator, or a puppet. Unfortunately, Stump had eradicated any evidence of her betrayal.

"This is nonsense." Fleur slapped her hand onto the table. The sharp clatter echoed. "My mother, the Queen, has been murdered and I demand the right to trial by arms."

"You'd face me?" Asti stiffened.

"You don't exist. I challenge her!" Fleur stabbed her finger at Maryan. She sprang to her feet, her swords already in her hands.

"Fleur!" Opella commanded. The warrior's hand shot out, her huge palm swallowed Fleur's shoulder, pressing her back into her seat.

The doors to the chamber burst open. "We're under attack! Thousands of goblins are swarming the gap. We need help."

The leaders of the castes exchanged glances, before Opella took control. "We need to command the defences." She squinted at Asti. "You'll help us?"

Asti nodded.

"Then, we'll debate your status another time. Let's get to the walls."

The city of Serenia nestled in a rugged crag on the coast. Protected by impassable mountains and the sea, the only place an invading army could effectively mass was the starward gap, a small, fertile, band of farmland. To get there, an enemy had to follow the long valley that provided the only route for overland travel into Serenia. The ancient walls of the city defences faced out overlooking the road and the plain.

"Permission to lead my troop?" Fleur asked.

"Of course, get to them," Opella replied.

Maryan followed Fleur as she sprinted from the refectory, crashing the doors open, making for the defences.

"They'll try to breach the gate," Asti shouted, running close behind.

"You're wrong," Fleur shouted back. "They'll go for where the cliff meets the wall. I've been fighting them out on the frontier. Goblins climb like nothing you've ever seen." They cut through a cluster of houses to a stone stairway leading up to the battlements.

"My troop will already be in position," Fleur said, her voice edged with pride. "We've a tactic for this."

Formed into a solid block of three ranks, Fleur's troop of thirty warriors waited with their bows poised, ready to draw. Instead of facing outward, they stood angled towards the cliff face.

Like a mass of evil red spiders, the goblin army swept toward the city. A large section of them peeled away from the main thrust. When they hit the base of the cliffs, they simply kept running, rank upon rank of goblins climbed high, their mass scribing an arc across the rocky surface. Like a red avalanche, the churning chaos of demons screamed as it descended towards them.

"Squad … release!" Fleur shouted. Thirty arrows picked off the topmost goblins. In their death, they swept the lower ranks from the cliff. The tumbling mass gathered momentum, but Fleur didn't stop to admire the effect. "Release," she shouted. Her archers stripped another rank from the cliff with devastating efficiency.

A grim smile twisted Asti's face. "Excellent! You have this covered. Now, where will they shift the attention? She rubbed at her chin as she surveyed the defences. "We'll be needed up there." She sprinted off along the battlements.

Maryan clambered onto the wall beside Asti. Hundreds of leering faces peered up at her. She swung her battle-axe to clear an arc beneath her feet. A hand grabbed her ankle, tugging her close to the edge. Trying to leap back, hauling the goblin almost onto the wall. Her sword went down its throat and a gush of blood spewed from its mouth. Another clambered into sight. A wave of screaming goblins bubbled over the crenellations, mercilessly trampling the broken corpse of the first beneath their horny-toed feet.

Despite still being unable to wield her twin blades, Asti leapt into the fray. Her leg swept out, tripping the leaders. At least a half a dozen goblins clambered over the fallen, clawing her to the ground. Sharp teeth in slavering mouths raked her naked thighs. She curled into a ball, her elbows breaking necks. Without pause, her long muscles powered her into a high dive exploding out of the mob.

Surprise filled the cruel faces as they found themselves facing the devastating power of Maryan's lion-paw axe, but not for long, Asti's blade flashed, hacking the life from their bodies, washing the walkway red with sticky blood. The awful stench of torn bowel spilled from the charnel heap.

"Don't gawp, watch the wall!" Asti shouted. She leapt onto the crenels, studded sandals stomping hands, her flashing blade, piercing flesh.

Maryan lost track of how many times the goblin horde attacked. Asti worked tirelessly, repelling the enemy. Always amongst the heaviest fighting, she became a golden beacon on the city walls.

A group of Serenian warriors struggled along the walkway with a steaming cauldron supported on wooden rails. They tipped hot oil over the parapet, washing the goblins screaming to the ground. A flaming arrow ignited the oil. In moments, flames licked around the base of the wall. The billowing, acrid smoke hid the killing field from view.

Without respite, the goblin army repeatedly threw themselves against the defences, rarely managing to crest the battlements. Every part of Maryan's body ached and she sighed when they pulled back leaving the foot of the wall scattered with their ruined dead.

Steppis approached, her face streaked with dirt, her grey hair smeared with blood. "What are these devils playing at? They know they can't breach the wall. It's as though they want to keep us pinned down." She glared out at the swirling mass of goblins in the distance.

Screams rang out from deeper in the city. Steppis and Asti exchanged puzzled glances. "Surely somebody sealed the labyrinth?" Steppis said. A crowd of red creatures burst into sight around the edge of the arena, scurrying into the civilian dwellings.

"It's the Queen's decision to drop the bolts and we don't have one." Asti set off like a cat down the stairs.

Maryan followed, pushing through the throngs of tired troops snatching a rest at the foot of the wall. Fleur was squatted amongst the wounded, smoothing a bandage into place across a woman's arm.

"What are you lot up to?" Fleur shouted. She passed the ministering work to a subordinate before sprinting to catch up.

Unable to spare the breath, Maryan remained silent as they ran wide of the arena, circling back to the double doors of The Academy.

"We need to block the labyrinth," Asti shouted. She crashed through the doorway, powering up the stairs. The deserted corridors were strangely silent. On they ran, quickly reaching the far side of The Academy. From a window above the kitchen, they watched the alien army vomit through the gateway in the courtyard.

"We've got to drop the bolts to seal the gate," Steppis said.

"That'll hold them, but we have to shut the gate first," Asti agreed.

"What are you talking about?" Maryan asked.

Asti pointed to the ornament above the gate. "It's not told to the girls, because they'd be forever activating it, but that pot releases a set of bolts to lock the gate. Once released, it's the work of Thrippas to get them open again." She shook her head. "But, the gate has to be shut before the bolts will drop."

All four surveyed the mass beneath them. Steppis grabbed Maryan by the back of her neck, almost pushing her out of the window. "You two go along this ledge as far as you can. Make for the rise. Asti, cover my back."

"But how are you going to shut the gate?" Maryan asked.

"I stay inside," Steppis said. The old warrior clambered through the window, paused for a heartbeat and then dropped into the mass of goblins.

"Steppis!" Asti followed the old warrior through the window. They worked in unison, turning and dipping. Dancing blades wielded by the best Serenia could produce carved their way across the courtyard.

"Well then?" Fleur allowed a wicked smile to crease her face. "Do you trust me to cover your back?"

How could she trust her school day nemesis, the woman who blamed her for the death of her mother? Maryan checked the courtyard. Without their help, Steppis and Asti would be sacrificing themselves for nothing. She weighed her options for an instant before stepping onto the ledge. Keeping an eye on the flow of goblins beneath her, she ran to the corner of the building.

"Over there." Fleur pointed to a place in the far wall where ornamental stones would provide narrow footholds.

Emulating Steppis, Maryan threw herself into the sea of red goblins. Her feet crunched enemies underfoot. Her sword and axe worked constantly. Fleur dropped close by and they started to hack their way across the courtyard.

Tiny hands clawed at her. A goblin leapt onto Maryan's back, but Fleur's blade instantly hacked it away. They struggled forward, wading ever closer to their goal.

Fleur shouted into Maryan's ear. "Climb up there and get ready to push the ornament over."

Maryan scrambled up the indentations, leaving Fleur to guard the bottom. The goblins clambered around Fleur, trying to overpower her, but her spectacular display of sword-work held them back. Maryan crested the wall and ran to the spot above Asti.

A quick glance upward told Asti that Maryan had reached the ornament. The older pair doubled and redoubled their efforts to clear the gateway. Unable to break through the flashing blades, the flood of red figures ceased. Gradually, the two warriors edged inside, vanishing from view.

In a sudden rush of snarling demons, Asti tumbled from the gateway. The solid gate clanged beneath Maryan's feet.

"Now!" Asti shouted.

Maryan pushed her weight against the ornament. Instead of it tumbling to the ground, she felt a latch release. Metal rasped against stone. Ancient iron slid through the frame of the gate, multiplying its strength and stemming the flow. She threw herself down from the arch in time to see Steppis swept under the mounting crush of evil creatures grinding against the gate. Times without count, Maryan thrust her sword through the bars to pierce the trapped demons.

"Help me!" Fleur screamed. The goblin horde threatened to swamp her. Maryan now fought alongside Asti to cut a swathe across the courtyard. Battle-axe and sword made short work of those attempting to overpower Fleur.

With the tide of goblins spewing from the labyrinth cut off, the remaining invaders scurried away from the warriors in search of refuge in the town. Asti cast a last glance to the gate where Steppis had made her sacrifice. "We need to get back to the walls."

Climbing back onto the battlements, they found a strange peace had descended. The goblins had fallen back leaving only six huge rocks in the middle of the field. The rock uncurled, resolving into trolls. Between them, they carried a battering ram slung on chains from their shoulders. On their outer arms, they wore shields the size of doors. Their glowing eyes surveyed the battlements. Moving as one, they stepped toward the main gate of the city.

A hail of arrows dropped from the sky, many of them striking, but none penetrating the rock-like hides. The trolls broke into a shambling run, covering the distance to the gate faster than a racing horse. At a shout from Opella, a battery of dragon-killer crossbows sprang above the battlement. Crews who could routinely pierce the sphincter of a moving dragon had no trouble hitting the chest of a troll. Leg-thick bolts punched through them, staking the trolls to the ground. Another volley from the dragon-killers tore away limbs, shredding them, ripping life from their rock-like form.

Asti pointed into the distance. Behind the massed goblins, black cloaked figures milled. "That's where our next problem will come from."

As she spoke, two fireballs arched through the sky, crashing onto the crossbow crews. Another two followed, seeming to hang at the peak of their flight before commencing a whistling descent to the wall. Like sparrows challenging eagles, two small fireballs leapt from the battlements. When they touched the larger ones, they exploded in a blinding flash.

"Gorath!" Maryan rubbed her eyes. Two, four and then six fireballs flew from the distance. Standing close to the giant crossbows, Bethan offered her reply. Tiny, but arrow straight, her response shattered the attack.

At a signal from Bethan, the remaining dragon-killers fired high over the goblin army. Her tiny fireballs streaked across the killing field shattering the bolts into a starburst of white-hot metal. Salvo after salvo flew, each chased by screaming fireballs and each showering deadly rain onto the foe.

Silence fell across the space. Both sides waited. Just before dusk, a single figure strode from the enemy lines carrying a flag of truce. Opella stomped out of the postern gate across the killing field to meet the emissary. After a brief exchange, she spun on her heel and returned.

"Now the battle starts for real. The politicians negotiate," Asti said.

Chapter 25

“**Finally!** This is where you’ve been hiding. I need you now!” Bethan’s voice snapped Maryan awake faster than a dowsing from iced water. The brown-clad healer’s tone brooked no argument.

Despite the warriors milling through the refectory in search of food, Maryan and Asti had managed to sleep on the hard benches. Torches illuminated the room and the high windows showed the full black of night. Maryan peered up at Bethan standing above her. “Why?”

“Because there is a ‘Peace Envoy’ standing in the middle of the killing field offering negotiations, but only if you are present.”

“I’m not a negotiator.” Maryan hauled herself upright. Aches forced her to ease her limbs straight before stretching. “Of course I’ll come, if it will help.”

“First, I have something to do.” Bethan laid her hands on Maryan’s shoulders. She felt her soul dragged from her. Leon was dead. She watched him die.

Kait snatched him from her arms to smother him beneath a pillow. All the while laughing as she held Maryan in magical ties. A halo of snakes writhed from Kait’s head. As they did, the binding force slipped away. Free to move, Maryan whipped the claw-axe from its holster. Pouncing across the room, she leapt at her old friend, crushing her skull with a single blow.

Agony wracked Maryan, her body shook with grief. Unable to stand, she curled into a sobbing ball on the floor. Why should she get up? Searching for compassion in those looking down at her, she felt their bewilderment.

"Now we are ready for the meeting," Bethan said. She held out her hand and tugged Maryan from the floor.

Somehow, Fleur had found time to polish her armour into a bright shine. She greeted Maryan with a grim stare before opening the postern gate. Opella led the council onto the field. A small detachment of Fleur's troop walked alongside carrying torches. The distant army lay hidden in shadow. The flare of campfires, shouts and harsh laughter betrayed them.

A hooded figure wrapped in a black cloak waited motionless in the centre of the empty space. Maryan tried to stop her legs shaking, but the weight of her grief threatened to rob her of any strength. Leon was lost forever. Her last link to the happiness she'd shared with Chentene had been erased. Asti took her left hand.

Fleur's lips drew into a thin smile. "You will survive," she whispered, slipping a supporting arm around Maryan's waist.

The negotiating party stopped to face the strange figure.

"We have an offer," the figure said. The harsh voice sounded female.

"Who are you?" Opella demanded, squaring to the stranger as if ready for a fight. "Why are you here?"

"My name is Nothing. We came expecting a better welcome than this." The figure raised an arm towards the battlements of the city. Her sleeve fell back revealing a skin covered in tattooed swirls. "We came seeking a homeland; a place to live without persecution. Surely, as women, you appreciate this."

The figure dropped its arms and the hood turned slowly to survey the council. "You may keep your lands. We need only one tiny concession." The hood snapped to face Maryan. "We want the baby. We shall depart, if you give us the false prince."

"The child never arrived," Bethan declared. "Probe my thoughts to see if I lie. He didn't make it through the caves."

"Dead?" The hood rustled. Two pairs of tiny red eyes stared out.

"My child is dead. Why won't you leave me alone?" Maryan choked. The stranger turned her full attention to her. The black hood expanded, blossoming like a storm cloud rolling from the horizon to blot out the night sky. It wrapped around Maryan. Desperate misery tugged her into the dark pit. Snakes pierced her, worming through her mind. She sagged. All of her memories cascaded wildly, love with Chentene, her flight from Manda Torre, the ordeal in the caves. Clutching her temples, she sobbed. "Stop, please stop." The snakes vanished, leaving her feeling violated.

"In that case, we shall claim this worthless husk and leave." The figure reached out to Maryan.

Asti stepped between them. "She stays. You depart."

The figure raised its hand. A seething fireball coalesced in the long-nailed fingers.

"Can you make two of those at once?" Fleur said. Ready to strike, the length of her sword glowed red in the light the fireball. "You heard. She stays."

Once more, worms writhed through Maryan's head rummaging through every dream, hope and fear. Merciless pain wracked her. Somewhere in the fog of agony, she heard the woman speak.

"This is not the one, she is no threat. You may keep your … burden." The figure swept the cloak around itself and strode away.

Silent and as unmoving as a statue, Maryan stood on the battlements high above the main gate. Although the horizon displayed a spectacular sunrise, it held no interest. She shivered in the ice-cold wind. Her son was alive! She'd grieved enough for a lifetime after watching him die. Bethan had saved the city and possibly Leon's life, but the cost to Maryan had been awful.

Her gaze traced the single road of hard-packed earth running across the fields to the border gap many leagues starward. Nothing moved between the walls and the point where it vanished into a fold in the land. The goblin horde had retreated, but the borders would always be a dangerous place. She stretched higher, hoping to see a flicker of movement.

If all had gone well, the party sent to collect Leon would soon be arriving back. She'd wanted to ride with them, but her presence would light a beacon, needlessly risking Leon's life. Instead, a barely recovered Sami had ridden out, leading Fleur's troop with the promise that none would stand against them. Fleur had passionately begged to go, but as a candidate in the election, the council had refused her the right to ride.

After the chaos of the goblin invasion, the selection of a new ruler had to be organised. The people had screamed for Asti's nomination. With little to gain by fighting against the tide of public opinion, the caste leaders had pardoned her banishment.

Hoping beyond hope, Maryan rechecked the road across the plain. It remained starkly empty. She turned from the cold heights of the walls, making her way down to the royal apartments for the next task of the day.

When Harlon had been released from the Infirmary, rooms were assigned to him a discrete distance from Asti's. The older warrior made no secret of her love and insisted on flaunting her twin braids. Maryan, prayed that today of all days, she'd find him alone in his room. She knocked and waited.

"Come in, I'll be there in a moment," he said through the door.

High-backed, red leather chairs stood either side of the blazing fire. The plaster walls were stained a pale mushroom. The drawing he'd carried from Manda Torre hung in the centre of one of them.

Harlon emerged from the door leading to his bedroom. He'd pulled on a pair of tight black breeches, his naked torso rippled with hard muscle as he rubbed a towel through the stubble of his red hair. He peeked out from beneath the cloth. "Have you come to declare undying love?"

"No, I've come to warn you that today of all days, you need to behave yourself. Has Asti explained this to you?"

"Naked! The entire city naked!" He dropped his towel around his neck, rubbing his hands in anticipation. "My, how invigorating."

“Behave! It’s to prove only women are voting.” Maryan grimaced, unable to remain stern when faced by his theatrical pose. “And that means you have to stay hidden. If people thought we had a man in the city today …”

“All that female flesh. All those untamed beauties. How can you ask a red-blooded man to restrain himself on such a day?”

“Harlon, be serious. We need to talk about you and Asti.”

He cocked his head, about to make a facetious comment, but her glare stifled the words. Instead, he smoothed his smile, motioning for her to sit.

“You realise that if you continue to womanise, you will hurt a woman who deserves better.”

“Deserves better than I?” He held his arms wide, allowing his annoying grin to tip the corners of his mouth.

“You know what I mean.” She banged her fist on the arm of the chair. “If you think of hurting her, you will feel the wrath of a nation. She isn’t wise in the ways of the world and won’t bear it the way those silly women in Garalandia did.”

“Hurt her?” He shook his head and pointed. “Do you see that picture, the one my brother gave me? I loved the image of the woman before I found the reality. When I did, the picture became a childish dream.”

He paused, a fervent gleam replacing his world-weary cynicism. “The grave might part us, but only if death can hold me.” His hands balled into fists. “To be a ghost forever at her side would be my chosen heaven.”

“What about her scarring? You’re obsessed with beauty.”

“That is her beauty. In every way, she is beautiful to me. I’m not going to hurt her.”

The door burst open and Sami marched in, a triumphant grin split her face. Close behind, Sophie followed carrying a bundle. Maryan rushed across to them, clasping Sami in a fierce hug before claiming Leon. “Thank you, thank you,” she muttered. She kissed Leon on his forehead, crushing his tiny body against her.

Sami embraced them both. “We’re home.”

“But only just in time. Shouldn’t you good Serenians be stripping off to make your way to the election?” Harlon twitched the keyhole medallion from his chest. Instead of raising it to his eye, he slipped the chain off his neck and lowered it around Leon. “Young man, Uncle Harlon is going to teach you a lot more than how to hold a sword.”

Having the only space large enough for a lion, the council had granted Maryan living quarters on the top floor of a warehouse close to the palace. It had a single flight of wooden stairs leading up from a cobbled courtyard.

The entire building reeked of warm lion. Mac padded into sight around the edge of a large wooden screen to snarl a greeting as they opened the door.

“You live here?” Sophie wrinkled her nose as she touched the rough stonework. Her head craned back to take in the open beams running overhead.

“It might be a little ramshackle, but I’ve never had a place to call my own,” Maryan said.

“Our own,” Sami corrected.

"One day, we might put some more permanent walls in, but look." Maryan guided Sophie through the maze of screens. "Here is a room for Leon and one for you to stay in as long as you wish. If it's not big enough for you, we can simply push the screens back a bit. Isn't it wonderful?"

Sophie grunted, following her through into the main space.

"In here we can train, or do anything." Maryan waved her arm to take in the expansive floor space. Four low sofas formed a square around a battered table. A large cargo door set in the end wall provided a spectacular view across the city.

"Stump won't be appearing through those, will he?"

"No, he's too big to fit now. The courtyard is easy for him to land in without damaging anything."

"Dining?"

"Have you tasted her cooking?" Sami laughed. "As honoured guests, we eat in The Palace, or The Academy." She nodded to a doorway. "In a real emergency, there's a small kitchen through there."

Sami thumped Maryan playfully on her shoulder. "Come on slowcoach, we have to get dressed for the election."

"Dressed?" Sophie said. "I thought you did this naked thing?"

"You'll see," Maryan explained. "As we can't show off clothing, Serenians tend to go over the top with makeup and theatricals. The whole city will be a circus."

"It's all too … barbaric. I'll never manage." Sophie dropped to the sofa.

They went through to the bedroom where Sami peeled off her riding gear. Maryan quietly admired her friend's delicious curves. Years of training had only made her more beautiful. She smiled as her friend began to apply a coating of makeup, starting with a cream of golden sparkles.

Sitting on the end of the bed Maryan undid her blouse. Leon nuzzled against her, searching for her nipple. Possibly in payment for the cruel mind trick, Bethan had helped her keep her milk flowing. Leon's mewling calmed and she closed her eyes, wanting to nurse him forever.

When she next looked, Sami had become a multi-coloured statue. A yellow lightning bolt crossed her face and she'd painted animal stripes around her ribcage and stomach.

"How on earth did you reach all around?" Maryan said admiring the way the patterns flowed perfectly from Sami's spine.

Sami raised her arms above her head, gyrating in a sinuous whirl ending with her hips swaying an arrogant invitation. Nobody could fail to be aroused by Sami's glorious body. Although large, her breasts were solid, with dark nipples. Her hips flared, flowing into perfect legs. She'd trimmed the tight curls at her crotch into a heart shape. "I'm very flexible."

"Let's get you ready to vote." She tugged Maryan into an embrace, closing her mouth over Maryan's.

Even though her memories of Chentene would never fade, Maryan savoured the kiss. Since her return, they'd not been physically intimate, but they would soon swear the blade-sister oath. Her love for Sami was different. The emotions she shared between

Sami and Chentene complimented each other, filling her with a reassurance of safety.

Partially trained in handmaiden skills, Sami quickly smoothed colourful patterns across Maryan's skin. Her eyes twinkled each time she stole the small kisses that told of her love.

They found Sophie resting in the main room. "Would you tend Leon for a short time longer?" Maryan asked. She reluctantly handed him back, feeling a pang of jealousy as he settled easily into the crook of the chubby woman's arm.

In front of the sparkling white façade of The Centre, workers had erected a series of marquees, filling the space with a riot of colourful fabric.

Clinging on to Sami's arm, Maryan gasped as they entered the market square. "Sionallus will be gathering some fools tonight, I'll bet."

With men banned and a rule of nakedness from dusk until dawn, the city became a crazy party. The council provided long trestle tables laden with beer, wine and food. Heat from stone-filled iron braziers warmed the air. All around, naked women laughed. Many had dyed their hair for the occasion, wearing it stiffened to great spikes or crests. Others had painted designs across their skin, baffling the eye with colourful swirls.

A low growl rumbled from Sami.

"Gorath, Sami. I thought Mac had followed us. What's wrong?"

Rose was pushing her way hunch-shouldered through the crowd. Her hand hovered covetously over her pile of food. She wandered across to lurk uninvited on the edge of a group of burly warriors.

“Easy,” Maryan whispered, checking her fiery lover. “Your flail? Where is it?”

“Somebody wanted to borrow it.” Sami winked. “Just wait and see.”

The main doors to the centre opened and Sheelan stepped out. Her unbound hair flowed in golden tendrils on her alabaster skin. Head high, she moved slowly, her pointed footstep pausing on each glistening white stair.

Walking just behind came her two assistants. A hidden drum sounded on each pace. In time with each thud, two more handmaidens emerged from the door. Spreading to either side, they formed a living train of synchronised, glorious beauty. Painted the colours of the rainbow their stride swayed musically. They performed a stately rotating dance, adopting the positions of allurement in time to the slow cadence of the drum.

The riotous chatter around the square ceased as everybody watched the stately procession make its way to the voting marquee. A blast of music shattered the hypnosis. Mighty drums from the jungles of Sudaland pounded out a wild rhythm. Squealing wildly, a tumbling mass of young handmaidens cascaded down the stairway, garish designs of every hue rippled and bounced.

As they danced, two of them spun long chains holding smoking burners over the heads of the onlookers. The purple fumes formed circles above the crowd. The people gasped in delight as the musky scent descended. Ridiculously expensive, the incense had a mildly intoxicating quality designed to enhance sensual memories.

After breathing deep, Sami squealed, dragging Maryan to the election tent. "Come on, through here."

The rules of the balloting dictated that each woman cast a voting stone at the feet of the woman they chose to be queen. There were two candidates facing each other across the space, Asti and Fleur.

The line of handmaidens wound through the crowd forming a queue that ended in front of Asti. "I place this stone in recognition of your sacrifice avenging Arlaine," each one said as they filtered past.

Despite the awful scar twisting her face and the marks of a thousand wounds marring her flesh, Asti appeared more beautiful than any of the handmaidens flowing past her. She tipped her head in dignified thanks to them.

The crowd on the other side of the marquee rippled with laughter and Sami dragged Maryan across to investigate.

"This is outrageous!" Opella stood with her hands on her hips, her solid square buttocks wobbled when she kicked the empty basket in front of Fleur. "Nobody is allowed weapons. It's the law."

As she noticed them, a conspiratorial grin split Fleur's face. "This isn't a weapon, it's a training aid, ask her." Fleur started to work the chain-linked flail. The lengths of wood blurred, vanishing under her arms, whipping around her waist.

A healer sporting her hair in a red crest tried to put her stone at Fleur's feet, but the flail swished so close to her head, she screamed. The healer scowled at Opella before scurrying away.

"You cannot avoid being voted for," Opella growled. "Queen Brakka was dragged to the booths in chains when she tried to escape. I won't stand any such foolery from you."

"I'm not avoiding being voted for, merely keeping warm. Any citizen has a right to exercise. I just happen to lose control of them occasionally." The flail whistled faster. Sweat glistened across Fleur's body, making her look like a warrior from stories. Years of training had spread her ribcage, flattening her breasts into muscle. Her washboard stomach tapered down to narrow hips. Every sinew of her body worked in harmony. White-skinned, her muscles rippled beneath the battle scars she'd acquired in service on the borders.

Opella spun on her heel and stormed off.

"I lent Sami my troop to collect your son, she lent me these." The flail snapped into Fleur's palm with a click. She adopted the casual ease of an officer in command. "Your child is safe?"

"Yes, thank you. What are you doing?"

"I'm not ready to be glued to a throne. My life is serving Serenia in my own way." Fleur nodded towards Asti. "Any who try to cast for me, I merely suggest they might want to vote elsewhere."

When they added their stones to the overflowing pile close to Asti, she bowed to hide her wicked grin. "I'll see you later," she whispered.

At the exit, Maryan dipped her hand into the tub of purple dye to show she'd voted. It stopped people from voting twice and proved that a woman had done her duty as a citizen.

The sounds of revelry rang through the night. A scuffle in the courtyard drew Maryan to the stairway outside their rooms. "Who's there?" she hissed.

She gasped, amazed at the sight emerging from the shadows. Working together, Fleur and Asti were struggling with something wrapped in a sheet. At the top of the stairs, Asti wrestled their burden on end before tugging the bindings away. The cloth dropped, revealing the painting from the hidden room.

"What?"

"We stole it." Asti held her arms wide. "A last irresponsible act."

"Not really," Fleur said. "One of us will be queen by morning." She nodded theatrically at Asti. "So we agreed we could give it away."

They hauled the painting close to the cargo doors and threw them open. Moonlight rippled on the distant ocean.

"Go on then, show us," Asti demanded.

Sami handed Maryan a candle. "Yes, go on."

She moved it across the arc of runes making them flow into words.

Now you are queen - forgive me, A.

A single tear ran down Asti's face, her fingernail traced the lines of Amara's features. Then, she stood back, turning to each of them.

"When I am queen, I'll need all of the guidance I can get. I want you all to be here to help me."

She reached out to Sophie. "A foreign noble." She held Fleur in her gaze. "Warrior perfection." Her grin blazed upon Sami. "A warrior who understands the handmaidens and of course you, Maryan."

"Who am I, apart from Amara's daughter?" Maryan asked.

"A princess."

"A mother."

"A lover."

Her friends replied without hesitation.

"The line of my blade-sister restored to Serenia. Plus, you're truly the greatest of treasures, a friend." Punctuating Asti's words, Mac roared in agreement.

Basking in the love from her friends, she glanced out across the sea shimmering in the distance. "So, mother, your friend will be where you wanted her. Am I?" The weight of a shadow lifted from her heart. She believed her mother had answered.

Printed in Great Britain
by Amazon.co.uk, Ltd.,
Marston Gate.